Clara Claus

Alexandra Lane

Clara Claus
Book One In The Snowflake Triplet

Alexandra Lanc

Also By Alexandra Lanc:

The Foxfire Chronicles

Shadows of Past Memories

Shadows of Past Memories: Brave Edition (Paperback Only)

Shadows at Midnight (2013)

The Snowflake Triplet

Clara Claus

Sugar Plum Dreams

THE PHANTASMAGORIA DUET

The Ending

The Beginning

Divide

Lyrics of the Heart

Made Of Stars (Coming Soon)

Clara Claus

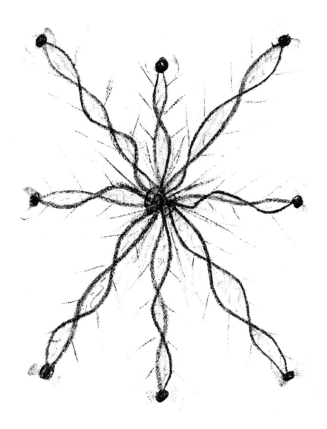

A Tale Of Frost And Snow

Copyright © 2010 - 2012 by Alexandra Lanc

All rights reserved. Except as permitted by the U.S. Copyright Act of 1976, no part of this novel may be reproduced or transmitted by any form or means -- electronic, mechanical, photocopying, recording, or by any information storage and retrieval system -- without written permission from the copyright holder. As it is a violation of the author's rights, please do not participate in copyright infringement.

Clara Claus, Third Edition. This novel is Young Adult fiction, and does not contain: sexual content, drug/alcohol abuse, or language.

This is a work of fiction. Any resemblance to actual persons, living or dead, events, or locales is entirely coincidental and not intended by the author.

Visit www.AlexandraLanc.com

For Mema:

Thanks for the inspiration. We miss you.

"Yet this I call to mind and therefore I have hope:"

Lamentations 3:21, NIV

Christmas' Tale

Buried deep in North Atlantic,
Is a place few people visit,
Clashed with ice and snow and sea,
Busiest on Christmas Eve.

Living deep in North Atlantic,
Is a man known, because,
Not only delivers gifts does he,
But also spreads joy and glee.

As you've guessed,
North Atlantic,
Is the home of Santa Claus,
But did you know his daughter also,
Lived there once upon a cause.

And return she did to North Atlantic,
On the day of Christmas was,
Amid the snow and ice and reindeer...
Born her girl, named Clara Claus.

Prologue

She could hardly bring herself to remember her mother on the best of days, and didn't even try to remember her on the worst. She knew that her mother had been kind and joyous and loving, and...a lot of other things.

But these things hardly mattered to Clara, because her mother wasn't there, and she knew that she never would be again.

She could never bring her back from that fateful night so long ago. She could never stop the shooter from pulling the trigger. She could never stop the blood that flowed from the open wound. She could never stop the killer from running off. She could never pound life back into her mother's heart...

And, perhaps worst of all, she could never erase the memories of that Christmas Eve...

Chapter One: Jack

The North Pole, One Week Before Christmas

If you would have asked Jack Frost what he wanted to be doing, right at that moment, he certainly wouldn't have told you that he wanted to be at a meeting with the Winter Council.

And yet, that's where he was.

Jack sighed loudly for what was probably the millionth time, drumming his fingers on the giant oval table he sat at, trying to keep his impatience from leaping out of his mouth and forming insults. The Winter Council had been sitting there for an hour, waiting on their newest member, who still wasn't there yet...

An hour! He was wasting an hour! Didn't they know how *important* his job was? No, of course not. No one cared. All Santa did was sit on his fat bum all day, drinking cocoa while his elves prepared toys for kids who didn't need them. And Saint Nick? It wasn't like he did anything special -- he was retired, for goodness sake!

And, Randoy, the Top Reindeer? Please, hadn't his team done enough test runs? How hard was it to fly, anyway? It was all the reindeer knew how to do. And Jack didn't even want to think about the Sugar Plum Fairy. He *hated* her.

No, no one knew how hard it was to have a real job. How hard it was to get your work done when you were constantly being called for pointless meetings. After all, if Jack couldn't complete his job, then it wouldn't be very frosty for the humans, and if it wasn't frosty, then it would hardly seem like Christmas...

Not that he cared much about Christmas.

No, the only one who knew Jack's pain was the North Wind, his best and only friend. "You're still drumming your fingers," Jack woke from his reverie when he heard North's voice, looking up at the navy-haired teen beside him. "Quit that," North's voice was monotone, as always.

Jack frowned at the order. "Why?" he asked, not really caring.

"It's an old table," North's frosty blue eyes turned towards the table as he took one of his leather gloves off, running a hand along the wood. "Made a long time ago. Renaissance period, I'd say. Truly priceless," he frowned as he looked over at Jack's fingers, which were still moving, drilling grooves into the table. "And you're ruining it."

Jack felt his eye twitch as he smirked at North, pulling a pen out of his pocket. He clicked the pen's top before reaching out and digging its tip into the wood, creating a long line of black ink as he drew the letter *L* on the tabletop.

North didn't look fazed. "Ever thought of anger management?" he asked, raising an eyebrow slightly.

Jack simply snorted, turning away.

He knew North wasn't being serious, of course. It was a long-running joke between him and his friend...even if it was annoying.

Jack and North had been friends for quite a while, both hating their place on the Winter Council, though Jack was the only one to ever verbalize the dislike. They'd become friends when they'd first met, both being dragged to the ridiculous meetings, both very much alike...and very different.

Jack was the "oldest" out of the two, forever nineteen, since he was Immortal (where as North would be forever eighteen). They were both considered the most eccentric out of everyone on the Council, choosing to wear what would have been considered a more Victorian Goth style (though they liked cobalt blue or navy, and neither minded accenting their wardrobes with contemporary styles). In matter of looks they were also very alike, both possessing frosty blue eyes, and haircuts that matched, though North's hair was a navy color, Jack's a snowy white.

Personality wise, though, the two couldn't have been more different.

No one was sure how to describe Jack's personality, other than "irritable, sarcastic, and generally unlikeable", but North was easy to describe. Jack found the words that suited him best were "boring, dull, and boring", though he did have many interesting qualities, and knew about a lot of different things...

Jack was pulled away from his thoughts as the door to the conference room opened, admitting the last of the Council members. Jack found himself frowning as a large, see- through freezer was ushered into the room, rolling towards the giant table on roller-skate wheels, a grinning snowman in it.

"Well, the fat man and the popsicle are here..." Jack said under his breath as the freezer came to a halt at the other end of the table, and Santa appeared, closing the door behind him. "Joy..."

North gave him a small smile. "Actually," he began, voice low as Jack's, though still monotone. "Chilly, the snowman, can't be classified as a popsicle, since he's not flavored or edible. And you can't call Santa 'fat'. The proper term is *'obese'*."

Jack grit his teeth as he shot North a glare. "Fine then, the obese man and the snow-freak are here. Is that better?"

"Actually..." North looked like he was about to say more, but he was interrupted by St. Nick, who cleared his throat, ready to start the meeting.

St. Nick pulled at his beard as he stood, everyone else sitting (minus Frosty, who was in the see-through freezer, tilting his head every few seconds). Next to him was Santa Claus, also known as Kris Kringle, whom St. Nick was commonly confused with. Of course, Jack knew better than the humans did. St. Nick and Santa weren't the same people at all -- well, not anymore...

Next to Santa sat the Sugar Plum Fairy, a woman in her forties, who was sipping tea from a teacup, nose held high in the air. Jack grimaced as he caught her gaze, and she frowned at him, obviously disapproving.

Next to the Sugar Plum Fairy was Randoy, the Top Reindeer, who was sitting on the floor, as tall as the Sugar Plum even though he didn't have a chair. He kept nodding his head along with Chilly, who was positioned next to him.

And then, on the other side of the table, across from everyone else, sat Jack and North, isolated as usual. Jack was going to point this out as St. Nick cleared his throat, picking up papers as if he were delivering a speech, but he decided not to, considering what they were at the meeting for...

"Καλωσο ρισμα. Let the five-hundred and fifty-sixth meeting of the Winter Council officially come to order," St. Nick announced in his bass voice, the beginning a welcome in Greek; it was his native tongue. "Now, I'm sure we all know why we're here. Sugar Plum," he nodded as he turned towards the woman drinking tea, "would you care to start?"

Sugar Plum nodded. "Of course, Nick," she said as she put down her tea, acting dainty, and Jack rolled his eyes again. "As you all know, this matter pertains to one of our Council members, Jack Frost..."

Of course. Jack thought, tuning out the conversation. *My time is up...*

It hadn't been his fault, not really. Okay, well maybe it *had* been his fault, but it wasn't like he'd done anything bad. All he'd tried to do was ruin Christmas. It wasn't like it was a crime...

Well, in Jack's book it wasn't a crime, but no one else went by his rules. Could he help it if they were all so stupid?

It had all started a month ago, just as Thanksgiving was getting ready to begin. He'd been on his usual rounds, frosting over planes and prairies and windows just like he was supposed to, when he'd had a brilliant idea -- another plot to ruin Christmas. This plot had been ingenious, and he was sure it would work, but somehow...well, it hadn't...and then St. Nick had gotten word of the incident.

And now he was in trouble. And not just *little* trouble, either.

The last Winter Council meeting had been held a week ago, St. Nick taking precedence as normal, being the head. It had been then that he'd accused Jack of trying to destroy Christmas -- and not for the first time, mind you. Jack hadn't been very surprised or worried about this, since it happened all of the time, but then St. Nick had said something to shake his whole world.

"Since you utterly refuse to stop trying to destroy Christmas, Jack, I hereby banish you from the Winter Council, and from Winter itself."

Needless to say, that hadn't gone over well with Jack. Banished? From Winter? That meant that St. Nick had wanted to take his job away. To take away the only thing in the whole world that he had left to care about. And the worst part was: there had been nothing he could do about it. St. Nick's word was law.

Strangely, it had been Santa who saved him, asking St. Nick to give Jack one more chance. It had shocked every one of the Council members, since it was Santa's holiday that Jack was trying to ruin, but that hadn't bothered the fat (oops, sorry, "obese") man.

He'd asked St. Nick to give Jack a week -- a whole week! -- to better himself, to turn a new leaf.

And St. Nick had agreed to Santa's request, giving Jack the most impossible, unattainable task to complete.

"*Alright,*" he'd said, fixing his all-seeing, creepy eyes on Jack. "*If Jack Frost can learn to love a human in one week, then he can keep his spot on the Council, and his job.*"

It was so crazy, Jack had nearly fallen out of his seat when he'd heard it.

A week! St. Nick had given him a week -- only a *week*! -- for such an impossible task. Jack was sure the old man had wanted him to fail.

And love? *Love?* What was that? Jack hadn't even known...

And, one week later, sitting at the Council meeting next to North, he still didn't. Instead of spending his week looking for "just the right human", he'd been looking for a way to destroy Christmas. Again.

And he'd failed. *Again.*

"...so, as you can see, it is time to banish the perpetrator," Jack sighed as he caught the end of Sugar Plum's sentence, knowing this was it. "And personally, I say good riddance," Jack glared at the woman as she shot him a smug smile, feeling his blood boil.

He couldn't believe it. After so many years -- after such a long time -- he was being banished. Banished! What was he going to do now? Where was he going to go? Who was he going to be?

Jack didn't know the answer to any of these questions. He wasn't sure he knew *how* to be anyone else.

Jack felt like he was suddenly suffocating as St. Nick nodded at Sugar Plum, sharing in her smile. Jack felt like the world was starting to spin as St. Nick opened his mouth, probably going to repeat Sugar Plum's "good riddance". Jack felt like he was going to pass out as Santa suddenly lay his hand on St. Nick's shoulder, asking him to sit back down--

Wait. Santa was doing what?

Jack felt his eyebrows arch as he stared at Santa, who was asking for permission to address the rest of the Council. Could the fat (obese!) man really be helping him again? He didn't understand it. What had he done to merit Santa's favor?

I can't think of anything. Jack thought as Santa cleared his throat. *All I've ever done is try and destroy Christmas.*

Why would Santa be happy about that?

"Dear members of the Council," Santa's speech was starting, so Jack ultimately decided to listen for once, since it concerned him. "I know as well as you do what Jack has done, but I think..." he looked at St. Nick pleadingly. "Why not give him one more chance? Christmas is a week away, and I need help preparing. Perhaps..." he let the rest of the sentence slip away.

St. Nick was the first to understand, of course. "You want Jack to *help* you?" he asked, obviously shocked. "Do you find that wise, Kris? After all he's done to try and destroy Christmas, you want to let him into the heart of it?"

The room was silent when Santa nodded, a smile on his face as normal. Shocked gasps followed the gesture, but St. Nick held up a hand, and silence once again reigned.

"Alright, alright!" the old man snapped, playing with his beard. "If Kris thinks this is a good idea, then I accept his judgement," he cast a weary glance at Jack as Santa laughed, and Jack smiled, putting on his most innocent face. "I hereby decree that Jack Frost will assist Santa with anything he needs in preparation of Christmas...However," the "however" made a few members lean forward in their seats, their eyes big. "I'm not waving his original task," he held up a hand before Jack could protest. "You will assist Santa this week, and then be free to complete your task by sunrise on Christmas morning. Meeting adjourned!"

Jack sat back in his seat as the meeting ended, and everyone started chatting, all casting him glares and looks of contempt.

One week. He had one week free, and then...

Why wasn't St. Nick letting him off the hook? Really, he had to find a human to fall in love with from midnight to sunrise on Christmas Eve?

That was all the time he got -- a few hours? That was impossible. *Impossible.*

Jack put his hands behind his head in a relaxed fashion as he gazed up at the ceiling, grinning mischievously.

But what did it matter, anyway? He would fulfill his one wish by Christmas Eve. St. Nick and Santa were idiots, because they'd let him have exactly what he wanted.

One week in the North Pole. One week to help Santa. One week to destroy Christmas...

From the *inside.*

Chapter Two: Clara

Clara felt her head spin as the plane rattled up and down in the cold and dark wind, and she looked out the window, not quite sure where they were going. They had been on the plane for hours.

Clara sighed as she put the book she was reading down, turning to the seat next to her, where her father slept, snoring slightly. She stared at him for a moment, feeling a sense of loss, before she gently shook him awake.

He gaped at her, bleary-eyed from lack of sleep. "Yes, luv?" he asked, his voice wavering a bit.

"Daddy, where are we going?" Clara asked as she took another look out the window, seeing nothing but white in the darkness -- was it snow?

Her dad yawned before shaking his head. "To see your grandpa, remember?" he said, closing his eyes again. "We should be there soon. Go back to your book."

This made Clara frown, but she didn't say another word as her father drifted off to sleep again. Instead she looked out the window, feeling cold.

She could hardly believe the events of the past few weeks -- the events that had seemed to change her life, and, if she wanted to be truthful, probably *had*. It had all been so easily done: the packing, the leaving, the door slamming. It hadn't taken much thought from anyone: her father, her stepmother, herself...

Clara felt her chest tighten as they started to descend.

It still made Clara sad, despite everything. She had never liked her stepmother, not even when her father had first met the woman, when Isabelle was nice. She had never wanted them to be married, even when her dad had seemed so happy, smiling like she knew he should have been. She had never wanted a new mother, even when Isabelle had promised that they would have fun, that she would take care of her. Clara had never wanted any of it.

But she had gotten it, anyway.

Her father had met Isabelle when she was thirteen, only three short years after her mother had passed. He had been at a coffee shop, grabbing a cup before work, and Clara had been at school. He hadn't seen the blonde-haired beauty as she came out of the restroom, headed straight for the door. He hadn't seen her flip her hair, trying her best to look attractive.

He hadn't seen her at all, in fact, until he was slamming right into her, spilling coffee all over her pressed pink dress...

Then he'd seen her, and he'd never looked away since.

They'd been married a few months later, tying the knot before Clara's dad left for a business trip to England, what had once been, and probably would always remain his true home. Clara had been the happiest she'd been since her mother's death at that time, though it had had nothing to do with her new mother, and everything to with her father's smiles. She'd been happy to see him happy, even though she hadn't been happy to acquire Isabelle.

But, things had been alright. They'd had family dinners and picnics and went to theme parks together. They'd smiled and laughed...until it was time for Clara's father to leave for his three month trip. Then things had changed.

Then Isabelle had turned into the monster she truly was.

But it didn't matter, not now. Not when her father and stepmother were getting a divorce, shipping her off to her grandfather's for Christmas so she didn't have to see their brutal fight back home.

Clara was jolted from her thoughts as the plane began to shake again, the seatbelt sign flickering, beneath them the plane's landing gear already in place. She turned her head to the window, looking out, trying to figure out where they were, but still all she could see was snow – though when she blinked at the snow, it appeared as if they passed through something nearly invisible, reminding Clara of a barrier of some sort, like one would see in a fantasy setting. Then, it was miraculously light, though still snowy, as if she'd just been shuttle from midnight to morning.

Clara furrowed her eyebrows at the strangeness, and shook her head, her mind reeling, but then she sighed as she grabbed her purse and shook her father awake another time, glad his seatbelt was already on as they landed somewhat roughly, and the plane came to a slow halt – she could worry about the light change later. "Daddy," her voice was quiet as her father groaned, swatting at her hand. "We're here."

That woke her father up. He shook his head as he straightened, yawning, blinking his bleary eyes. "Already?" he asked, ruffling his grey-streaked hair. "Are you bloody kidding me?"

"No," Clara said, staring at him. "You're the one who said 'we should be there soon'."

Her father looked perplexed. "Did I now?" he asked, blinking again. "I don't recall..."

Clara was about to calmly remind him when the flight attendant appeared, all smiles, just as she had been when they'd boarded. "Need help with anything, Mr. Williams?"

"No, no. We're fine, thanks," Clara's father shook his head as he stood, motioning for Clara to do the same. "Ready to go, Snowflake?" Clara nodded as she stood, shouldering her bag, smiling at the nickname.

Her father had been calling her that for years. It was no news to Clara that she had been named after a certain heroin in *The Nutcracker* ballet, so she found it rather funny, considering there were snowflakes in said ballet as well. She was sure her mother had probably called her by the same nickname, before—

Clara shut her eyes as the thought came, willing it away.

No. She told herself, her shoulders hunching as her father turned to exit the small plane, the only other passenger besides her. *Don't think about it. Not now.*

She couldn't afford to lose herself in the past, not when she was being given a new beginning, a new future. Not when she was offered the chance to finally meet her grandfather, who had always been a mystery.

"Clara, luv, are you coming?" it was her father's voice that snapped her out of her depressing thoughts, and she smiled again, looking up at him. He was waiting at the end of the plane, ready to step out into the cold. "If you are, you'd better hurry. It's cold out there, and I'd rather get inside as fast as possible," as if to reinstate his point he shivered, grimacing.

Clara nodded, following him to the exit door. "Okay, Daddy. I'm coming."

Clara took a moment to examine her father before they stepped out into the snow, the wonder of where she was still lingering in the back of her mind. He looked different than he used to look when she was a child...

Older, more seasoned, more wrinkled, tired. He was a shadow of his former self — especially now that Isabelle was producing problems with the divorce papers — but Clara still found comfort in his angled features. She still found comfort in his short, choppy hair, and his blue, misty eyes. She still found comfort in the way he walked, always rushing, always busy. She still found comfort in the way he talked, so commanding yet gentle.

As Clara looked at her father, striding ahead of her in the snow, pushing against the wind purposefully, she instantly knew why her mother had loved him.

If only I could have known her longer. Clara thought as she fought the cold behind her father, grabbing his hand when he offered it. *If only she could have told me what she saw...what she felt...what she wanted for me.*

But she couldn't. She *wouldn't*. She would never be able to.

Clara pushed that thought aside as her and her father slipped into a building, the cold and snow vanishing from around them. Her breath was momentarily stolen as she looked around at the room she was in -- a wide, high-ceilinged room, probably the end of a building, all decorated and ready for Christmas -- but her attention was stolen a moment later when she heard a voice.

"Ho, ho, ho," the voice said, loud and booming, overly cheerful. "I was wondering when you'd arrive..." Clara nearly fell over when she saw the voice's owner, who stepped into the room from a hallway, smiling at her and her father.

He was taller than her, rounder, his huge belly taking up half of his form alone. He had sparkling eyes and white hair, and a long white beard to match, which he was thoughtfully stroking. He wore a strange suit of red and white, though it was missing its jacket. In his free hand was an ornate silver goblet, which was holding a steaming liquid -- hot cocoa, from the looks of it.

In short, the man looked exactly like Santa Claus.

Clara felt her mouth drop when she saw him, but her father didn't look fazed. "We're precisely on time, Kris," he said, drawing a pocket watch from his trousers and flipping it open. "I told you we'd arrive by noon."

"Is it noon already?" the Santa-man looked confused, stroking his beard again, but then he pulled out his own pocket watch, checked it, and nodded. "Ho, ho, ho. Of course. You're right, Sebastian. Silly me!"

Clara's father sighed, putting his watch away. "Of course I'm right," he said rather curtly as the Santa-man "ho, ho, ho"ed again. "Now, Kris, if you would be so kind...I have a plane to catch..." Clara watched as the Santa-man nodded, her father turning towards her.

"Snowflake, here's your stop," he said, smiling as he hugged her. "Be a good girl, and I'll see you soon," he stopped for a moment as Clara frowned, hating the way he was talking to her, and then he laughed. "Alright, alright. I know you're a big girl, but give your daddy a break? I'm not--" he stopped before he could say it, and Clara's frown deepened.

She knew what he'd been about to say, and she knew it wasn't true. He'd been about to say "I'm not used to leaving you like this", but the truth was, he was used to leaving her. He'd been doing it for years, leaving on business trips, ever since her mother died...

But she wasn't mad at him. She still loved him. She knew it was the only way he'd been able to cope with his loss, even after he'd remarried. She knew it was the only way he felt like he was worth something -- by providing her with everything she needed.

But she also knew that it wasn't enough. It never had been, because the only thing she'd really needed was her father.

"I have a present for you, Clara," her dad cleared his throat as he opened up the briefcase he carried, pulling a square box out. "Isabelle tried to steal it, but I...well...here you are..." he cleared his throat again as he handed the package to Clara.

She took it without a thought, opening it. What was inside was the last thing she'd expected to see, but it was a welcome sight--

A small, plastic nativity scene, all one piece, hand painted with child's paint and glitter. It smiled at Clara as she looked at it, holding it in her hands, and she smiled back. Such a simple gift, but much appreciated.

"Thank you, Daddy," Clara felt tears well in her eyes as she hugged her father, balancing the plastic scene. "I'll miss you."

"Miss you, too," her father said, clearing his throat once again. "Ah, yes, Clara..." he looked suddenly nervous as he turned towards the Santa-man, who was watching them, a strange smile on his face. "Let me introduce you. This is your grandfather..." Clara felt her throat tighten. "...the one and only, abso-bloody-lutely real Father Christmas -- well, Santa Claus to you, I suppose. Welcome to the North Pole."

Chapter Three: Jack

Jack's eyes darted to every nook and cranny as he walked down the hallway, trying to memorize all of it.

He couldn't believe it. He was in Santa's workshop. Santa's *workshop*!

The "heart" of Christmas. The big circle. The toy factory. Headquarters. He was in Santa's workshop!

And he was loving every second of it.

"Hmm...door here, ten paces to the left, another door...three paces down, a closet," Jack made a mental note of everything and, feeling overwhelmed, withdrew a small pad of paper from his suit pocket, writing everything he saw down. "This is perfect. Absolutely perfect."

"What's perfect?" a voice asked from behind him, making him jump.

Jack whirled around to face the figure, annoyance written on his features. If he hadn't recognized the voice he would have been worried, since he didn't want to get caught while planning another sabotage, but since he did know the voice, he didn't worry about being worried...

Instead, he worried about what North would ask him. "Hmm?" Jack decided to play oblivious. "Whatever do you mean?"

North wasn't fooled.

"Don't play dumb," he said in his monotone voice, clapping a hand on Jack's shoulder. "You're as see-through as glass."

"Great..." Jack groaned, eyeing North as he frowned. "Just great..." He hadn't planned on letting North in on his little scheme just yet. He had wanted to wait until he began to initiate his plans before he asked North for his help, but decided to just tell his friend his plans now, to make things easier.

North had been granted access to Santa's facilities as well, and was helping map out the obese man's Christmas Eve flight, so Jack knew his company would be helpful...

That, and North was his best friend. He may have been boring and dull, but Jack was glad that at least one person was on his side.

"So, what are you planning now, Jack?" North asked expectantly as they continued down the hallway. "Are you going to blow up the sleigh? Overfeed the reindeer? Break the toy machines, perhaps?"

Jack shook his head as they walked, the hall turning from red and green doors to long, observatory windows, through which they could see the elves, working away. "No, no," he scowled. "Those things are much too obvious. What I'm planning is a lot more...*devious*," he grinned on that note, looking decidedly, well, devious.

"Really?" for once North's voice wasn't monotone -- it had something...a hint, a spark of curiosity in it. "You know, I've never really been one for mischief, but I do find it interesting. Will you 'count me in', as they say?"

Jack nodded as they stopped in front of a blue-lined glass window, past the elves now, in a more deserted part of the workshop. "Of course," he said, shaking North's hand. "Of course."

Now, if he could just initiate his plan...

He'd been thinking about it ever since that afternoon, when he'd talked to Santa. The jolly old roly-poly had been glad of St. Nick's decision to let him help, and he'd shown it, giving Jack a bright smile...and Jack had tried not to wince from the brightness, smiling back as best he could.

Santa had led him on a short tour of the main building then, grinning from ear to ear like a little toddler as he'd pointed out happy elves and toys and other things that Jack had found repulsive. And Jack had smiled through the whole thing, pretending to be taking notes about the elves performances, when he was really jotting down blueprints to use for his plot.

Last but not least, Santa had led Jack to his office -- a large, round space filled with a multitude of Christmas decorations and tins of cookies -- and told him about his job.

"*Now, Jack,*" Santa had started as they'd sat down on surprisingly comfy chairs, and a little elf girl had come shuffling into the room, carrying hot cocoa. Santa had taken it with delight, sipping the frothy drink with ease, but Jack had been a little more hesitant. He'd always liked tea best. *"I'm sure you're wondering why I spoke up for you at the meeting."*

If Jack hadn't been listening before, he'd been listening then. *"Why, yes, Santa. I was wondering that..."* he'd said, taking the cocoa before the elf girl could throw it at him.

"Ho, ho, ho," Santa had laughed, and Jack had cringed at the sound, finding it nearly impossible not to. *"As I said at the meeting, I need some extra help preparing for Christmas this year. So many boys and girls..."* Jack had tried to nod sympathetically, but he was sure he'd scowled instead. *"And this Christmas I have an extra load, which I am appointing to you..."*

Jack had hardly been able to contain himself then. He'd nearly jumped, sitting on the edge of his seat, staring at Santa like a puppy stared at his owner when he wanted to be petted. His mind had automatically jumped to conclusions, big jobs that Santa would give him.

Would he make Jack head of toy production? Reindeer watcher? Head of sleigh maintenance? Any of those jobs would make destroying Christmas easy.

The obese man was practically begging him to ruin the holiday.

Santa had seen Jack's impatience. *"Of course, of course. I'm sure you want to know what your job is...I was getting to that..."* he'd taken a long swig of cocoa then, guzzling the drink for nearly a minute, and in his impatience, Jack had wanted to drown him in it.

Finally, Santa had set the mug down and explained…

Jack was pulled back to the present by North, who slapped the side of his face just then, trying to gain a reaction from him. Jack glared at him as he pulled away, but North didn't look the slightest bit fazed.

"Are you still in there?" North asked, cocking his head ever so slightly, his navy bangs falling into his face. "Or has that devious mind of yours left you immobile?"

Jack simply rolled his eyes, walking over to the hallway's glass window, peering at the wall on the other side of it, not even looking down into the room below. "Of course I'm here," he snorted. "I was just thinking about my 'job'."

"Oh, yes. *That*," North's eyes concentrated on Jack's face as he strode over to the window, too. "What is it that Santa wanted you to do, exactly?"

Jack grimaced as he looked through the glass, not really wanting to answer. He couldn't believe the task that Santa had given him -- the task the obese man had called the "most important". Jack had been expecting something exciting, something more useful -- and something that hopefully didn't require much of his time or energy, all of which he would be putting towards destroying Christmas…

But no, Santa had surprised him, that lying cheat.

The "most important". Hardly! Jack's new job was the "most annoying" maybe, but certainly not the most important.

"*Well?*" North prodded, his eyebrows raising now, a sure sign that he was deeply interested. "What is it? It can't be that bad."

Jack wanted to hit him. "Of course it's that bad!" he snapped, turning towards a not-so-shockingly-unshocked North. "That idiot wants me to show his granddaughter around, like some stupid babysitter! I didn't even know he had a granddaughter…" Jack took in a deep breath, trying to calm down.

He supposed it wasn't so bad. After all, if he worked things right, he could use this granddaughter of Santa's to help destroy Christmas.

"Hmm," North looked thoughtful. "Granddaughter, eh? She must be Clarice's girl."

Jack raised an eyebrow at that. "Who?" he asked, somewhat interested since it concerned him.

"Santa's daughter," North explained, nodding. "She left before you arrived. Gave up her immortality to become human, got married, and had a kid, obviously. She was nice…interesting…had a good singing voice. She could have been on Broadway."

Jack's eyebrows furrowed as he stared at North in disbelief.

He could care less about Broadway, but a daughter? Santa had a *daughter*? Why had he never heard of her before?

Jack's thoughts were interrupted when the air around him was suddenly penetrated by a lovely sound — coming from the room below them, just beyond the glass window. Jack felt himself relax ever so slightly, a strange sort of smile on his face. He liked very few things, and out of those few things, music was his favorite.

But why was someone playing music now? Shouldn't the elves have been working? Maybe one of them had skipped on doing their job?

Jack grinned at that, wishing more elves would skip work.

"Music," North stated, looking into the room beyond the glass. "Grand piano. *Think of Me. Phantom of the Opera*. Nice fluidity, too..."

Jack rolled his eyes, annoyed with North and his vast expanse of knowledge. Why did humans feel the need to name things? Couldn't you just call a song *"song"*, and leave it at that?

Jack shook his head as he suddenly heard words, drifting up along with the notes of the song.

Someone was singing.

Jack saw North lean in towards the glass. "She has a lovely voice, too," he commented, and Jack rolled his eyes, looking down at the girl along with North.

The piano's back was facing them, so that they could see the girl sitting behind it, singing as she played.

She was young, but not so much "younger" than Jack himself, probably sixteen or seventeen -- though she looked younger because of the strange, white and blue ruffled dress she wore, which made her resemble a porcelain doll. Her dark brown hair was the color of chocolate, swept back from her face into two curly pigtails, furthering the doll look. Though she was as pale as a doll, there was some color to her cheeks, her doe eyes focusing on her music...

Jack took one look at her and turned away, sneering, disgusted by the girl's doll-like appearance. She should have at least *tried* to look her age.

But North didn't turn away. He kept looking at the girl, glancing at the disgusted Jack every few seconds.

Finally, he said: "Jack, how old did Santa say his granddaughter was?"

"I don't know," Jack growled grumpily, waving it off. "She's probably some snot-nosed little brat. Six, or something. Why?"

North took his arm and turned him back towards the window. *"That's* why," he said, pointing to the doll-girl.

"That can't be her," Jack grimaced again at the stupid girl, who had just finished playing, depriving him of his music.

"What was her name?"

"I don't know."

"You don't know?"

"Fine, fine. Santa said it was something..."

"Her name is *'Something'*?"

"No! It started with a C. Caroline...Christie...Kyle..."

Suddenly, the doors to the room below them opened wide, admitting one obese and laughing man...also known as Santa Claus.

"Clara!" he boomed cheerily, addressing the doll-girl, who stared at him blankly.

Jack clapped his hands together. "Yes, that's it!" he said, all grins. "Clara. The brat's name is Clara..." Jack stopped abruptly as North gave him a rare, smug smile, pointing at the glass next to them.

Jack's head turned towards it just as Clara took her grandfather's hand, walking out of the room with him. Jack groaned as he watched her leave, knowing that he would meet her face to face soon enough.

Because, the doll-girl was none other than Clara, Santa's granddaughter. The doll-girl was the one who he would be showing around the North Pole, who he would be babysitting. The doll-girl was the one who he would be stuck with for the next week, following those stupid bouncy curls of hers around.

She was going to ruin all of his devious plans--

Now, he'd have to think of new ones.

Chapter Four: Clara

Clara shivered as the cold wind hit her, her teeth chattering, her muscles sore and aching from the shivers.

She had only been in the North Pole half a day, just having had lunch, and she was already miserable. Strangely, the actual North Pole Town -- where Santa had his workshop -- wasn't as cold as it should have been. It was purposefully kept a little warmer, Santa had explained, for the elves and everyone else. But, being from Florida, Clara was freezing, since it rarely got below thirty in her home, and the Pole was much colder than that...

Enjoying your time, Clares?" Clara blinked when she heard the new nickname, looking up at Santa, her grandfather. "I suppose it's a bit chillier than you're used to, but it won't take long for you to grow accustomed to it. And don't worry, thanks to the magical barrier surrounding the town and matching area, the days change like they normally would – instead of that constant daylight and twilight between the Equinoxes, like outside the barrier. If you look extremely hard, you can see the real sky outside, but it takes a special eye," he sent her a smile as he "ho, ho, ho"ed.

Clara didn't say anything in response, though she did marvel at how easily he could mention magic. She had been wondering why the sky had become light all of a sudden, where before it had been dark – outside of whatever barrier it was that Santa was speaking of; she was glad that the days would continue to go by in twenty-four hour periods, as far as light was concerned. Clara simply followed the man's back as they walked along in the chilly snow, headed towards a bright red building, where Santa had said she'd meet her "tour guide", the person who would show her the North Pole's best sites while she was there.

Clara was still getting used to the idea that Santa Claus was her grandfather. Her father had never mentioned the man before, and she couldn't remember ever seeing him, and if Santa was her grandfather, then--

Then did that mean that her mother had been his *daughter*?

Clara had never met her father's parents, and she knew she never would, because they had passed away long ago, and her father had no siblings. She supposed that she'd thought her mother was the same, with no siblings and no parents...but obviously she'd been wrong, because here her grandfather was -- Santa Claus.

But how could this be? How could her grandfather be Santa?

I thought Santa wasn't real. Clara frowned as they finally reached the red building, Santa holding the door for her. *I thought he was just a story. How can I believe this?*

She had to have been dreaming. This couldn't have been real. She was probably still back at her house, sleeping, waiting for her father to wake her, tell her it was time to leave, time to board the plane to see her real grandfather. Yes, she *must* have been dreaming.

Clara's eyes widened as they entered the red building, and she saw her tour guide.

But, at least it was a *good* dream.

"Ah, there you are, Jack," Santa seemed pleased as he stepped into the room, which resembled a large café, Clara following behind him warily. "You're early."

The man -- or was he a teen? -- that he addressed nodded. "I'm always early," he said rather icily, casting Santa a cold glance, but then his eyes flickered, as if he'd suddenly remembered something, and he smiled. "But that's alright. I don't mind waiting," Clara could tell he was lying.

But, Santa couldn't.

"Good, good," Santa was as jolly as always as he lumbered over to take a seat near the stranger named Jack, turning to look at Clara. "Coming, Clares?" he asked, once again using the nickname he'd much-too-quickly given her, a secret sort of smile on his face.

Clara cast a weary glance at Jack, who glared at her while furiously stirring the contents of the mug he held, before she nodded at Santa. "Of course," she said, sitting beside him.

It was the moment she sat down that she finally allowed herself to get a good look at Jack, glancing at him wearily again. He didn't look at her as she scoped him out, talking frankly with Santa about something, and she was grateful for that, because he kind of scared her.

There was something fierce about this figure named Jack, even though he was obviously trying his best to look nice when Santa glanced his way.

Clara could tell that he was taller than her even though he sat in a comfy Christmas chair, back as straight as a rail. She could tell that he liked old-fashioned things because of the clothes he wore, and that he didn't mind new fashions by the way his hairstyle sat...

And, perhaps the thing that Clara noticed most was the coolness of Jack's eyes. She'd felt their chill when they'd landed on her, like she'd stepped back outside.

That's almost...frightening. Clara thought as she fidgeted in her seat. *That man, he's almost—*

"Clares!" Clara jumped when she heard Santa's voice, Jack's eyes sliding to her, making her shiver. "I'm sorry. I haven't properly introduced you," he laughed, "ho, ho, ho"ing like there was nothing wrong.

"This," he finally said, motioning towards the figure whom he'd dubbed Jack, who was now drinking whatever he had in that mug of his, still staring at Clara coolly, "is Jack Frost. You know, the one who makes those nice patterns on windows," Clara almost wanted to laugh then as Jack cast the unknowing Santa a glare, obviously insulted. "He's going to be your tour guide, show you around town."

Clara felt her chest constrict as Jack looked away from Santa, his frosty eyes connecting with her stare.

She couldn't believe it. Her dream had turned from nice to naughty, happy to mildly scary, and this was only the beginning.

If only she could wake up. If only she could move on with her life, get back to reality. If only--

But, Clara knew she could do none of those things. Reality had ended for her the day her mother had died. It had shattered, her world had, and no matter how much she searched, she would never be able to pick up all of the pieces, put it back together again...

And maybe it wouldn't be so bad. Her tour guide, Jack, he looked kind of scary and cold, but maybe he would turn out to be alright, and maybe they could become friends. Clara was going to try her best to make that happen.

Because, even if her mother was dead, and her life was in shambles, she still refused to give up on *Hope*. It was all she had left.

Clara pulled a smile to life, like a magician pulls a rabbit out of a hat, beaming at Jack as she spoke. "It's a pleasure to meet you," she said, hoping it was true. "As I'm sure you've guessed, I'm Clara Williams, but," she glanced at Santa, "here I'm Claus, I guess. Clara Claus," the name felt strange rolling off her tongue, but right at the same time.

"Clara?" Jack laughed in a stiff way as he sat his mug on the table next to him, a Cheshire Cat grin spreading across his lips. "Oh, no. The pleasure's all mine, Miss Clara. *Believe* me."

And Clara did believe him. Because, as he smiled broadly at her, she could see Jack's thoughts behind his eyes; they were turning, turning, turning, moving like the gears of a clock…

Chapter Five: Jack

Jack sighed into the tea mug he held as he waited for North to arrive, mind still swimming over the meet-and-greet he'd had with Santa and the doll-girl that afternoon. He was more than glad to be rid of the annoying pair for the day.

Jack sighed again as the door opened, and in walked North, as unfeeling and uncharacteristic as ever.

Now he would have to prepare for tomorrow, the first of his five days of showing the doll-girl around.

How *fun*.

"So, have you come up with a plan yet?" North wasted no words, sitting across from Jack, folding his hands in his lap as he studied his friend's face. "Or are you still brooding over it?"

Jack ignored the stab at his pride and shook his head. "I'm still *thinking* about it," he said in a gravelly tone, glaring at the floor. "There has to be some way..."

He had to be able to use the doll-girl -- Clara -- for his own purpose of destroying Christmas. The question was: how? She wasn't a little six-year-old brat like he'd thought -- she was older, wiser, and less impressionable. She wasn't going to do whatever he said -- not without asking questions, anyway. He wouldn't be able to steer her against her grandfather as he'd planned...

Or, would he?

Jack's eyes lit as he looked up at North, who was staring at him with raised eyebrows, expecting something. A slow smile spread across his face as he got an idea -- a wonderfully horrible, utterly atrocious, evilly luscious idea.

"Of course," Jack breathed, wondering why he hadn't thought of it sooner. "My old plan still applies! I can still turn her against Santa!"

North's eyebrows returned to their normal, unfeeling state. "And how is that?" he asked in monotone, cocking his head ever so slightly.

"It's very simple, really," Jack felt his evil grin widen as North stared at him blankly, attention focused on Jack's plan. "The doll-girl--"

"--Clara," North corrected. "Her name is *Clara*."

Jack waved a hand. "Whatever!" he snapped. "The point is that I can still use that stupid girl to destroy Christmas. As I said, my original idea was to turn her against Santa. I had planned on accomplishing that by playing the role of 'nice babysitter'," Jack grimaced when he said the word "nice", shivering as if he'd just been hit with the world's largest snowball. "However, since the doll-girl--"

"--Clara," North corrected again.

Jack glared at him this time, grabbing a pillow from the nearby couch and throwing it at his head. "Whatever!" he repeated. "The point is--"

"--Are you almost finished?" North interrupted yet again, checking his icy blue watch. "Because I have an appointment with Santa in a few hours -- you know, about that whole 'mapping out Santa's flight' thing -- and I wanted to acquire some dinner beforehand, maybe attend a movie--"

Jack tried not to strangle North. "Alright, alright!" he snapped, sitting back in his chair, sighing as he rubbed his temples. "The point is, as I was saying, that since Clara -- " he cringed as he said her name, liking her even less. " -- isn't six, and isn't stupid -- at least, I assume she's not stupid. I could very well be wrong, judging by that ridiculous dress she had on -- she's not going to fall for the 'nice babysitter' act. However..." he trailed off purposefully, grinning at North, trying to make him guess.

"However?" North yawned, looking almost uninterested. "Don't try that 'hook, line, and sinker' with me, Jack. It doesn't work."

Jack glared at North again as his friend yawned another time, knowing he was purposefully being a pain.

North loved to do that -- make you think he wasn't interested in something when he was -- and it annoyed Jack to no end. But, North had always been that way, ever since Jack had met him, all those years ago...

They'd met at Jack's first Winter Council meeting, sitting next to one another without even thinking about it. They'd both been relatively new to the North Pole, and they'd both been a little nervous, as well as excited, since they'd both longed to map out the place, though for different reasons (of course, they hadn't been able to, because they'd been given a guided tour after the meeting. Santa always gave them one, after every meeting. That was how they knew the North Pole so well.)

The topic that day had been *"Global Warming"*, which both Jack and North hadn't been the least interested in, since Jack didn't give a hoot, and North already knew everything there was no know about it. They'd resorted to sleeping through the meeting, and, with a sharp glare from St. Nick, had been sent to "North Pole Community Service" as punishment.

Needless to say, this had furthered Jack's detestation of Christmas, not to mention reindeers (since they'd had to clean the reindeer stalls, much to Randoy's amusement). But it had fueled his friendship with North, the most interesting uninterested person he'd ever met...

Jack was drawn back to the present as North threw a pillow at his head, hitting his target dead on.

"You really have to stop that 'zoning out' pastime," North shook his head as Jack glared again. "It can't be healthy."

Jack threw the pillow back. "I was *thinking*!" he said, glaring at North again. "Is that so bad..." he saw North's mouth open again.

North could be so annoying.

"Never mind," Jack grimaced, sitting back in his chair. "The point is, I can still turn that doll-girl -- I know her name's Clara, and I don't care -- against Santa. Not because she's young and naïve," a grin crossed his face, one that could be labeled dastardly, "but because she doesn't trust Santa. She doesn't even *know* him."

Since learning that afternoon that it was the doll-girl who he was going to be chauffeuring around the North Pole, Jack had snuck into Santa's office, looking for a file on the obese man's only grandchild. He'd found the file tucked away, safe and sound.

He hadn't been able to cover all of the large file, but he'd learned the basics about the doll-girl, and that had told him enough.

1.) Clara had lost her mother (Santa's Christmas-loving daughter) at a young age.

2.) Her father had remarried only a short amount of time after.

3.) Her father was always away on business trips, leaving her with her stepmother.

4.) Her stepmother was not the nicest of people (after all, Jack had learned, she'd refused to let Clara see her grandfather, even when Clara's father had explained to her about Santa Claus, and she'd met the obese man.)

5.) Clara's father and evil sounding stepmother were now going through a divorce, which is why she was at the North Pole.

These key points may have not seemed like much to others, but for Jack, who had always prided himself in his ability to read people, it seemed like a lot. And, from what he'd seen of Santa's granddaughter, it was a lot.

He almost felt bad for the girl, even though he knew he shouldn't have. She'd lost her mother at age seven, and she probably didn't even remember the woman that well, considering how she'd died; Clara had to have been in shock, and may have repressed some things. Then she'd acquired a new mother who was a beast, being "left" by her father, who was always away at work. It was a wonder she trusted or cared for anyone. No one had given her a reason to trust...

Which was just what Jack was counting on.

A small, single part of him was beating against his plan, telling him it was wrong, but for the most part he didn't care. He needed to destroy Christmas, if it was the last thing he did, and Clara would be the perfect fire to light the rockets of Christmas' demise.

After all, the girl had been abandoned and mistreated by everyone she knew, why would she trust Santa Claus, a grandfather who she had never even met, never even known? Yes, Jack was sure that she'd heard the stories about Santa -- but stories and reality were two different things. If he could convince her that Santa was bad -- not the perfect grandfather she had always wanted -- then Santa would break down because of it. He would lose it if his granddaughter started to hate him...

Yes, it was a perfect plan, but...Jack still felt that grading feeling, that feeling that was telling him: *"No, let's think of another way. We can't do this. It isn't right."*

But Jack refused to listen to that feeling. Even if -- even though -- he felt sorry for the doll-girl Clara, he couldn't allow himself to get attached to her.

It was bad enough that he was attached to North, his best and only friend.

Jack shook his head, trying to clear it.

He had promised that he would never get attached to anyone ever again -- and he intended to keep that promise, even if it meant shattering a young girl's dreams, clutching them until they broke.

Chapter Six: Clara

Clara sighed as she stepped into the cold, shivering for what was probably the billionth time. Her first day (well, technically her second) in the North Pole, and already she was wondering what she was doing there...

Clara shook her head as she tried to focus on what the day would bring. She had slept in late that morning, not used to the time change between her home and the North Pole, and had woken up well into late afternoon. Mrs. Claus had been there when she'd woken, smiling at Clara as she'd offered her an early dinner, before bustling off to help Santa, who'd been at the toy factory, overseeing preparations for the "big day".

Clara felt suddenly stiff as she looked up to see Jack, who was waiting for her, leaning against a lamppost, looking dejected.

She would have to spend the whole evening with her "tour guide", Jack Frost.

Clara willed herself to speak as she stopped in front of him, feeling suddenly nervous. "H-Hello," she managed, shrinking back as he glared at her.

"You're late," Jack said gruffly, not wasting any words, and then: "Where would you like to go first?" his cool eyes regarded her as she bit her lip. "What do you want to see?"

Clara blinked at him, surprised (and a little miffed that he hadn't had the decency to even say hello). "Well..." she debated.

Truthfully, she didn't know where she wanted to go. The North Pole was so much bigger than she had anticipated. She'd always thought it was rather small, like in the Christmas movies, housing nothing but Santa's toy shop and maybe a few cafés and apartments for the elves, but she had been wrong.

The North Pole Town -- located in the middle of the Pole itself -- was huge, holding a shopping mall, town-homes, bookstores, and even a movie theater -- not to mention the local museum -- so she didn't know where to start. After all, it wasn't like she'd been able to plan her trip or anything. She hadn't even known she was coming to the North Pole. She hadn't known *anything*.

Besides, as her "tour guide", shouldn't Jack have been planning the schedule? Clara glanced at Jack, who was still waiting -- impatiently -- for her to answer. She didn't know why Santa had picked him, of all people, to be her "tour guide". He didn't look the least bit interested in showing her around, and all he'd done so far was grimace.

Maybe Santa hadn't been able to find anyone else? Maybe Jack really had wanted to do the job, and was just having a bad day? Maybe--

Maybe Santa didn't care if she enjoyed her time in the North Pole. Maybe he was too busy, and it didn't really matter.

Clara felt her heart sink at that thought, her shoulders hunching. Even though she didn't know him very well, and even though she had never seen him before, she wanted to like Santa, her grandfather. She wanted to be close to him, and have him care about her. After all, he was the only living thing (other than Mrs. Claus and her father) that she had left to connect her to her mother. If she were to lose him, she would be left with nothing. She would be truly alone--

And that wasn't something she wanted.

Maybe she just hadn't given Santa enough time. He'd been nice enough to her so far -- letting her stay in the North Pole right before Christmas, opening up his home, finding a "tour guide" for her (even if he was kind of frightening). Maybe he was just as afraid that she might not like him, as she was that he might not like her. He had to have been a good guy, a good grandfather -- he was *Santa Claus*, after all!

"Fine!" Clara was pulled from her reverie by Jack's harsh snippy tone, Jack standing to his full height as he turned away from the lamppost. "Since you're not making a decision, and I'm tired of waiting, we'll go see a film," he crossed his arms over his chest as he glared at her icily, Clara feeling like she was being stabbed with a frozen stake. "I'm bored, and it's cold," he glared at the air around him as he said the word "cold", growling like he was facing some unseen enemy.

Clara glanced at the air before her eyebrows rose. "But you're Jack Frost," she said, and Jack rolled his eyes. "Aren't you supposed to like the cold?"

"I do like the cold!" Clara flinched as Jack turned his icy eyes back to her, glaring again. "I like the cold a lot. But this cold," he glared at the air again. "*this* cold I hate. This is the cold that only comes around once a year -- around *Christmas*," his lip curled in disgust as he said "Christmas", but before Clara could ask him about it, he started to walk off, turning towards the town.

Clara gaped at him in shock before she started to run after him, a frown playing on her lips.

Why was he being so mean? Couldn't he have waited? Was she really that much of a pain?

And what had he meant by *"the cold that only comes around Christmas"*? Did he not like Christmas?

Clara almost wanted to laugh when she thought that, finally catching up with Jack, who didn't even glance at her, hands in pockets, looking bored once again.

How silly! Jack couldn't have hated Christmas! He was part of it, after all. And not only that, but he was working -- or was it *with*? -- Santa, and she didn't think that Santa would trust anyone who didn't like Christmas, especially with the Holiday right around the corner.

But, still. Clara felt herself frown again as they neared the movie theater, a long, red and green building with flashing lights. *That doesn't explain why he's so...cold.*

Yes, *cold* was a good word. It suited Jack perfectly. Clara could tell that, even though she'd just met him.

Yes, there was something cold about Jack Frost, and Clara had a feeling that it wasn't just because of his occupation. There was something else -- something in his persona, his very being -- that was cold. Colder than the ice around them, colder than the North Pole. It was almost as if--

Clara's breath caught in her throat as they finally reached the movie theater, and Jack stopped, turning to glare at her again.

It was almost as if he had undergone some horrible tragedy, and his heart had frozen over because of it.

But what could have happened to make that a reality? What could have happened to make Jack so cold -- on the inside and out? What could have been that horrible?

Clara shook her head, deciding not to think about it anymore. She really shouldn't have been making such assumptions.

She barely knew anything about Jack Frost. How could she judge him when she had just met him?

No, it was probably nothing. He was probably just having a bad day, or a bad week, or a bad month. He was just grumpy because it was almost Christmas, and he was being taken away from his job to play "tour guide" for her. He was just miffed.

Probably.

"I'll pick the movie," Jack said, bringing Clara from her thoughts, not even bothering to ask what she wanted to see. "Since this is the North Pole, Santa doesn't allow those horror flicks, but we should be able to find something worthwhile," he grimaced again. "Hopefully."

Clara barely heard the end of his sentence, however, because just then she felt something land on her face -- something wet and cold and...beautiful.

"*Snow*," Clara breathed, turning her face towards the sky. "It's snowing." Jack turned back towards her with another frown, obviously unimpressed. "So it is," he said. "It tends to happen around here -- shocking, I know," he laughed to himself, probably expecting Clara to glare at him, but she didn't turn her eyes away from the sky. This annoyed Jack, and he grimaced again. "Yes, yes, it's very interesting! What are you, five years old? Come on, let's *go!*"

But, Clara didn't budge. She continued to stare into the sky, eyes transfixed. She had never seen snow before.

Well, not like this, anyway.

She had seen snow the day before, of course, when she'd arrived in the North Pole, but it hadn't been a gentle, calm snow. It had been a snowstorm. And she had barely been able to glance at it, anyway. She'd been too busy following her father to go meet her grandfather, Santa. And later, when it had been snowing again, she'd been too busy following Santa, to meet her "tour guide", Jack Frost.

So, really, she had never *experienced* snow before--

But she was experiencing it now.

Clara smiled even wider as she tilted her head back some more, flake after flake of the icy snow landing on her face, her jacket, on her curls. She reached her hand out to catch it as it floated, curling her fingers when it landed in her gloved hand, wishing she could keep it.

Snow. She was really seeing snow.

Finally.

I made it, mama. Clara thought as another flake of white landed on her cheek, and she tried not to cry, an overwhelming sadness overcoming her. *I made it to see snow.*

The memories came flooding back as Clara stood there, in front of the movie theater, in the North Pole, oblivious to everything but the falling white around her. They were precious memories -- so precious -- kept for years without fading. They were few memories, old and worn from many times of remembering, but they were still fresh in Clara's mind.

Her mother.

Her mother, she had been tall, tall and thin and perfect, with blue eyes and blonde hair that curled in ringlets just like Clara's. She had had a smile, a perfect smile, one that always eluded Clara's memories -- there, but fuzzy, as if it had been blotted out. She had had a laugh, a laugh that had been more familiar than the singing of the birds, more beautiful than the loveliest violin playing.

Her mother.

"*Promise me something?*" The words rang through Clara's head as she gazed up at the snow, feeling something long and warm on her cheek, something just as wet as the snow.

"*Of course.*" She wanted to reply. "*Of course.*"

But she couldn't reply, because the voice was only a memory.

"*One day, when you're older, and you finally find your place in the world...leave this state and find some snow, and watch it. Watch it until you can't watch it anymore.*"

"I'm watching," Clara whispered as the last flake landed on her face, melting, and she was pulled back to reality, a harsh gust of wind blowing through the air.

It wasn't until she looked down that she realized she'd been crying. It wasn't until she looked down that she realized it was late, the sun starting to set already. It wasn't until she looked down that she saw Jack staring at her, standing in front of the door to the theater, hands in coat pockets, wind ruffling his strange white hair.

It was then that Clara realized something -- realized just what it was about Jack that made her so uneasy--

It was those eyes of his -- those blue, icy eyes, which were both penetrating and distant, looking at her in the most strange way, as if they were...confused, sad -- *something*! It was those eyes of his that stared at her, holding her there, trapping her in an icy chain.

It was those eyes of his that scared Clara to the very core -- chilling, and yet so enticing.

Chapter Seven: Jack

Jack paced back and forth along his room, trying to sort things out in his mind.

He just didn't understand! It didn't make sense! Why had Clara cried when she'd seen the snow? It wasn't that beautiful! And why had he suddenly stared at her like that, the urge to rush into the movie theater gone?

Did he feel *sorry* for her? Maybe, though he didn't know why. Had he thought that she would break down and tell him why she'd been crying? Maybe, but she hadn't, not even when he'd asked her about it. Had he just been so transfixed by her fascination with the snow that he hadn't been able to leave, let alone stop staring at the doll-girl? Well...

Jack stopped in his tracks as North entered, a mug of tea in his hand.

Yes. As much as Jack hated to admit it, the answer was yes -- he *had* been transfixed by Clara's adoration of snow.

Jack had never thought of snow as anything great. It was cold, it was wet, and it fell from the sky. So what? Who cared? Certainly not Jack.

It wasn't *his* area of expertise, after all. He was Jack *Frost*, not Jack *Snow*. All he cared about was, as Santa so lovingly put it: *"those nice little patterns on windows"*. He could have cared less about the white stuff that fell from the sky. Why, frost and snow weren't even the same thing, and though they were similar, Jack preferred the frost...it was easier to handle. Snow was harder -- all those little snowflakes, each cut in different designs. Such a bother!

But, Clara -- Clara was something else. When she had seen the white, wet stuff, she'd lit up like a Christmas tree, and even though Jack hated Christmas trees, he'd been strangely enthralled by the way she'd lit up.

Though he didn't understand it.

What's so great about snow? Jack thought furiously as he paced some more, ignoring North as his friend sat down on a chair, sipping his tea daintily. *All it does is fall, and melt, and block driveways, and -- what's so great about snow?*

And not only that, but why had the snow turned from wonder to horror for Clara? Why had she been smiling one moment and crying the next? Why had what she'd deemed as beautiful a moment before suddenly turned to ash in her hands?

Jack just didn't understand it. It didn't make sense!

But, oh well. He couldn't think about it now. So what if the stupid doll-girl had cried over the snow? So what if she'd been upset? What did he care? She was just a pawn to him, anyway -- a tool in his diabolical Christmas-destroying plan. Why should he care what happened to her? Why should he care what she felt?

Why should he care?

Jack shook his head as he thought this, still pacing, not liking where his thoughts were going. Truthfully, he *shouldn't* have cared about Clara at all. Truthfully, he should have just dragged her into the movie theater, tearing her away from the snow. Truthfully, he shouldn't have gazed at her at all while she was watching the snowflakes, transfixed as he had been.

But.

He hadn't done any of the things he was supposed to have done, and now he was paying for it. Now he was curious about Clara. Now he *did* care, if only a tiny bit...

I have to stop that before it starts. Jack scolded himself, turning towards North, who was waiting patiently, a rare, bemused smile on his otherwise uncaring face. *From now on, I'll treat that girl like the pawn that she is.*

He would get his revenge. He would destroy Christmas. Even if it was the last thing he did.

"So?" North finally spoke, his voice monotone as always, and Jack shook his head, clearing away his thoughts. "How did it go? Have you professed your love to poor Clara yet?"

Jack stopped in his tracks when he heard that, glaring at North.

Even though he knew his friend was joking, he couldn't stop a burning blush from spreading across his cheeks. "Of course not!" he snapped, glaring at North harder. "Why would I do that?"

"I don't know," one of North's eyebrows rose at Jack's answer, and he looked slightly shocked, which was big for him. "Why *would* you?"

Jack forced himself to calm down, sitting in a chair across from North, taking in a deep breath. "I wouldn't," he concluded, crossing his arms. "Now, why don't you ask me a useful question?"

"I already did," North replied, face returning to its normal unfeeling state. "I believe I asked you *'how did it go?'* first. You just didn't hear because you were so busy blushing over the other question."

Jack's face lit up with red again. "I wasn't blushing!" he countered, though he knew it was a total lie.

"Yes, you were," North knew it was a lie, too. "You were blushing madly, just like you're doing now."

Jack wished he had a pillow or something to hide behind at that moment, but, seeing as he didn't, he simply glared at North again before looking away, not wanting to discuss the matter any further.

He knew North was only poking fun at him, hoping to get a reaction, but he also knew that his friend had no idea what was going through his head, what he was struggling with at the moment -- and Jack certainly couldn't tell him. He knew North would understand -- in fact, he'd probably stop poking fun and help

Jack assess the...*situation* -- but that didn't mean that he wanted to tell him.

Jack had never had this sort of problem before. He'd always known what he'd wanted and gone for it. Nothing had ever gotten in the way. Even when...

Jack shut his eyes tight before he could think of it -- think of the memories he had locked away, deep inside of himself, never to see the light again. He couldn't afford to lose his head now. Not when he was so close.

He had a promise to keep. He couldn't back down. It was a moment before Jack could think clearly, but when he could he looked up at North, who was once again waiting patiently. "It went fine, if you must know," he said in an agitated voice, referring to his first day of playing tour guide.

"She showed up late and had no idea what it was that she wanted to see. I don't know why she didn't just pick something. It's not that big of a town. She could have spun in a circle and pointed to a random building, but -- " Jack stopped himself, knowing he was ranting. "But anyway, it went fine, as I said. We were going to go see a film, but she got...distracted"

"Distracted?" he should have known North, of all people, would pick up on the waver in his voice when he said that one word. "Distracted by *what*, exactly?"

Jack glared at him again. "I don't know!" he snapped, shoulders hunching. "She just got distracted. She looked up, and it was snowing, and..." he trailed off, the events of earlier playing in his mind.

How many times, he wondered, would he see Clara's smiling face turn to tears before the night was over?

Chapter Eight: Clara

Clara sat on the couch in Santa's living room, staring straight ahead at nothing, not even hearing the tolling clock above her chime.

She had been sitting there for about an hour now -- amidst the decorative Christmas figures and Christmas tree, and all the other things that made Santa's living room feel like, well, Christmas. Ever since coming home that day -- after practically running away from the movie theater -- Clara's mind had been in nothing but jumbles.

Cry. He'd seen her *cry*! Jack Frost had seen her cry...in front of a movie theater...over *snow*.

Clara buried her head in a pillow, groaning at the embarrassment. She couldn't believe she'd been so stupid! She should have known that the sight of snow would remind her of her mother, and that the memories of her mother would make her cry.

She should have ignored the snow as soon as she'd seen it, not looking up, not staring at it, not catching it in her hand. She should have just gone into the theater, following the bossy Jack. She should have been smarter.

But, she hadn't been, and she couldn't take it back.

She would just have to live with the fact that Jack, an almost stranger, had seen her crying over snow. She would just have to forgive herself for being so foolish. She would just have to ignore him if he asked about it. She would just have to forget about it -- forget about the snow, about the tears, about her mother.

No. Clara thought, clutching the pillow she held tighter. *I can't forget about her. Not ever.*

Even though she could barely remember her mother, she could never forget her. Clara's mother was as much a part of her as her hair was, as her voice was, as her father was, as--

"Santa," Clara breathed the word as she jumped, the door that led to the kitchen opening, admitting a humming and smiling Mrs. Claus.

Yes, Clara's mother -- and Clara's memories of her -- were as much a part of her as Santa now was.

"Hello, dear," Mrs. Claus greeted, smiling even wider as she sat down next to Clara on the couch, offering her a plate. "Would you care for some cookies? They're chocolate chip. I had to make a fresh batch just now -- you know how Santa loves his sweets," she chuckled at that, and Clara gingerly took a cookie, smiling as well.

Even though she didn't know her very well, Clara rather liked Mrs. Claus.

"Yes, I know," Clara replied after a moment, savoring the cookie's taste as she bit into it, and it all but melted in her mouth, hot, warm, and decadent. "Every time I've seen him he's been drinking cocoa..." she drifted off as her smile warmed, and she took another bite.

He's just like Daddy. She thought, a sigh escaping her lips. *He loves cocoa, too.*

It almost made her laugh, thinking about it. Even though they were polar opposites, Santa and her father were very much alike in some aspects -- especially when it came to sweets. Clara remembered how, on the days her father had been home, he would beg Isabelle to make him one of her famous sweets, and, when she did, would eat nearly all of them at once, barely saving a crumb for Clara -- let alone Isabelle, who would always frown at his appetite.

Over the years, the baking and making of sweets had passed from Isabelle (who was tired of never seeing -- or tasting -- the fruits of her labor) to Clara, who had been more than delighted to make her father whatever sweet he desired when he came home -- as long as he came home.

Clara shook her head, coming back to the present, feeling a pang in her chest as she thought about her father, who, at the moment, was probably in a courthouse back in Florida, fighting it out with her stepmother.

Clara was sure that Isabelle would want everything -- the house, the car, the pool, the dog -- but she honestly hoped that her father could manage to hold onto what had once been "theirs". She would hate to see everything fall into the hands of Isabelle and her new boyfriend, Frank.

Clara shook her head again as she pictured Frank, the tall, thin, oily man her stepmother had been seeing for half a year now, cheating on her father for all that it was worth. She hated the man and the way he smiled, looking like a snake with lips. What Isabelle saw in him, she didn't know, but then again, she didn't care much either, since she had never liked Isabelle.

I should call Daddy tomorrow. Clara thought then, pushing the image of Frank from her mind as she ate the last bits of her cookie. *To see how things are.*

Maybe the "negotiations" would end early, and he would be able to come to the North Pole for Christmas, finally getting to spend some time with her.

Clara sincerely hoped so, because Christmas was her favorite day of the year -- just as it had been her mother's.

"So, Clares, how did it go?" Clara was shocked from her thoughts by none other than Santa, who entered the living room just then, looking as bright and merry as ever.

Clara had to blink a few times before she could see him clearly; she was feeling tired all of a sudden. "How did what go?" she asked, confused as to what he meant.

"Your first day in the North Pole, of course," Santa laughed merrily at this, and Mrs. Claus joined in, and to Clara the two sounded like a collection of bells, synchronized perfectly.

But she wasn't offended. She knew they weren't laughing at her. She knew they weren't making fun. They were just merry people.

How lucky.

Clara felt her face flush slightly when she answered. "Um...it went..." she was having a hard time finding the right word. "...fine."

Truth be told, she wasn't sure if "fine" was a good word to describe her day with Jack Frost, but it was the best she could come up with at the moment. She was still having a hard time deciding what exactly she thought about their day together.

"Just *fine*?" Santa asked as he stopped laughing, stealing a cookie from Mrs. Claus' plate, earning a sly sort of grin from his wife. "Really? Well, I suppose that's good," he "ho, ho, ho"ed as he bit into his cookie, smiling at Clara. "So, what do you think of Jack? Isn't he an interesting fellow?" Clara felt her cheeks redden as she thought of Jack, her "tour guide", and she looked down, not quite sure what to say once again.

"Interesting" wasn't exactly the first word that came to her mind when she thought of Jack Frost. "Cold" was a good word, maybe, but not "interesting".

It wasn't the description of Jack that bothered her, however, it was something much, much more complicated than that.

Clara had felt scared of Jack when they'd first met -- mostly due to his cold eyes and glaring looks -- but now, now she didn't know what to think of him. She'd felt strange when he'd stared at her earlier, and she still felt strange, blushing now, though it wasn't for the reason most people would have thought.

It wasn't like Clara *liked* Jack -- she'd only just met him, after all. Her life wasn't one of those romantic comedies where boy meets girl, and girl suddenly likes boy, and gets jumpy when she's around him or thinks of him. No, this was something different. Something much more personal--

He'd seen her *cry.*

It may not have seemed like a big deal to an outsider, but to Clara, it was a big deal. Jack had seen her cry, and no one had ever seen her cry before. Not her father, not her stepmother...no one. No one had seen her cry but Jack, an almost complete stranger, who seemed to hate her for reasons unknown.

He'd seen a side of her that she showed to no one, a side that she didn't visit until she was alone in her room. He'd seen a side of her that she disliked, that she wasn't proud of. He'd seen a side of her that was weak and vulnerable and altogether falling apart. He'd seen a side of her that no one saw, that no one knew about...

He'd seen the most secret side of her, and she barely even knew him.

And now they shared a connection, whether they wanted to or not, and Clara wasn't sure what she thought of that. She wasn't sure she wanted any kind of connection with Jack -- the cold, cynical, rude maker of frost -- let alone a connection as deep as that.

And what about Jack? What did he think of what he'd seen? She knew he wanted to know why. He was curious.

Clara felt her shoulders hunch as she fought the strange new feeling inside of her.

If she were to tell him the truth, would he understand? Would he laugh at her? Would he make jokes? Would he use the information for some evil purpose? Or...would he be interested and understand? Would he be able to relate? Would he feel sorry for her?

Clara wasn't sure, but she knew that she didn't believe that Jack was a horrible person. She *couldn't* believe that. He may have been hard and cynical, but she had seen something in his eyes -- something horribly sad -- that told her he wasn't as unfeeling as he appeared to be.

That sadness in his eyes had told her that he had a heart, even if it was frozen at the moment.

"Clara," when Santa's voice broke through her thoughts, it was soft, sounding strange compared to normal, and Clara had to wonder if she reminded him of her mother, his daughter.

She'd never thought of that, but it must have been true. She knew she looked a lot like her mom had.

When Clara blinked and turned towards Santa and Mrs. Claus, she noticed that their smiles were sad, and that they were looking at her with empathy in their eyes. It was a strange sight, compared to their normal jolly, merry demeanors, but Clara was almost glad to see it, though she didn't know why.

She'd been thinking so hard about Jack, she had almost forgotten they were there, but now their presence was comforting, wrapping around her like a soft, old blanket. And for the first time since she'd arrived at the North Pole, they almost felt like family.

Almost.

"I know how hard this must be for you, coming here," Santa started, sighing as he sat down next to his wife, who took his hand. "But, we want you to know that we're here for you if you need anything, and that," Santa cleared his throat as he laughed merrily, smiling his jolly smile, "and that we love you, Clara."

Clara felt another blush escape as she looked up at her grandparents, her heart feeling warmer. "T-Thank you," she managed to spit out, feeling overwhelmed by both their kindness, and the thoughts that still lingered at the back of her mind.

It had been so long since she'd heard a sincere *"I love you"* from anyone. Sure, her father had said it when he'd left, and she knew that he'd meant it, but it had been short and brief, and his voice hadn't been very bright -- not like Santa's.

Maybe Santa wasn't so bad, after all. Maybe she just needed to give him more time. After all, she'd only been in the North Pole for a short time. They were still getting used to one another.

Clara still wanted to believe in him. She had always wanted to believe in him.

"Oh, that reminds me," Santa "ho, ho, ho"ed again as Mrs. Claus stood, making her way to the kitchen for some more cookies. "I have something for you, Clara. An early Christmas present."

The mention of Christmas made Clara's heart leap. Strangely, even though she was surrounded by toys, and colors, and by Christmas trees, it didn't quite feel like Christmas yet.

Maybe it was the absence of her father, who had always been home for Christmas, even if he were a little late.

We still have a few days. Clara reminded herself, not wanting to give up on a perfect Christmas just yet. *Maybe he'll be able to make it...*

And even if he couldn't, she had a new family now -- the best family in the world to spend Christmas with. She would make sure she enjoyed it. After all, Christmas was a gift.

The *greatest* gift.

"Um..." Clara cleared her throat. Speaking of gifts. "You didn't have to get me anything."

She had just met her grandfather. She felt bad that he'd gotten her a Christmas gift -- and so early, too.

But, then again, he was Santa Claus.

Santa chuckled loudly. "Why, of course I did! I'm Santa Claus, after all," he said, practically reading her thoughts. "Plus, with everything going on, I figured you could use some good cheering up," he chuckled merrily again as he waddled over to a cabinet near the couch and drew a thick, rectangular package from one of its drawers. He handed it to Clara with a warm smile. "Go ahead," he said. "Open it."

"Alright..." Clara did as she was told, ripping into the reindeer paper gently, staring at what the wrapping revealed. "Oh," she was nearly lost for words. "Thank you."

What sat in her now paperless hands was a thick, leather journal. It was indigo in color, and had a light blue snowflake imprinted on it, sitting in the middle, tilted at an angle. All around the large snowflake there were small flakes, scattered across the cover like birds, all different colors. Clara smiled as she opened the journal up, untying the woven ribbon that held it together, staring at the snowflakes printed on the paper inside.

How had her grandfather known she liked snowflakes so much?

Oh, of course. He was Santa. She kept forgetting.

"Well?" Santa leaned towards her a little, anticipation written all over his face. "Do you like it, Clares?"

Clara looked up from the journal and nodded, smiling as best she could. "Yes," she answered truthfully. "Yes." It had been a long time since she'd had a journal to write her thoughts in.

At first, Isabelle had been fine with things like that, but after she'd been married to Clara's dad for a little while, she'd changed her mind, not allowing Clara any time or space to write.

"Thinking too much is bad for the young child," she'd said, hiding all of Clara's writing utensils. *"If you need to know anything, I'll tell you."*

Clara had spent a long time listening to those words, but now...she was starting new. She was getting a new chance at life, a chance to live without Isabelle and her rules...a chance to finally be herself, to finally grow. And she intended to take that chance, even if it was hard.

She wanted to grow. She wanted to learn. She wanted to become her own person, feel her own things.

She was tired of living someone else's life.

"I find journals to be one of man's best inventions," Santa mused as Clara blinked away her thoughts, running a hand over the cover of her new journal, smiling at every bump and bend. "It allows thoughts and feelings and truths to flow. It's the best way to discover yourself," he smiled a knowing smile as Clara looked up at him, mouth falling open, surprised he knew just what she'd been thinking again. "After all, out of the pen flows the words, and out of the words flows the heart."

That phrase continued to ring through Clara's mind as she got ready for bed that night, saying goodnight to her grandparents before making her way to the room they'd provided for her -- a small, cozy, blue room.

In fact, it rang through her head so much that, just as she was about to climb under her covers for the night, Clara picked up the journal she'd been given, opened it up, and started writing.

Her first entry was simple, small, and incomplete:

About Jack Frost...

Chapter Nine: Jack

Jack was waiting at the lamppost again the next day, staring into the dreary, snowing sky...dreading the moment he would see Clara.

North had drilled him on the events of the previous day the night before, wanting to know every detail, every account. It had exhausted Jack to even begin to talk about what had happened, and had put him into an extremely bad mood -- and not just because he felt odd when thinking of the annoying doll-girl.

There was something else. There was something about Clara that intrigued him. Something that made her stick to his mind.

Was it because he had seen her so upset, seen her *cry*? Maybe, but Jack kind of doubted it. He'd been bewildered by the crying, which had come so suddenly, but that wasn't what had interested him the most about seeing Clara and the snow. No, it had been her *smile* that had interested him.

It was that soft, tranquil, lit-up smile. How could she smile like that -- so freely, so truly -- when her life was in shambles? Jack shook his head as he groaned, not wanting to think any more of it. The Claus girl simply didn't make sense -- he should just leave it at that. There was no use in getting suspicious, or trying to figure it out. He had other things to focus on.

Like implementing his plan to destroy Christmas.

"Sorry I'm so late," Jack nearly jumped as Clara appeared, looking slightly out of breath. "I just..." she trailed off then, noticing that he was staring at her.

Jack really couldn't help it. His jaw dropped as he peered at the doll-girl, who suddenly didn't look so much like a doll anymore. He felt his shoulders start to hunch as he tried to fight the strange feeling growing in his chest, the feeling that had started yesterday, when he'd seen Clara smile.

What was *wrong* with him?

"Um...are you alright?" Clara asked after a moment, her brown eyebrows raising as she cocked her head. "You look...did you catch a cold or something?"

Jack shook his head, trying desperately to only look at her face. "Of course not!" he snapped, returning to his normal, rude self. "I'm *Immortal*. I don't get colds," he shivered then, shaking his head again, and said: "You look different."

"Different" was quite an understatement as to how Clara looked today, although it was the best word Jack could come up with at the moment (besides "hot", which he certainly wasn't going to use, appalled at himself for even thinking of the word).

Clara had thrown aside her doll clothes for a more modern, yet still wonderfully snowy look. Her curly brown hair wasn't in pigtails anymore (thank God), and instead hung from her head in ringlet curls, flowing out across her shoulders. Instead of her ruffled, high-cut, simply atrocious blue and white doll dress, she now also wore a long wool coat, and peeking out from under the coat near her stylish boots, Jack could glimpse the bottom of a wintry blue dress.

Jack had to manually turn his head to quit looking at her, feeling suddenly nauseous, though not in a bad way.

How had she changed so suddenly, overnight? Where had the annoying doll-girl -- who looked more like a six-year-old than an adult -- gone to? How had she vanished so suddenly? And where -- pray tell *where* -- had this girl come from? This lovely, beautiful, serene--

Okay, okay. That's enough! Jack scolded himself, still not looking at Clara. *Get your head back on straight, Jack, before you lose it.*

He couldn't afford to lose his head, especially not over the ex-doll-girl.

After all, no matter how different she looked, she was still Clara Claus, and there was certainly nothing interesting or desirable about the obese man's granddaughter.

Well, nothing aside from looks, anyway.

Jack rubbed his temples in frustration, trying to concentrate on his evil plan, before Clara spoke again.

"Oh...yes," her voice was as small as it had been the day before, as fragile. "It was the strangest thing -- I woke up this morning, and I couldn't find my extra suitcase. I guess it must have gotten misplaced. Luckily, I found some clothes in the closet of my room. My grandmother said they belonged to my mother," it was the moment she stopped speaking that Jack finally looked at her again, catching the pained look on her face.

He didn't like that look one bit. Just seeing it made him want to run over to her, rip that frown off her face, and replace it with the smile he had seen yesterday -- wait, no, scratch that, it sounded violent. What he *really* wanted to do was make her smile again, but since he had (a) no idea how to do that, and (b) no idea why he felt the desire to cheer her up, he decided to just stand there and stare...

At least now he had something nice to stare at.

"So, where are we going to today?" Clara's voice cut though his thoughts (and his gape) when she spoke, taking a step towards him. "Or do you want me to decide?"

Truthfully, Jack had no idea where they were going to go, and, since he was having the hardest time thinking right now, he couldn't seem to come up with a plan.

He decided to let Clara choose. "Go ahead," he said rather gruffly, at least wanting to keep up his image. "Pick a place."

"Well..." Clara looked thoughtful for a moment before her eyes suddenly lit up, and she grinned, and Jack felt like he was melting into the snow. "I haven't had lunch yet, and the map I have of the North Pole says that there's a café that serves crepes. Could we go there?" she smiled up at him pleadingly, the blowing wind ruffling her curly hair.

Jack couldn't stand that smile. It was too pretty.

He stood there for a moment, trying to compose himself yet again, before he suddenly turned and started stalking off towards the café, highly annoyed with himself. "I'm hungry," he said loud enough for Clara to hear. "Let's eat at the café, shall we?"

Even if he was dazed by Clara's new appearance, he couldn't let her get to him. He had to stay himself -- his annoying, rude, cynical self.

"Alright," strangely, Clara didn't seem fazed by his rudeness. She ran to catch up with him, stopping by his side, not at all bothered. "Sounds fine to me."

Jack couldn't help it then.

He turned his head towards her, grinning from ear to ear. "I was hoping you'd see it my way."

****

"So, Jack, do you mind if I ask you a question?"

Jack blinked and looked up from the menu he held in his hands, staring at Clara's face. Truthfully, he hadn't needed to look at the menu, since he'd been to the Hollytop Café before and already knew what he wanted, but he'd been trying to avoid Clara, and that annoying yet so irresistible smile of hers.

Needless to say, it hadn't worked.

Jack put down his menu, propping his arm up on the table, putting his head in his right hand. "Ask away," he said glumly, frowning.

"Well, I was wondering..." if Clara was appalled by his lack of enthusiasm, she didn't show it. It seemed that more than just her appearance had changed. Maybe she was used to him already? "Why aren't you blue?"

What?

Jack found himself bewildered by the question, and he didn't know why. Had she honestly just asked him why he wasn't blue? "Um..." Jack's mouth couldn't find the words to say -- a strange thing for him. "What do you mean by that exactly?" his tongue felt tied even uttering the words.

He didn't understand at all.

Clara looked a little embarrassed now, her cheeks turning slightly pink, but that didn't stop her from pressing on. "I mean," she said, brushing her bangs from her face, "that all of the other Jack Frosts -- like in movies and books -- are usually...well...*blue*," she looked a little uncomfortable with the word now, and Jack almost wanted to laugh--

Because now he understood what she meant.

It was true, after all. In all of those stupid human Christmas movies, Jack Frost was always blue -- as in he had bluish skin, like he'd been frozen over after being left outside at a particularly wild Christmas party. But Jack wasn't that way -- not in real life.

Because in real life, Jack looked exactly the same as he did when he'd been human.

"I'm not blue," Jack emphasized the word, and Clara's blush deepened, showing off her obvious discomfort as Jack smirked at her expression, "because I'm not *frozen*. I do have powers and I am able to deal with frost, but, other than that, I'm pretty much just like you," he scowled then, adding as an afterthought: "I think those ridiculous human screenwriters love making me look like I'm permanently suffocating."

Clara seemed to absorb this for a moment, a varying display of emotions crossing her face as he watched her reaction, but then she laughed, and everything seemed to be okay.

She seemed to *understand*.

So, he was Jack Frost, but that didn't mean he was an alien or anything. He was normal, just like her, despite the fact that he lived pretty much indefinitely and had powers to *"make nice patterns on windows"*. His skin may have been pale, but it wasn't blue; he may have worked with frost, but that didn't mean his touch felt like an icicle.

Clara cocked her head at him as she asked another question, barely skipping a beat. "So, then..." her eyes were lighter now, bright like a fire of curiosity, "are you always going to be Jack Frost?"

The question hit Jack hard, and he almost coughed as his breath hitched. Why was she asking him that? Why had it suddenly popped into her mind? And, why did he have the sudden urge to tell her?

It was a confusing topic, one that Jack didn't like to think about, especially since St. Nick had "sentenced" him, but he would explain. He'd learned about it many years ago, on his first day at his new job, from none other than Santa… Jack settled back into his seat, sighing.

"Funny thing about employment up here," he said, grinning at Clara, "it *lasts*. It lasts so long, in fact, that the job openings only come up every once in a long while."

"Pardon?" Clara looked confused, which strangely amused Jack to no end.

He couldn't blame her for being baffled, though. It wasn't like the *IJEM* (Immortals Job Employment Market) was an easy thing to understand. It had taken Jack a few hours to understand it fully, and North a few minutes (which, for him, was a long time to process something).

Jack's smug grin didn't falter as he looked at Clara, feeling more comfortable now that he'd gotten used to her new look and wasn't ogling at her anymore. "Think of it this way: You've heard of St. Nick, right?"

Clara nodded. "Yes, he's Santa Claus."

Jack snapped his fingers, and she jumped. "Wrong," he said, fixing her with a dead stare. "He *was* Santa Claus — or, well, what you think of as Santa Claus, the equivalent of Santa, the original. But, he's not anymore. That's the way it works," he wanted to laugh as Clara's eyebrows pulled together in a line, and he smirked at her again, enjoying her confusion. "St. Nick started the whole Santa business, and he was so good at it the Big Boss-man gave him immortality, so that he could continue to do his job through the ages, spread Christmas cheer — blah, blah, blah, blah," he rolled his eyes, hating the Christmas bit.

"But, as with any job, poor old St. Nick got sick of it after a while. So, he asked the Boss-man to find some schmoe to replace him. After a few years, they found someone else, and St. Nick retired, choosing instead to head the Winter Council," Jack frowned as he thought of St. Nick, who he was still convinced was out to get him, and then grinned again as Clara gasped, finally getting it. "And as you know, the schmoe they replaced him with was none other than Kris Kringle, your grandfather."

Okay, so maybe it wasn't such a complicated setup. Every once in a long while, one of the Immortals (Santa, The North Wind, Jack Frost, etc.) would get tired of doing the same thing over and over again, and put in for retirement...and then some newbie would be hired for the job, undergo training, become Immortal themselves. When this happened, the old Immortal would either fly up to Paradise or live what would have been the remainder of their life out on earth (usually with a good sum of retirement money).

That was the way the world worked, whether you were Immortal or not. Maybe.

"So, you're not the original Jack Frost, then?" Clara gazed at him in a way that made his skin crawl -- curious, attentive. Maybe she wasn't so bad, after all. "There was someone before you?"

Jack nodded as the waitress came to the table (a short little elven girl, who was wearing Christmas colors and smiling brightly), and asked them what they wanted. Jack barely paid attention to her, pointing to something on the menu, instead focused on Clara.

He was actually having an interesting time explaining things to her -- which was strange, considering.

Clara ordered and the waitress stalked off, looking offended as Jack all but threw his menu at her. "No, I'm not the original Jack Frost," he finally answered Clara's question, smug once again. "The original is now retired and dead. I'm actually the third in the line, though Jack Frost *is* my real name."

When Jack had first acquired the job, everyone had been shocked by his name, the same as the title of the job he was to perform. Jack had always found it rather humorous, considering he'd never dreamed of becoming anything more than...well, *nothing*. He'd never really dreamed of becoming anything, and yet he had achieved so much.

Not everyone could say that. Not everyone got to fulfill their dreams -- even if they did know what they wanted -- and even less people achieved greatness if they didn't set out for it.

Jack had just been lucky. He'd been in the right place at the right time, gotten the right job, done the right work. Ever since the day he'd become the official Jack Frost, he'd had everything he could have ever wanted, and he hadn't even asked for it.

Clara was staring at Jack now, waiting for him to continue.

Well, he had *almost* everything he could have wanted, anyway.

Jack shook his head before the memories could come, and decided to keep talking about the Jack Frosts, a safe subject. "The first Jack was actually kind of a loser," he admitted, and Clara laughed, making him smile for reasons he couldn't quite comprehend. "He didn't even keep the job that long. A hundred years or so, and the Boss-man made him quit, hiring a new Jack, the second Jack...now, *he* was amazing. If I could become half as amazing as him, my life would be complete," Jack felt a strange drumming echo in his chest as Clara laughed again, obviously amused.

But, somehow, he didn't think he minded so much anymore.

So what if Clara's smiles and laughs made him feel strange? There was nothing wrong with enjoying her company while he could, right? It would help him get close to her, help him accomplish his goal. If he could get Clara to trust him, then he could use her to destroy Christmas.

If he could get Clara to trust him, then he could break her heart.

But if he did break her heart -- make her hate Santa -- she wouldn't smile anymore, would she? She would be just like she had been when she'd come to the North Pole, just like she had been the day before, before she'd come out of her shell -- lost, confused, sad, and alone.

Could he really do that to her? Could he really take away that smile of hers -- the smile that was now making his heart beat faster, even though he'd promised himself he wouldn't get attached to it, to her? Could he really erase her happiness now, without also erasing his own?

No. Jack had to admit, feeling his heart sink as Clara asked him another question, unable to answer at the moment. *I can't take her smile away without feeling miserable myself, but...*

But, he couldn't give up now. He still had to destroy Christmas. He *had* to. It was what he'd been working towards all these years, what he'd been planning for. If he didn't destroy Christmas now, then his revenge would never be complete, and he couldn't allow that.

He had promised himself that he would avenge Molly, and he fully intended to do it.

Jack looked up at Clara again, and felt his heart sink even further, landing at the bottom of his chest.

What was *wrong* with him? Why did he suddenly care so much about the Claus girl? He didn't know her very well -- he'd just met her two days ago! He'd spent barely any time with her. He'd thought she was repulsive until this morning. He'd been nothing but nasty to her, and yet she still--

That was it!

Clara had *talked* to him. Clara was talking to him, right now, right this very moment. She was talking to him, even though he'd been nasty to her, even though he'd snapped at her, even though he'd seen her cry the night before -- seen something that he knew he shouldn't have.

She was still talking to him. She wasn't afraid to talk to him, ignoring the glares she got from everyone else at the café, all of who hated Jack with a passion. She wasn't afraid to ask him questions, even though he might snap at her or turn her away. She wasn't afraid to laugh in front of him, or to smile.

She wasn't *afraid*.

Jack and Clara sat in that café the rest of the day, talking back and forth until the sun was low in the sky, until their elven waitress was tired of seeing them.

They sat in that café until everything else evaporated, until Jack was so caught up in listening to Clara that he forgot nearly everything else.

They sat in that café until Jack had memorized all of Clara's gestures -- the way she smiled when talking about her father, the way she grimaced when talking about her stepmother, the way her hands moved animatedly when she spoke of her friends.

They sat in that café for a long time, until Clara noticed exactly what time it was.

"Oh!" she nearly jumped from her seat, staring at the watch on her wrist. "Is it really that late? My grandfather must be wondering where I am."

Jack felt something pulling on his mind as Clara stood up, smiling apologetically. "I'll walk you back," he finally said, getting the hint, understanding what his brain was trying to tell him.

Of course. *Santa.* He still had to get her to turn against Santa.

This was his chance. If he walked Clara to her grandparent's abode, then he could talk with her more, tell her about the evils of Santa. Surely now that she had spent so much time with him, she would listen, though he kind of hated to tell her.

Just when he'd been starting to like her. Just when she'd finally decided that he wasn't so bad.

But, it didn't matter. He had to do it. He couldn't back down. He was so close--

Too close.

"Would you really walk me back?" Clara inquired, smiling brilliantly again. "Thank you."

Jack had the urge to say *"you're welcome"*, but he didn't. It was bad enough, what he was about to do. Why make it worse? Instead, he just nodded. "Of course," he said, following her out the café door.

A moment later they were outside, Clara looking towards the sky, towards the soft snow. Jack caught her brilliant, illuminating smile when she saw it, but this time he beheld no tears. Whatever had made Clara cry the day previous, she had obviously gotten over it now. Perhaps she had talked to her grandfather, sorted her feelings out...

Though Jack sincerely hoped not. If she had talked with her grandfather, that would make his job all the harder.

But he knew that something must have happened to Clara. After all, she hadn't been like she was now the day before. She'd still been cheery, yes, but she'd also been scared, like she might say the wrong thing or act the wrong way.

Perhaps she was so used to her life back home -- her life with her evil, brooding stepmother -- that she was still having a hard time adjusting. Perhaps now that she'd spent a little time in the North Pole, she was feeling more herself.

Jack didn't know, but he resolved not to think any more about it, though he was curious. Whatever had happened he was glad for it, because he preferred the Clara he saw in front of him now to the Clara he'd seen crying in the snow the day before. He liked her much better, even if he was going to smite her dreams.

Jack was just about to open his mouth -- ask Clara what she thought about Santa -- when she started to talk.

"You must like being Jack Frost," she said softly as she glanced at him, looking down from the sky. "You get to be part of Christmas."

Jack felt himself stiffen when he heard the "*C*" word, fighting the monster in him that wanted to rip it apart.

Of course. He should have known. As much as he liked Clara, she was still a Claus, which meant that she loved Christmas. They *all* loved Christmas. They loved it so much that they wanted to burst, and it was all so--

Revolting.

Jack felt his icy side come back, and he glared at Clara, unable to help it. "What makes you say that?" he asked in a cold tone, watching as she gaped at him in sudden shock. "What makes everyone *assume* that I love Christmas?"

"Don't you?" as shocked as she looked, Clara still spoke to him, still wondered. "Don't you like Christmas?"

Jack could have laughed at the irony of it all. Of all the things to break him and Clara apart after their short time together (so to speak), this was it. Christmas, it ruined everything, even the things you never thought you'd have.

Jack *tried* not to mind, though.

It didn't matter much, did it? It wasn't like he'd been planning on staying by Clara's side. It wasn't like he'd been planning on staying her friend -- he didn't need her. He didn't need anybody.

All he needed was to destroy Christmas, to break apart the thing that was so secretly evil. Then he would be done. He didn't care what happened to him after that. He didn't care who he left behind, as long as Christmas disappeared with him.

It's not like I have anybody left to leave behind, anyway. Jack had to remind himself, scowling as he stepped away from Clara, who looked almost hurt now. *Molly's already gone, so I have no one.*

He was completely *alone.*

"I don't understand," Clara's voice was pleading now as she stared at him, her eyebrows wound together. "Are you telling me that you hate Christmas? How is that possible?"

If he hadn't been so angry, Jack could have laughed at that, too.

But, he was angry. Just the thought of the cursed holiday made his blood boil, and not only that, but…Clara was treating him like everyone else, and he wasn't everyone else.

She was grouping him with all of the other losers who relied on Christmas to bring them happiness, who fed themselves with the lie of peace and joy. She wasn't taking into account his feelings, his very person, and for that he couldn't forgive her.

He didn't want to be like everyone else. He wanted to stay himself. He always wanted to stay himself. "Of course you don't understand!" Jack didn't even try to calm himself. He knew he didn't need to. He'd been stupid to think that he could become even tentative friends with the Claus girl. It was better she hated him. He would just have to find some other way to destroy Christmas. "No one understands anything that is out of the ordinary!"

Clara looked completely confused, and she was starting to back away now, scared as well. "*Out of the ordinary*?" she quoted. "What do you mean by that?"

"'*What do you mean*'? What do I mean! Is that all you can do -- ask questions!" Jack was more frustrated now than angry, though the anger spark was still there. "What I mean, Clara, is that you can't understand what I'm saying because it's different from what everyone has been telling you."

That was the way it was. That was the way it had always been. No one ever understood Jack's view of things -- understood how he could hate Christmas -- because they didn't even *try*.

They just assumed that, like everyone else, he loved the holiday. They just assumed that, like everyone else, he couldn't wait for Christmas to roll around. They just assumed that, like everyone else, he was totally and completely blind.

They just assumed. They never *asked*.

But even if they did ask, they wouldn't understand. Jack sighed then, his fists balling, his shoulders hunching, his chest aching with pain.

He would never let anyone understand. He would never let anyone in. He would never tell them the truth. He would never give away his secrets.

Clara was staring at him now, tears threatening to fall from her big doe eyes.

He would never tell his secrets, even if it was the one thing that could have saved him.

"But *why* do you hate Christmas?" Clara's voice was small when she spoke, her eyes searching his face, pleading, hoping for some sort of solid answer, something she could hold onto; something that made sense. "It's such a wonderful, beautiful time of year."

If Jack hadn't felt his anger ignite again at the word "beautiful", he may have been impressed by Clara's intentions. She was trying, though it was obviously hard for her, to understand. She was actually asking him *why*, a question that no one but North had ever bothered to ask.

She was actually trying to see his side of the argument... But Jack did feel his anger ignite when he heard the word "beautiful" -- that cursed, cursed word that was the exact opposite of his rendition of the Christmas holiday -- and all his sympathy and calm went out the window, replaced by malice and spite.

Jack knew his eyes were blazing when he glared hard at Clara, who flinched once again, but his heart felt as cold as the frost that it was his job to form. "Wonderful? Beautiful? Christmas is a *horrible* holiday!" he shouted in fury as Clara stared at him in horror, not caring who heard. "It takes everything away, and it's so commercial! Christmas is all about toys and gadgets and -- and *stuff!* People are so greedy, always wanting what they don't have," Jack saw Clara's eyes turn from frightened to empathetic, and that made him even more angry.

Why did she suddenly look like she felt sorry for him?

"And the worst part of Christmas is, the people who really need things spend the holiday in their one bedroom, slum apartments, or in homeless shelters -- or on the street. They spend Christmas hungry, shivering, weak, dying -- while everyone else opens their presents and awes at the gifts they won't even use in a few months!" Jack was nearly out of breath then, gasping, but he managed two last spite-filled sentences. "So, no, Clara, I don't love Christmas. I don't even like it -- I *hate* it!"

The words seemed to echo off the walls as Jack stood there, snow swirling around him.

It was a moment before he realized how truly angry he'd been, how loud, how worked up. It was a moment before he realized that he was now shaking, all of his fury leaking out of his system in a rush, making him feel lightheaded. It was a moment before he realized just how quiet it was without his voice echoing off the walls, penetrating the otherwise serene night...

And, also, it was a moment before he realized that Clara was now standing in front of him, completely fearless.

Jack felt his breath catch in his throat as he looked at her and her doe eyes, which were focused on his face, trying to find something beneath the surface. He watched as her eyebrows furrowed slowly, the wind whipping her hair, before she reached up, touching his cheek with her hand.

Her voice was soft when she spoke, crystalline. "What *happened* to you?" the question was so simple, yet so difficult, so many things rolled up into one little sentence, so many feelings tied to those four little words.

Jack stared at Clara for what felt like hours, relishing and yet detesting the feel of her hand on his cheek, before the whole world seemed to shatter before him, his mind not able to compute what was happening. He felt his eyes widen, horrorstruck, as one word played over and over in his mind:

Why.

He didn't understand. Why was she still there? He had yelled at her, shouted, scared her, glared, and done so many other things, and yet she wouldn't leave his side.

Why.

It didn't make sense. Yesterday she'd been quiet and pathetic, today she had changed, and now she had changed even more. She had asked him questions.

Why?

It was crazy. He'd told her that he hated Christmas -- the holiday that her family practically lived for -- and she hadn't shunned him for it. She hadn't pushed him away. She hadn't left. She hadn't run away, but--

WHY!

Jack couldn't grasp a single coherent thought as he gazed at Clara, his emotions conflicting inside of him.

What was he going to do? This had never happened before. No one had ever asked him questions like this. No one had ever stood there while he'd yelled at them, ranted about the reasons (that he shared) that he hated Christmas.

Not even North had stood there and listened to him. He'd turned and walked away at first, approaching Jack about the subject later on.

But, not Clara. No, Clara was still there, standing in front of him, waiting...

Jack pushed Clara away from him then, the snow around them starting to spiral into a blizzard, not knowing what else to do.

He'd done enough already. He'd gotten too attached to her, and after he'd promised himself he wouldn't. He'd lost his head.

But he was going to get it back.

Jack's voice was full of ice when he finally spoke, glaring at the shocked and hurt Clara once again, pulling on his mask of malevolence. "Don't ask me that ever again," he said coldly, fists balling, referring to Clara's ill-thought question. "Don't ever ask me that again, or I'll--" he stopped abruptly after taking a step towards her, finally seeing the thing he wanted to see in Clara's eyes, the thing that would keep her a safe distance from his heart--

Fear.

If he could push her away with nothing else, he could push her away with fear. It wouldn't be hard for him to hurt her, and Clara knew it.

After all, his powers as Jack Frost weren't limited to windows and plant-life (as the idiotic Santa thought). They reached far beyond that. He could easily use his powers on people too, on humans...like Clara.

Though he knew in his heart he could never do that--

Not anymore. Not now.

Jack looked at Clara one last time -- regretting the fear he saw in her eyes, the fear he himself had placed there -- before he turned and started to run, not caring if it looked cowardly or not. He simply had to get away from that face of hers, the face that he knew would now haunt him, just as it had the night before.

Only this time, it was a face riddled with fear, not sorrow, that would haunt him.

Chapter Ten: Clara

When Clara shut the door to the Claus' house behind her, she was still shaking, snow clinging to her hair and jacket. She stood there for a few minutes, eyes closed, unable to move, before she finally stepped away from the door, heading towards the couch. She fell onto it without another thought, her face landing in a big, red, Christmasy pillow.

So many things had happened that day, none of which she could sort out.

Thought after thought echoed in her mind as she lay there, sometimes crying, sometimes not. But one thought stuck out from all the rest -- one scene from that day stayed in her mind until she finally fell to sleep--

Regret. The word rang through Clara's mind like a warning bell, alerting her to something she didn't quite understand. *Before he ran off, his expression was full of regret.*

But, regret over what? Over yelling at her? Over scaring her? Over threatening her? Over spending time with her at all?

Clara wasn't sure, but, as her eyes darkened into a lulling stupor, she found that it was all she could think about.

****

Clara woke sometime later to the sound of her grandfather's voice, coming from somewhere nearby. He was saying something -- saying her name, perhaps? -- but she couldn't quite make the words out. Clara felt a groan escape her lips as she shook her still half-asleep mind and sat up, feeling like she'd just been run over by a large truck.

When she blinked, the world came into view, and she saw Santa sitting across from her, staring at her worriedly.

"Grandpa?" Clara asked in a sleepy tone before she yawned, rubbing her eyes. "What is it?"

He took a moment to examine her face before he spoke, and when he did speak, his voice was less cheery than normal. "Clares, just how long have you been lying there?" he asked, just as Mrs. Claus came into the living room, carrying a steaming mug on a tray.

"I don't..." Clara tried to awaken her still sleeping brain as Mrs. Claus sat down next to her, handing her the mug she'd been carrying, filled to the brim with peppermint tea. "I don't kn--"

And then it hit her, the memories flooding back to her conscious mind like water flowing from a waterfall. Mrs. Claus had to catch the tea mug as Clara gasped, her hands flying to her face as tears pricked at her eyes.

Of course! How could she have forgotten?

"I see..." Santa sounded sad as he blinked at her, sighing. "I was afraid this might happen."

Mrs. Claus set the tea mug down and put a hand on the now sobbing Clara's shoulder. "What might happen?" she asked her husband quizzically, raising an eyebrow.

"You know..." Santa sighed again as Clara tried to wipe her tears away, "*Jack.*"

Mrs. Claus was on her feet as soon as she heard the Immortal's name, the tea tray she'd carried held out like a weapon. "He didn't hurt her, did he?" she asked Santa in a roar, and then turned her fury towards Clara. "He didn't hurt you, did he? Because if he did--"

"Clara's fine, dear. Please, calm down..." Santa tried to stop Mrs. Claus' anger, but she simply waved the tea tray at him threateningly.

Clara was wiping away the last of her tears when she looked up at her grandmother, who now had her hands on her hips defiantly. "Don't you tell *me* to calm down, Kris!" she snapped, glaring at Santa. "I told you that you shouldn't have let that sneaky, conniving, malicious man come here, and you didn't listen to me! And now look what's happened! We have Clara crying, and--" Mrs. Claus continued to raise a fit as she looked at Clara, who's face was still red, and then she seemed to think better of her ranting and went to sit down, sighing fitfully. "I really think we should just fire that—"

"Wait! *Please*!" Clara's voice sounded rather breathy when she spoke, and her grandmother stared at her in shock. "Please, don't take it out on Jack. I just...I think...I think that I may have said something to upset him..." she trailed off as she looked down, lost in memory now. "Yes. I'm *sure* I upset him."

She had never meant to upset him, of course. All she had wanted was to get to know him better, to hopefully find out what it was that tormented him so, to find out why it was that he sometimes looked so sad.

She had decided to do it after receiving the journal from Santa, while she was writing. She had known from her first day with Jack Frost that there was something about him -- something hidden, something that he didn't seem to show the world -- and she'd wanted to know what it was.

She had known that he was cold and cynical and mean and many other unpleasant things, but she'd also known that that wasn't his only side.

The look he'd given her when she'd been crying in the snow had proved that.

So, from the very last word in her journal, she had promised herself that she would try to get to know Jack, even if she had to work hard at it. After all, she'd been given a new chance upon coming to the North Pole -- a chance to start life over again, to break away from the bonds of silence she had endured with her stepmother...why not live her new life to the fullest? Why not try and become the caring, smart, interesting person she had always dreamed herself to be?

And, it had been fun! When she'd been talking to Jack, trying to get to know him, it had been fun. She'd found that she actually liked him, even if he was a little strange.

After all, he'd actually *talked* to her. He'd sat down and talked with her nearly all day, in fact. No one had ever done that before.

The kids back home had either ignored her, or made fun of her and her love of snowflakes, which didn't even occur in Florida. At school she'd never gotten along with many people, much too frightened that her stepmother would disapprove of her taste in friends, though she had had a few secret friends. And when she'd been home with her family...well, most of the time it had been Isabelle, whose favorite voice to hear was her own.

But Jack had been different.

He hadn't minded talking to her at all -- and when she'd been saying things, he hadn't minded listening, either. In fact, he'd looked like he'd been enjoying their conversation, too.

And, so he was a little...was *blunt* a good word? Jack didn't care about sugar-coating things, or about beating around the bush. If he thought something, he came right out and said it, even if it was unkind. But strangely, Clara found that instead of annoying or bothering her, she rather liked this trait in Jack Frost. It made him interesting, and funny, even if it was at other's expense.

But, all of that had been erased now. Clara had done something horrible -- something she'd never, ever intended to do. She'd made Jack upset -- upset enough to threaten her.

What am I going to do? Clara thought, eyes wanting to shed tears again. *He probably hates me now...*

But she didn't blame him, not really. Everyone had sore spots, though Jack's seemed to be overly awful, which had Clara wondering what it was. It had to have been something unspeakable for him to react like he did. It had to have been something more than painful, something sad, just like--

His eyes.

Of course! Whatever had triggered Jack's defensiveness must have been what made him look so sad at times, so torn. If Clara could only figure out what it was, then maybe she could--

"Clara, dear...are you alright?" it was Mrs. Claus' voice that broke through Clara's thoughts, once again soft and concerned, all of its anger gone.

Clara had to blink before she could focus. "Um, yes..." she finally answered, looking up at Mrs. Claus and Santa, who both looked worried. "I was just thinking."

"Thinking?" Mrs. Claus sniffed at that, though Clara didn't think it was because she disapproved of thinking in general. "Not about that annoying Jack Frost, I hope," she sniffed again at Jack's name, and Santa patted her arm, as if to calm her.

Clara blushed ever so slightly, not wanting to admit that Mrs. Claus was right, but knowing she should. "Um, yes, actually. I was thinking about Jack..." she trailed off, trying to find the right words, but hurried on when she saw Mrs. Claus frown. "I was just thinking that...well, did something happen to him?"

Truth be told, Clara already knew the answer to that question.

Of course something had happened to him! Otherwise he wouldn't look so sad at times.

But she knew that Jack wasn't going to tell her -- she had already tried asking him, and he'd gotten mad at her, threatening to practically turn her into a popsicle -- so she'd figured that maybe her grandparents knew.

Whatever it was that had happened to Jack, it had to have happened after he'd gotten his job as the official Jack Frost, because otherwise he wouldn't have been hired. And judging from what Jack had told her about her grandfather becoming Santa, Clara assumed that he'd started work after Kris Kringle had been hired; both of them had been hired by the previous "Santa", St. Nick, who was the head of Winter.

If anyone could tell her what had happened to Jack, Clara was sure it was Mr. and Mrs. Claus.

Mrs. Claus had a fit as soon as Clara asked her about Jack, jumping from her seat, wielding her tea tray again. "Of course something happened to him!" she barked, and Santa sighed, rubbing his forehead. "And ever since then he's been causing us all sorts of trouble, the evil little devil! Do you know he's tried to destroy Christmas at least a *dozen* times already? You can't imagine the break he's had on poor Santa and I," she sat down again at the last part, sighing wearily, though she didn't put her tea tray down.

Clara felt shock as Mrs. Claus' words sunk in, her doe eyes widening.

He's tried to destroy Christmas? She thought, nearly gasping. *I didn't know that...*

She'd known that he hated Christmas -- he'd made that more than clear -- but she hadn't known that he'd tried to destroy it. It made her sad to think that Jack hated something that much, especially Christmas. Christmas was such a wonderful and enjoyable holiday, why had he excluded himself from it?

What had happened to him to make him hate Christmas so much?

"Um, grandpa?" Clara looked at Santa as she continued her questioning. "Do you know why Jack hates Christmas?"

Santa stared at her for a moment before a frown took over his face, and he sighed again. "Unfortunately, yes," he said, confirming Clara's theory. "It happened before you were born. Jack had been working with us for not even a year..." his frown turned into a saddened face as he looked down, his bushy eyebrows bunching.

"But what is it that *happened* to him?" Clara pressed, dying to know. "What made him hate Christmas?"

If she could figure it out, then maybe she could become friends with Jack.

Santa looked back up at her, and his eyes seemed to twinkle. "You really want to know that badly?" Santa asked, and Clara thought she heard a hint of amusement in his voice. "You'll pursue your question till the end?"

Clara didn't even have to think about it. She simply nodded. She wanted to know what had made Jack so sad inside. She wanted to know more than anything else at the moment. She didn't know why she wanted to know so badly, but she figured that she could figure that out later, after she had sorted everything else out.

After all, she was just now getting to know her real self; she still needed time to figure out her real feelings.

"Well, if you're that set on knowing," Santa "ho, ho, ho"ed as he stroked his beard, and Mrs. Claus frowned, not approving one bit, "I *could* tell you, Clares, but I think," his eyes twinkled again, and Clara felt her heart sink, "it would be better if you found out from Jack."

Clara groaned, shaking her head. "But he'll get mad at me if I ask him! And I don't want that. Can't you tell me, grandpa?"

"Like I said, I could," Santa "ho, ho, ho"ed again and then chuckled, smiling widely at Clara. "But the truth always sounds best when it comes from the right person. If you really want to know about Jack's past, then you should ask him. He may get angry with you, like you said, but that's just a step on the road to learning more about him."

Santa's smile widened as he patted Clara's hand. "But, I must say, I'm rather surprised by you, Clares. Not many people want to know what's wrong with Jack Frost."

Clara felt suddenly sad when Santa said that, though she knew it was true.

She was sure that a lot of people avoided Jack, and not just because he was cynical and mean (though she was sure that played a big part in it). Anyone who looked hard enough could tell that Jack had some deep issues, and not many people were willing to help him sort through them, or stay by his side while he sorted them out.

But, Clara was -- well, she was willing to try, at least.

"I know that everyone thinks he's a horrible person," when Clara spoke again her voice was small, thoughtful, sad, "but I don't think that's true at all. And I know Jack hates Christmas," Clara glanced at Mrs. Claus quickly, and her grandmother sighed again. "But, maybe if I can figure out what happened to Jack, then I can get him to see the *real* Christmas."

Santa smiled at her, beaming like an angel, but Mrs. Claus frowned again, standing and heading towards the kitchen. "Good luck," she muttered, before disappearing.

Santa laughed an unrealistic laugh when he saw Clara's hurt. "Don't mind her," he said, motioning towards the kitchen door. "She's had a lot of trouble with Jack. She doesn't want to dislike him, but it's hard on her since she's seen firsthand all that he's done to destroy Christmas. She just needs some time to see how great your plan really is," he beamed again, and Clara felt her heart lift an inch, smiling back at him.

She only hoped that her plan was good. Sure, she had good intentions, but--

But how was she going to get Jack to talk to her again? He'd been so angry with her when she'd seen him last, surely he wouldn't want to play her "tour guide" anymore -- or even see her for that matter.

And if he did talk to her, then how would she ask him about his past? She had barely even touched the subject during their last talk, and he'd all but blown up.

What was she going to do?

I'll have to think of something. Clara tried to solidify her resolve, putting on her brave face. *I just can't let this go.*

And she couldn't. Not now. She cared too much.

"Oh, that reminds me," Clara nearly jumped when Santa spoke next, uttering one of his famous "ho, ho, ho"s. "There was a letter at the door this morning. Must've been left there sometime last night, while you were sleeping. I didn't get in until a little while ago and am about to head back. We had a hard night at the factory, preparing for the big day."

Clara was shocked by the news. "Last *night?*" she squeaked. "Do you mean to tell me that it's morning?"

"Of course," Santa chuckled as he pulled an envelope out of his pocket, handing it to Clara. "You must have passed out on the sofa," he "ho, ho, ho"ed again as Clara gaped at him. "It's nearly noon."

Clara gasped when she heard that.

Noon! She had wasted half the day! She had to find Jack and tell him she was sorry for upsetting him, and ask him again about his past, and all of the other things she wanted to know.

Clara shook her head as she tore into the envelope Santa had given her, getting the strange feeling that she knew who it was from. It read:

~~Dear Clara,~~

~~Clara,~~

Dear Clara,

By now you've probably realized that I'm absolutely horrible at writing letters, something you will hopefully try to ignore.

Anyways, I'm writing to tell you that...well...Okay, I'M SORRY! There, I said it. Now you can't say I didn't. I know I overreacted and that I shouldn't have and that you're going to tell me it was all my fault and th

Now I'm ranting!!!

Okay...starting over...

Clara, I'm sorry for getting upset with you, and I would really appreciate it if you would let me make it up to you by completing my role as tour guide. If you don't completely hate me and my letter writing skills by the end of this message, then please meet me at Holly Street Park at noon tomorrow (or today, depending on when you get this).

Jack

P.S: Also, could you not tell Santa about the whole bad-at-writing-and-ranting-in-letters thing. It's kind of embarrassing. Just torch this thing when you're done reading it...

Jack

(Yes, I know I signed it twice. Get over it.)

Clara was giggling and laughing so much by the end of the letter that she barely caught its mention of time.

Finally, she asked Santa: "Grandpa, what time did you say it was?"

"Almost noon, Clares," Santa said, smiling again as he stood from his seat. "Like I said, time for me to get back to the workshop. Those toys don't build themselves, you know. I need to be there to supervise."

Clara barely heard him, however. She was too busy rushing towards her room, nearly tripping over her feet. "I'm going to be late!" she shouted as she shut her door behind her, panting heavily.

She couldn't miss this meeting. She wanted to see Jack. She wanted to tell him she was sorry. She wanted to talk to him. She--

Suddenly, Clara wanted so many things.

Chapter Eleven: Jack

Jack felt nervousness build in him as he paced back and forth, back and forth across the snow, leaving a deep groove in it. It was nearing twelve-thirty in the afternoon, and he was growing antsy, sure that he looked like an idiot with all of his pacing. He stopped once, glancing out at the road that led to the park, and seeing nothing sighed, pacing some more.

He couldn't believe it.

He couldn't believe he'd been so stupid! How on earth had he written that horrible letter? It wasn't as if she was going to show! She had to have hated him by now! She'd probably seen the letter was from him and torn it to bits, telling her grandfather to fire him.

There was no way she was going to show.

I should have left it alone. Jack grumbled to himself as he continued to pace, his mouth in a tight line, his shoulders hunched. *I should have stayed mad at her, found some other way to destroy Christmas.*

But he hadn't, and now he was paying for it with an empty street.

When Jack had come "home" the night before, he'd immediately been confronted by North, his caringly-uncaring friend and North Pole roommate wanting to know everything that had happened that day. Jack had of course told him to get lost (though not as politely), but North had ignored him, instead choosing to sit and wait for Jack to finish fuming.

It had taken a while, since when it came right down to it, Jack had been angrier with himself than he had been with Clara.

Sure, he hadn't liked thinking of the questions she had asked him -- especially the question about what had happened to him -- but in the end he'd known that she'd only been trying to help. In the end he'd known that what Clara had done had really helped him more than hurt him, because she'd shown him a kindness that many others didn't.

So, no, Jack hadn't been overly mad at Clara. In fact, when he'd thought about what had happened, he'd been more than ashamed by the way he'd reacted, which is what had started his anger towards himself. Not only had he been unfair to one of his new and only friends, but he'd also been unfair to Santa's *granddaughter*.

Jack had told these things to North when he'd finally calmed down, needing a level head to help him sort out his problems.

"*So, how are you planning on destroying Christmas now?*" North had asked as Jack had mentioned the last part -- about threatening to turn Santa's granddaughter into a frozen statue. "*From the way you reacted, she probably won't want to see you again. She probably won't even want to hear your name--*"

Jack had snapped at that. "*Alright, alright!*" he'd all but yelled, knowing that North was just trying to get under his skin. "*Don't you think I know that she probably hates me?*" he'd sunk into a chair then, sighing as he'd hit himself in the head with a pillow.

He'd been so unused to the feel of regret that he hadn't known what to do.

All his life, Jack had never regretted much. And even if he had regretted something, it had never been anything big, only little things -- like not charging more for the cookies he'd stolen and sold in kindergarten, and never trying out for the "mock the football" team.

He'd never regretted anything big -- well, only *one* thing.

"*You know, it's strange, Jack...*" North's voice had been less monotone and less loud when he'd spoken next, as if he were telling a heartbreaking secret, "*I don't think I've ever heard you sound bothered by the fact that people don't want to see you.*"

Jack had known North was right -- in fact, the annoyingly annoying best friend was always right -- but he'd wanted to deny it. "*So what?*" He'd asked, throwing his pillow aside. "*It's not like I care what she thinks, either! I'm just...tired, is all!*"

"Hmm, yes. Tired. I can see that," North had smiled one of his smug smiles as he'd leaned back in his chair. "*You know...I almost think you're beginning to like Miss Clara.*"

Jack had sat up immediately upon hearing the word "like", his face turning red. "*I do not!*" he'd shouted, shaking his head fiercely. "*That's just ridiculous!*"

"*I find the word 'ridiculous' is too prominent in your vocabulary,*" North had replied calmly, cocking his head at Jack, looking secretly thoughtful as his navy bangs fell into his eyes. "*Try replacing it with another term...you could use...oh, I don't know...accurate, factual...correct, perhaps,*" North had smiled evilly then and, other than realizing that his friend had had more facial expressions in the last week than in the last year, Jack had realized that he was still talking about Clara.

Jack had simply glared at him. "I. Do. Not. Like. Clara. Claus," he'd said it slowly, hoping North would get the hint. "*What? Do I have to spell it out for you! I-D-O-N-O-T--*"

"*Alright, alright. Don't pop a vein,*" North had sighed, making Jack glare all the more. "*But if you don't like Miss Claus, then why haven't you used that oh-so-devious mind of yours to turn her against Santa?*"

It had taken Jack a moment to answer that, and when he had answered, he hadn't known what to say.

And he still didn't know. Not even now. Not even a day later, while he was furiously pacing the entrance to the park, hoping to goodness that Clara showed up.

Why haven't I turned her against Santa yet? Jack wondered as he continued to pace, lost in thought now. *I was going to try last night, but then--*

At first they had been talking, which had distracted him. And then they'd been walking back to Santa's, and then Jack had blown it. He'd yelled at her, and now she was never going to talk to him again, and he wouldn't get to say anything to her -- let alone try and convince her of the evils of Santa Claus.

He had blown it. He had blown his chance...

And now he would never get another one.

Jack sighed as he stopped pacing, the wind kicking up, ruffling his spiky white hair. He was about to just give up and leave when he heard it--

"Jack!"

--Clara's voice, calling his name.

Jack turned just in time to see her running towards him, a strange smile on her face. She stopped just in front of him, panting, out of breath, but after a moment she straightened, smiling wider.

"Sorry I'm so late," she said, brushing her curly brown bangs from her face. "I've had a crazy morning," she sighed as she said "crazy", looking him straight in the face as she waited for a reply.

Jack simply stared at her, not sure what to say.

How had this happened? How had he been wrong? He'd been sure that she was going to desert him -- to leave him standing there! He'd been sure that she was going to stand him up -- to stay at home instead of meeting him like he'd hoped.

Clara cocked her head at him as he gaped, blinking her big doe eyes.

But, he'd been wrong. Clara had come. She was there, standing in front of him, waiting for him to answer yet again.

She really came. Jack thought in astonishment, still shocked from words. *I can't believe it!*

Why was she there? Wasn't she still mad at him? Wasn't she upset because he had yelled at her and shouted at her, and glared at her, and *threatened* her!

Wasn't she upset that he had treated her that way, when she'd only been trying to help? Wasn't she afraid that he would do it again?

Why was she there? What could she possibly gain from meeting him?

And why was he so *happy* to see her?

Sure, Jack had written her the letter, come to meet her that afternoon, but most of that had been North's idea. After they'd had their little spat the night before, North had been the one to suggest that Jack write Clara the letter, that he not give up on turning her against Santa (though Jack was beginning to wonder if North cared about destroying Christmas at all, or if he was just trying to prove his "you like Clara" theory).

Yes, maybe if Jack thought about it, he had wanted to come see Clara...just a little bit -- but mostly, it had been North's idea! So why did he feel so rejoiced when he laid eyes on the ex-doll-girl?

Jack shook his head, not wanting to contemplate this development any further. He had enough mixed emotions as it was. He still didn't know why Clara's smile made him feel so weird, or why he liked talking to her so much, or why he had been upset with himself when he'd yelled at her. He didn't need to complicate things any further.

After all, Clara was there now, and that was all that mattered.

"Jack?" it was Clara's voice, soft and sweet, that broke him from his thoughts. "Are you alright?"

Jack shook his head, frowning at her. "I'm fine!" he snapped, but seeing Clara's face, calmed himself. "I'm just a little...tired. I've been waiting for a long time," he felt stupid as soon as he said it; he was sure that Clara was going to laugh.

"Oh. I'm sorry," but Clara didn't laugh. Instead she smiled at him apologetically, her head tipping down. "Like I said, things have been crazy this morning. I kind of lost track of time," her face turned slightly pink when she admitted her lack of time management skills, and Jack suddenly grinned.

For reasons he couldn't completely understand, he rather liked that look on her.

Jack stuck his hands in his trouser pockets and shrugged. "Not much harm done, I suppose. You're here now, so I can get on with what I wanted to say," he looked away then, clearing his throat, trying to remember what he had rehearsed. "Well, Clara...I guess I should say that I'm..." his eyes traveled back to Clara, who almost looked like she was laughing, and suddenly he felt flustered. "Okay, okay! I'm -- I APOLOGIZE!"

"You already said that," Clara did laugh then, making Jack feel even more flustered, since he wasn't used to apologizing to anyone -- especially to a member of the Claus family. "In your letter."

Jack wiped away his embarrassed face and shook his head, wagging a finger at her. "No, no," he said in a reprimanding tone. "I believe I said *'I'm sorry'*, which is completely different from *'I apologize'*. The word *'sorry'* isn't as meaningful if you ask me, which is why I wanted to meet you," he stopped speaking as Clara stopped laughing, smiling at him funnily instead.

Was there a legal length for how long eyelashes could be? Jack wasn't sure, but if there wasn't one, he was going to protest -- because Clara's were much too long, and the way they moved when she blinked bothered him, giving him butterflies he couldn't ignore.

What was this girl doing to him? He couldn't even begin to understand it.

Was it possible that maybe North was -- God forbid -- *right*? As much as Jack squirmed at that idea -- and squirm he did -- he couldn't help but think of it now that he was around Clara. And if North were right, well, then what would that mean?

He can't be right! Jack concluded, angry with himself for thinking of things that shouldn't have crossed his mind. *I do not like Clara! I'll never like Clara!*

He couldn't afford to like Clara.

"Well, if you're sincere, then I accept your apology," it was once again Clara's voice -- riddled with something that was almost like laughter -- that broke through Jack's thoughts, sending another violent thud through his heart. "*If* you're sincere."

Jack actually laughed at that, confusion pushed aside for the moment. "Sincere?" he laughed again, throwing Clara a smug (if not evil) smile. "My dear Miss Claus, I am *never* sincere. I hardly know the meaning of the word."

"Oh," Clara blinked at that, which made Jack all the more amused. "Well..." she suddenly looked lost for words, her too-long eyelashes playing with Jack's pulse.

Jack's smug smile turned strangely soft as he took a step towards her, focusing on her face. "I may not be sincere," he said, "but I'm always honest, as long as it serves my purpose. So, you can trust me," his voice was strangely quiet when he spoke to her, staring into her eyes. "I have no reason to lie to you."

It wasn't until the words left Jack's mouth that he realized the truth of them.

He had no reason to lie to Clara. He didn't even want to lie to her, which was strange for him.

Was it because she was so different from everyone else he'd met? Because she was so understanding? Because she tried to see --

and *did* see -- him as no one else did? Was that why he didn't want to lie to her? Or maybe--

It was in that moment that Jack realized...she was having a profound effect on his heart.

Chapter Twelve: Clara

"So...you had something to tell me?"

Clara sighed as she looked at the sky, catching the snowflakes as they came down in clumps -- not really a heavy snow, but not quite a light one, either. They were still standing in front of the park, and she wasn't sure what she wanted to say yet.

Truthfully, she did have something to tell him -- something to explain, really -- She wanted to tell him the truth about her mother. She didn't know what had prompted her to want to tell him, but she knew that she wanted to now. Perhaps it was because they had become friends, or perhaps she felt that she owed it to him -- that, because she wanted to know something about him that was so personal, the least she could do was extend the gesture, tell him something personal on her end.

But she couldn't tell him yet -- not now, while they were in the park, and the afternoon was so young. Not when they still had some sunlight to spend together, continuing their "tour" of the

North Pole. She *would* tell him -- she had promised herself she would -- but not right now.

Right now was for fun, not tears.

Clara felt herself smile as she glanced at Jack. "I'll...tell you later," she said, hoping she sounded at least somewhat mysterious. "But first, can we continue with my tour?"

"Your tour?" Jack seemed a little miffed at first -- probably wanting to know what it was she had to say -- but when she blinked at him, his annoyed expression vanished, and he shrugged. "Why not? I have nothing better to do," he pretended to sigh as he started to walk off, but then he stopped, turning towards Clara. "Where were we going again?"

Clara had to laugh at his expression, which was almost smug now, in a joking sort of way. "Well, I was thinking that since we're right here, we could go to the park," she said, pointing to the park entrance next to them, the sign above which said *Holly Street Park* in bold, curved letters (that resembled candy canes).

"The park?" Jack's nose wrinkled ever so slightly when he looked up at the letters above them, but then he looked back at her, and a grin spread across his face. "I suppose nature does deserve my attention," he said, and Clara started to laugh, her cheeks turning red from the cold.

Jack didn't say anything about her laughing at him -- in fact, he almost looked happy about it -- as they stepped into the park, walking under the candy-cane-like sign. They were perhaps twelve or thirteen steps in when Clara felt the breath rush out of her, staring up into the trees.

Holly Street Park was a giant patch of winding, snow covered roads, and tall, towering trees. Everywhere they stepped there was snow -- on the ground, in the trees, in the air -- and Clara felt herself become mystified by it. She watched as the snow fell down, hitting the tree branches before dropping to the road beneath them, falling downward and downward until it finally hit its destination.

Never in her life had she seen so much snow, and, never in her life that she could remember had she been so happy.

It almost didn't seem fair.

I love this place. Clara thought as she looked behind her, spotting their footprints. *And I love...*

She wasn't sure what it was just yet, but there was something else she had grown to love recently, too.

"All this snow..." Jack seemed to be as mystified as she'd seen him as he looked around, a crooked smile on his lips. "I may not love the stuff, but it's almost pretty."

Clara barely heard his last sentence, too enthralled by what was around her. "Isn't it beautiful?" she asked, giggling as a few flakes hit her nose.

"You really like it all that much?" this question made Clara pause, turning her head towards Jack. They stopped walking as he stared at her, now in the middle of the park, near a bench and some snowbanks. "It's just snow."

Clara could hardly comprehend the words he was saying.

Just snow? *Just* snow?

There was no such thing as *just snow*.

Snow to her was like clouds, like water, like frost was to Jack -- something so vital and necessary that you simply couldn't live without thinking about it. Sure, she had never seen snow before she'd come to the North Pole -- at least, not in person -- but it had always been on her mind. She'd constantly been reading about it, pinning homemade snowflakes up in her room, watching the weather channel just to get a glimpse of the white stuff.

Snow had always been important. It had always been a part of her. It had always been something she loved.

And it had always made her feel connected to her mother.

Clara relayed these feelings to Jack. "Yes," she said, her expression softening. "I love snow. I always have," she laughed as she thought back to her middle school days, sure she saw Jack's cheeks turn slightly pink. "I used to carry this giant book about snowflakes with me around school. All of my classmates would make fun of me for it," she frowned on that note, no longer finding it funny.

Her classmates had never understood, never tried to see things her way. They'd simply laughed at her differences, never trying to understand.

But she didn't mind so much anymore, because now she had people who she knew she could count on -- people who she knew would understand, who would stand by her no matter what.

She loved her new family -- the jolly Santa, and the sweet but cranky Mrs. Claus. She loved the North Pole, with all of its strange yet interesting sights. She loved--

"Jack," Clara bounced out of her reverie, a question popping into her mind. "If you're responsible for the frost, and Santa's responsible for the toys, then who," her eyebrows raised. "makes the snow?"

Truth be told, she had never thought about it before -- but then again, before coming to the North Pole, she hadn't truly believed that Santa Claus or anyone else existed, not since the day her stepmother had come into her home.

One of Clara's few memories of her mother was that she'd been very into Santa. Her mother had simply loved the fatly obese man. She'd put up Santa decorations, and sent Santa cards, and Santa had been so much a part of Clara's life that she'd fully believed he was real, just like the rest of the kids her age.

Now this wasn't to say that Santa was the only thing her mother loved about Christmas -- Clara could never forget her mother's nativity scene, which her father had given to her before leaving the North Pole -- but she had really loved Santa.

And, so had Clara.

But then Isabelle had come into the picture, bringing everything that was about her (what she liked to call the "ME network") along for the ride. Suddenly, Christmas had been different. Instead of putting up a normal Christmas tree and hanging ornaments, they'd gotten a fake, plastic tree, and hung pictures of Isabelle on it (although they had been kind of Christmas-like, since they'd been photos of her at Christmas parties). And instead of watching Christmas movies to prepare for the holidays, they'd watched old movies of Isabelle, as a young girl, in different Christmas pageants. And instead of wrapping presents and opening them on Christmas day, Isabelle had pouted and wanted to go out shopping by herself, to make sure that she got what she wanted.

When Clara had asked her dad about this anti-Christmas behavior, he had either become angry with Isabelle, getting into all sorts of nasty fights that would keep Clara up at night, or he was too tired to care, coming home from his business trips just in time for Christmas.

So, gradually, Christmas had gotten pushed to the side, nearly forgotten, and though Clara had kept up her Christmas spirit (refusing to forget what Christmas -- the Christmas her mother had known so well -- was all about), she'd all but given up on anything Santa. At first she had kept believing, wanting to keep her childhood as best she could, but then she'd gotten to the point where she hadn't wanted to believe in Santa anymore, and then, eventually, one day, she'd found she hadn't believed in him at all.

But, she'd been wrong. She could see that now. Santa, the elves, Mrs. Claus, the flying reindeer, Jack -- they were all real, not just a fantasy. They may not have been the people she'd thought they would be, but they were still *real.*

And maybe, just maybe, the fact that they were real proved something. Maybe it proved that believing in something you couldn't see wasn't foolish, just difficult.

"The Snow Queen," it was Jack's voice that snapped Clara from her thoughts, and she turned towards him, puzzled.

Had she heard right?

"The *Snow Queen*?" Clara echoed, the name sounding strange on her tongue. "What do you mean?"

"The answer to your question," Jack said, shaking his head, as though it were obvious. "Don't tell me you've forgotten it already?"

Clara had to shake her head before she realized what he meant.

Of course. She had asked him whose job it was to make snow, but she hadn't really expected that to be his answer.

The Snow Queen? Was she real, as well?

"The Snow Queen was hired by the Big Boss-man some time ago, to design snowflake patterns, which she would then send to special Snow Elves to manufacture," Jack explained everything with an almost grim expression, his normal grinning, mischievous face gone. "But, as with the story, she got kind of...well..." he coughed inconspicuously. "Let's just say that St. Nick had to fire her for certain 'circumstances'. There hasn't been a new Snow Queen since then, so the Snow-elves do all the work. They're really quite lazy, and use the same patterns over and over, but since snowflakes are so small, you humans never seem to notice."

Clara sighed, thinking of how weird it was that Jack always called people "humans" instead of just "people". She knew that he had once been a "human", too, before he'd become the official Jack Frost.

She supposed now he wasn't quite human at all -- at least, he lived longer. He was still like her in every other way, though.

I wonder why he separates himself. Clara thought as Jack glanced at some falling snowflakes, probably trying to see if they were poorly made (as he had accused the Snow- elves of being lazy). *I wonder why he doesn't consider himself to be human...*

There had to have been some reason, some thing that made Jack so against humanity. Perhaps it had something to do with his past, with the thing that he wouldn't tell Clara about?

Perhaps.

She didn't know -- Though she wanted to find out.

"So, they still need someone to take the Snow Queen's place?" Clara finally concluded, looking to Jack for an answer.

It was a moment before he looked away from the snowflakes, but when he did, seeing her face, he started to laugh. "What, do *you* want the job?" he asked, grinning at her devilishly. "Oh, that would be great, now wouldn't it? Then you could see all the snow you want," his tone was so taunting, Clara wasn't sure whether he was serious, or if he was just making fun of her.

She decided to give him the benefit of the doubt.

"I would *love* that job!" Clara exclaimed, giving Jack a challenging smile before she looked up at the sky again. "If I could design snowflakes...well, I can't think of anything else I'd want to do."

She saw Jack frown out of the corner of her eye, but this time she could tell that he didn't mean it. "Yes, you'd be Miss Clara Snow," he chuckled then. "Imagine that."

Clara nodded, closing her eyes, trying to envision herself as "Clara Snow".

What would it be like, she wondered, to design snowflakes? She had always been good at drawing and painting, so she was sure that she would enjoy it. And even if she wasn't good at it at first, she was sure that she would get used to it, grow better over time. After all, no one was good at something when they first started.

Yes, it would be a wonderful life. She was sure of it. She would get to see her grandfather every day, her grandmother, and the elves.

"It must be wonderful to live in the North Pole," Clara said, opening her eyes, staring up at the sky again. "I'd love to be in this place every day."

To her surprise, Jack snorted, frowning as he glared at the ground. "What are you talking about?" he asked in a cold tone. "We don't live here."

"You *don't?*" Clara was shocked. "Then why are you here now?"

When Jack looked at her, his eyes were just as cold as his voice had been, and his expression just as cold as his eyes. "Didn't

Santa tell you?" he asked, and Clara could tell that it wasn't something she wanted to know.

Though, she was curious.

"No," Clara's voice was small, breathy when she spoke next, a sudden shiver enveloping her. Though she wasn't terrified of Jack -- though she probably should have been -- she couldn't stand it when he gave her that look -- the look that was cold, cold as ice.

Truth be told, Santa hadn't told her much at all about Jack -- other than the fact that he was going to be her tour guide while she was at the North Pole. He hadn't told her what he was like, where he'd come from, if he liked Christmas or not, and when she'd asked him, he hadn't told her about Jack's past (well, not really).

The only real thing Santa had told her about Jack was that he'd tried to destroy Christmas numerous times -- a fact that she still couldn't believe.

Clara felt her heart drop to the bottom of her chest as she looked back at Jack, who still wore his cold expression. *I don't really know anything about him.*

It was true. She didn't know anything about Jack.

Not really.

Sure, he'd told her that he used to be human before he became the official Jack Frost, and she knew that he hated Christmas, but other than that...nothing. He'd only told her unimportant things when they'd been at the café that day, things he probably didn't think she would remember.

He hadn't told her anything important--

But then again, he didn't really know anything about her, either. She had told him about her stepmother, and about her father, and the fact that her real mother had passed away, but other than that...nothing; she'd told him no intimate, important information, nothing to really grab onto and hold.

He didn't know about her dreams. Her fears. Her regrets.

He probably thought she was a simple girl without faults. He probably thought that she had never hurt anyone, never caused pain. He probably thought--

But he was *wrong*.

He was so wrong.

She had caused the worst of all tragedies. She had caused death.

Jack seemed to lose his cold expression as he sighed, looking more annoyed now than anything. "It doesn't matter," he finally said, running a hand through his spiky white hair. "The fact is that I don't live here. None of us do -- save Santa and the elves. They're the freeloaders. We only get to come here when we have meetings."

"Meetings?" Clara caught onto the word immediately. "Oh," then she remembered -- the Winter Council. Jack had told her about them.

Jack's annoyance evaporated, and he looked smug once again. "Yes," he said, fixing his eyes on her face. "I hate meetings, but I have to attend. I guess they just can't do without me," he sounded anything but sincere when he said it, and Clara laughed for the first time in minutes. "Although I normally only get to see North at meetings, so I guess that's an incentive to go..." he trailed off, and his eyes seemed to glaze over, losing focus of her.

"North?" that was a name Clara had never heard before.

Jack snapped out of his glazed state and blinked at her, grinning once again. "Oh, yes, North," he said, and then he grimaced, as if he'd remembered something he'd rather forget. "He's my friend -- my *only* friend, I guess you could say. He's also the North Wind -- you know, that annoying gust that makes everything cold? He's monotone and obnoxious and infuriating, and I hate him!" Jack yelled just as Clara jumped, and then he laughed at her. "But, he's still a friend."

He trailed off for a whole minute before he blinked again, and then checked his watch, frowning. "Speaking of the intolerable, he asked us to meet him for lunch at the café, if you showed today. He wants to meet you for some ridiculous reason," he grinned at Clara then, grabbing her hand, starting to drag her off.

Clara's heeled boots dug into the snow beneath as they walked along, going further and further into the park, leaving trails behind them in the snow. As Jack slowly dragged her along, Clara stared at the back of his head, thinking.

North. She was going to meet North, Jack's best friend.

I wonder what he's like. Clara thought as they passed a few snow-mounds, the trees starting to thin out. *I wonder if he'll like me?*

She certainly hoped so. After all, Jack liked her, so North probably would, and--

Did Jack like her?

Clara wasn't really sure. He had been spending an awful lot of time with her not to like her, yet he never said anything about liking her at all. He never called her his friend. So, maybe he didn't like her after all. Maybe--

"Jack, what kind of girls do you like?" the question popped out of Clara's mouth before she could catch it, having been sitting just on the edge of her tongue.

Jack dropped her when he heard that, turning red as he rounded on her. "What!" Clara noticed his shoulders hunch as he tried not to look at her. "Why are you asking me *that*?"

"Um..." why was she asking him that? "I don't know. It's just that..." Clara stopped, trying to find a good excuse, brushing snow off of her dress. "Well, I'm a girl. We tend to think about these things."

It was in truth the most pitiful excuse she could have had -- "I'm a girl"? Who said that? -- but, it was also the best she could come up with at the moment.

Jack's eyes narrowed as he crossed his arms over his chest, but he was still beet red. "Fine," he said. "Who am I to question what goes on in a woman's mind?"

"So?" if Clara hadn't been suddenly curious, she probably would have been annoyed with the "woman's mind" crack, but she was curious, so she let it slide. "Aren't you going to tell me?"

Clara couldn't explain it, but sometimes Jack looked...*strange* when he gazed at her, as if he couldn't control his face muscles. Like right now, he was staring at her but not staring at her — almost like he was trying not to look her in the face.

That had never happened to her before.

Everyone else she had met -- every *guy* she had met -- had always been able to stare at her straight (if they were staring at her at all, which many of them hadn't). Why not Jack?

What made him so different?

He's probably just embarrassed by what I asked him. Clara concluded, deciding not to read into the subject. *I guess it did come out of nowhere.*

She couldn't do that again. It was too embarrassing.

"Well..." Jack was still trying to find words, looking at the ground now. "I don't really know."

Clara blinked at his answer, puzzled. "What do you mean you don't know?" she asked, the wind around them starting to pick up. "You don't know what type of girl you like?"

"Not really," Jack shrugged then, and the red on his cheeks lessened a bit. "I guess I've never really thought about it. I'm always..." he took a deep breath, sighing. "I'm always traveling. I go from place to place, city to city, plane to plane, bad coffee shop to bad coffee shop, never stopping. I go all over the world to complete my 'job', and I hardly get a break," he shrugged again, and Clara felt her heart sink. "So I've never really had time for the 'dating' thing. And no woman wants to be dragged around like a suitcase -- and besides, I'm *Immortal.* That kind of puts a damper on things."

Clara stared at him as he relayed this to her, her heart sinking even further into her chest, landing somewhere near the bottom, all welled up and saddened.

She'd had no idea. She hadn't known what Jack's job entailed, the extents he went through to complete it.

Now that she thought about it, it made sense, though. Of course he had to travel the world, going from place to place. Of course he never got a vacation. She was sure that there were times when he got a bit of a break -- when it was summer, and the world didn't need as much frost -- but it couldn't have been very often. He had to have been on the move all of the time.

But, planes? He used *planes?* Clara supposed that was an easy way to travel...But how did he get everywhere in time? And what if people -- humans -- saw him? What would they think? And how did he make everything frosty? Was it like what the Snow Queen had done? Did he just distribute frost to some sort of Frost Elves, or did he do everything himself?

Clara didn't know, and she was sure that even if she did know, she wouldn't understand. These things were so complicated -- Jack's frostline, Santa's delivery, reindeer's flight patterns -- that she could never hope to understand them.

But, that was alright. She didn't have to understand them to know that they happened. But there was something that she did want to understand. "You mean...you're alone?" the words flew out of Clara's mouth before she could catch them, sounding much worse than the ones she had uttered a few moments ago. "You've been alone all this time? As long as you've been Jack Frost?"

If Jack's demeanor had been shrugging and nonchalant a moment ago, it turned icy again now, his eyes narrowing rigidly. "Yeah," he said, as if he didn't care. "So? What difference does it make?"

What difference did it make? Clara was sure it made all the difference. After all, no one wanted to be alone -- not even Jack Frost. "Is that why you look like you're not paying attention a lot of the time?" something had just occurred to Clara, and she felt her forehead crinkle in thought. "Because you're not used to talking to people -- because you're alone all the time?"

Clara had never really thought about it until now, but it was true -- Jack was always staring off into space, looking like he was thinking, making conversation a bit awkward. But did that mean that he didn't talk to people much, didn't get to interact? Did that mean that the only person he got to share his feelings with was himself?

What a lonely existence.

Jack's icy rigidness increased, and he grimaced. "I guess," he admitted, looking like he'd swallowed something foul. "I know I tend to 'zone out', as North has put it before, but I don't see where it matters much. I travel a lot, like I said, so I really only get to see people I know at the Council meetings, and then North...well, he's the only one that really talks to me," Clara felt her chest ache when he said that, and then Jack shrugged again. "But it doesn't matter much. I don't care if I have anyone around."

He didn't *care*? How could that be? How could he stand such a lonely life, without friends or family or--

"But don't you want to fall in love, have someone else there with you?" Clara couldn't help but ask the question, stepping towards Jack, feeling pained as Jack stepped back, defensive all of a sudden. "Isn't that important to you?"

It had always been important to her. She'd always wanted to find true love, get married, travel the world, see the sights, and spend time with her new and old family. She'd always thought that it would be great, that it was something to look forward to, that when she did find love and get married, she'd get her very own happy ending, just like you were supposed to.

But Clara had seen what "happy endings" amounted to. Though her parents had been immensely happy (from what she remembered, and what her dad had told her), they'd still had fights and arguments, and had even hated each other at times. And then her stepmother -- well, Clara wasn't sure if her stepmother had really loved her dad at all, or if she had just been faking it.

But either way, "happy endings" weren't guaranteed in real life, like they were at the end of every storybook. Not every marriage, friendship, or even acquaintance ended in happiness -- at least, not if you didn't work for it.

But, oh, if you worked for your happy ending -- worked to keep it safe and sound -- Clara was sure that it was possible.

Though Jack didn't seem to think so.

He scoffed at her questions, his blue eyes just as cold as they'd been the first day she'd met him. "*Love?*" he asked, scowling as if it were a curse word. "What do I care about love? I don't need anyone. And besides," he crossed his arms in a challenging way, his icy eyes shooting stakes through her. "I don't think love is real, anyway."

"You don't?" Clara was completely shocked, her doe eyes widening. "What do you mean by that? How can you not believe in love? I mean--"

Jack cut her off, his fists balling slightly. "This is what I mean!" he all but shouted. "This is what's wrong with the world! You always *assume* everything! You assume that you know everything about me, and you assume that I love Christmas, and you assume that I want to find that oh-so-special someone to spend the rest of my life with. You spend all your time assuming, and yet you're never *right* about *anything*!"

The words hit Clara like a slap, and she stumbled back, staring at Jack in shock. As much as she hated to admit it, he was right. She did assume all of those things. She didn't know everything about Jack and his past -- even though she desperately wanted to know -- but she had already made assumptions about it. She had already decided that something sad had happened to him in the past -- something that had made him into the irritable person he was today, something that had made him hate Christmas.

She hadn't asked Jack what he'd thought about her favorite holiday. She had just assumed that he loved it as much as she did -- as everyone else seemed to -- even though she'd been completely wrong.

And love, she had just assumed that Jack wanted to fall in love with a nice girl and stay with her forever, just like most guys (secretly) did. She had never even thought that he would be repelled by the idea of love. She had never even thought that he would hate it.

But...I don't understand. Clara's thoughts were spinning now, making her feel dizzy. *How can he not believe that love is real? Hasn't he ever felt it himself? Hasn't he ever received it?*

Maybe not. Maybe he hadn't been loved by anyone before -- by family, by friends. Maybe she had just assumed yet again.

These thoughts made Clara feel even more dizzy, spinning until she nearly fell, losing all control of her balance. Just as she was about to collide with the ground, she felt a hand wrap around her arm, holding her up. When she looked up, all she could see was Jack's face.

"I'm sorry," his voice was strangely quiet now, so different from the shout she had heard not a moment before. "I don't mean to explode, it's just..." he sighed as he helped her stand, never letting go of her arm. "It's just that, sometimes, I don't know what to make of you, Clara. Your ideas are so different from mine, and I feel like no matter how hard you try, you'll never understand me."

Clara had to blink before she could see him clearly, but when she met his eyes, she suddenly felt dizzy all over again.

What was he saying? That she could never understand him? That they could never understand one another? That she would always be standing there, on the other side of the gate, trying to get into his prison, but never able to find the key?

Clara didn't want that. She wanted to be able to understand him, if only a little bit.

She was trying so hard to understand.

"You're not all bad, though," Jack tried forcibly to smile then, his hand still on her arm, part of him still touching her. "At least you *try* to understand. Most people just look the other way, as if they can't see me," he smiled wryly on that note, all force gone. "But we only have a few more days together, so quit trying so hard..." he trailed off as his eyes darkened, and he finally let go of her, stepping back.

Clara suddenly felt as heavy as a rock as she stared at him, wanting nothing more than for time to rewind, for him to never let her go. She wasn't sure why she felt this way, but she knew that she did, and that alone confused her.

What was going on? What was happening to her? She couldn't understand it.

Jack was about to turn and start towards the café again -- for their lunch date with North -- when suddenly he caught her eyes another time, and stopped. When he smiled, it was the gentlest smile she'd ever seen him share.

"You know," he said, suddenly conversational, "I've thought about it. If I knew what type of girl I liked...well, I'd have to say, she'd probably be something like *you*," and with that said, he turned on his heel and started off, reminding her of their lunch date with North, telling her that they'd cut through the *Empty Flake Pass*.

But Clara, Clara couldn't move. She stared after him as he started off, her chest feeling like it would burst at any moment, so full of emotion.

Chapter Thirteen: Jack

It happened at the Empty Flake Pass, on the way to their lunch date (if you wanted to call it that) with North...

Jack and Clara were walking towards the pass -- Jack relating to Clara various illegal uses for Christmas tree tinsel -- when a snowball came soaring through the air, hitting Jack square in the face.

Now Jack, being the oh-so-patient person he is, simply sighed, tearing the snow away from his face. He waited about five seconds or so -- *maybe* six -- before yelling: "Who threw that?" his shoulders already hunching in annoyance.

The forest around them was silent as Clara secretly giggled, obviously finding this abuse funny. Jack scanned the trees and snowbanks as Clara laughed next to him, but he didn't see anything...

So he turned towards Clara, a giant grimace on his face. "What's so hilarious?" he asked darkly, though he already knew the answer.

"Nothing," Clara replied, stifling her laughter, plastering on a lovely, innocent smile that didn't fool Jack for one moment -- though he did like looking at it. "Nothing at all."

Jack gave her another grimace before he turned back towards the trees, still searching for his assailant. It had been quite a long time since he'd last been hit with a snowball...since he'd first turned against Christmas.

When he'd first "gone evil" (as Mrs. Claus so lovingly put it), he'd tried to destroy Christmas just as he was trying presently, only he hadn't been as smart then. He hadn't taken many things into calculation. He hadn't come up with a brilliantly evil plan -- in fact, he'd just attacked Santa, right in front of everyone, trying to get his frustrations out. He hadn't been thinking clearly then, having just lost Molly, and the fatly obese man had overpowered him, not surprisingly.

And then everyone had ganged up on the "evil" Jack Frost, throwing snowballs at him, trying to get him away from Santa. Jack had disappeared for a year after that, plotting his revenge on Christmas, waiting.

Jack heard Clara shriek as a snowball hit her, landing in her hair.

He was still waiting, waiting for Christmas to be gone.

"*Ha*! See how it is?" Jack couldn't help but shout as Clara clutched the side of her head, obviously not used to snowballs. "How do you like--" Jack didn't have time to finish his sentence, because just then another snowball came flying towards him, hitting his arm. Jack growled at the impact as another came flying towards Clara, who was still getting over her first attack. Jack found himself strangely angry when the second snowball hit Clara, a third following in its footsteps, barely missing the brunette.

How dare they attack Clara! Once was bad enough -- funny almost, considering how she'd shrieked -- but an all-out attack was uncalled for! Jack was angry enough that someone had attacked him -- but Clara, too? That was too much!

Jack stepped forward as the snowballs continued to rain down, barely missing one as it flew past him, hitting Clara in the leg. "Alright!" he shouted to a particularly large snowbank, where the snowballs seemed to be coming from. "Show yourself!" he felt his fists ball as he glowered at the bank in rage.

It was a moment before anyone appeared, but when four little beanie-capped heads poked over the edge of the snowbank, Jack wanted to smack himself.

Of course. Elven children.

If the life of an elf was spent making toys, running the North Pole, and drinking hot cocoa, then the life of an elven child was spent playing with toys, making model cars, and of course, throwing snowballs.

Over the years, the elves had developed an intense dislike of Jack (which almost-but-not- quite rivaled Mrs. Claus'), wishing he would never visit the North Pole. And it seemed, from the way the elven kids were glaring and sneering, that this dislike had been passed down to the elves' children.

Jack watched as the extra-mini children stared at him, jeering at first, but then screaming as Jack glared at them threateningly. They put down their snowballs as they slid off the snowbank, heading for the trees, running before they could get caught.

Jack didn't follow them, but he shouted words of warning.

"Yeah, you'd better run!" his voice was like ice as the elven kids ran, a few of them tripping. "Or else I'll catch you, and you'll be frozen until--"

Jack was cut off by none other than Clara. "Can you really do that?" she asked, dusting the remaining snow from her blue dress and cloak. "Can you really freeze people?"

Is she asking because of the threat I gave her the other night, or because she just wants to know? Jack wondered, feeling a sudden ache in his chest as he thought about the threat he'd given her. *I guess she doesn't really know much about my powers.*

She had to have asked because she wanted to know. She wasn't frowning or scared or anything -- merely curious, her doe eyes staring at him. She couldn't have been asking him because she was still afraid he might freeze her. She had already forgotten that, or at least pushed it to the back of her mind.

Despite his mental reassurances, Jack couldn't shake the ache he felt when thinking of the threat he'd given Clara. There was no way he'd be able to take it back. And even though they were back to being friends now, and Clara was nothing but curious looking, she had to have still thought about it, even if it was in the back of her mind.

She would always think about it now. She would always be afraid of him -- at least somewhat. His words would always be there.

Even if he didn't -- and *hadn't* -- meant them.

"My powers aren't exactly limited," Jack started to explain, trying to push his past threat from his mind. "So, yes, I can freeze people. I can freeze anything, anything at all, but," he smiled mysteriously at Clara as they started walking again, nearing a frozen lake. "that isn't all I can do. I do have other talents, aside from just freezing things," he grinned at her then, starting towards the lake, Clara following slowly.

Jack didn't tell others about his abilities very often, mostly keeping them to himself. The only person who really knew about his talents was North, and that was only because he'd happened upon them by accident, following Jack to a frozen lake one day when he'd gotten upset.

Jack smiled broadly as he fished a long, blue, pen-like object out of his coat pocket.

But, today he was going to show Clara what he could *really* do.

"What is that?" Clara asked, pointing to the pen-like object that Jack held, which, when he'd pressed the silver button at its end, had grown a curved, blade-like tip.

Jack smirked as he held up the pen. "This?" he asked innocently. "This is what you call a carving tool."

"A *carving* tool?" this seemed to be new to Clara, who gaped at the object as if it had two living, breathing heads. "For carving what, exactly?"

Jack felt his smirk widen as he stepped out onto the ice. He didn't slip or slide, much too used to the frozen surface, feeling strangely at home on it, laughing to himself as he remembered the time North had suggested he become a figure skater (though Jack hadn't found it at all funny at the time).

Jack walked until he was about at the center of the little lake before he looked up at Clara, who was watching him quizzically. He found himself immersed in her questioning stare, almost entranced by the concentration and curiosity on her face.

She smiled at him as she cocked her head, and Jack looked away, down at the ice beneath his loafer-clad feet.

"This," he finally said, holding up the carving-tool pen, "is used for carving ice," he smirked again as he saw Clara's confused expression reflected on the ice's surface, bending down towards the frozen lake. "The head is made of diamond, the sharpest gemstone. It's been specially made for this…" he stopped speaking for a moment as he touched his hand to the ice below, studying it.

Jack could hardly remember the day he'd first been introduced to carving. It had been so long ago, when he'd still been human.

But, from what he did remember of it, it had been his father who had shown him the basics, on one of the rare days he was home.

It had been a simpler time in Jack's life -- before all of the tragedies had happened, before he'd become the official Jack Frost. It was one of the few happy memories he had of his father, and despite everything that had happened afterward, he still cherished the memory--

Well, he cherished it as much as he cherished anything, which usually wasn't much. Jack tried to stay away from emotions, though he'd been having too many lately.

Jack found himself smiling strangely when he finally stepped off of the frozen lake, back onto the snow-covered ground, holding a huge chunk of ice in his hand. He showed it to the intrigued Clara before he set to work carving it, holding the ice block with one hand, the carving-pen with the other.

It had never taken Jack long to finish a carving -- an hour at the most -- and it didn't take him long that day, either. In less than five minutes the ice block was carved to perfection, and he was looking at his finished work, more than satisfied.

Out of the corner of his eye he saw Clara staring at him, mystified as he gently blew on the work of art, creating an icy cloud around it, solidifying his sculpture.

When he was finished, he offered the newly carved carving to Clara, grinning like the Cheshire Cat. "Here you are, then," he said, mock bowing as he beamed. "A rose for your thoughts, princess?"

Clara took the sculpted rose with a smile, trying to cover her laugh.

Jack rolled his eyes. "Alright, alright. That was corny, wasn't it?"

"It was sweet, though," Clara admitted, staring down at the glistening rose he'd given her, and Jack felt his insides buzz. "And it's also...*amazing*," she gave him a shy smile before she looked back down at the sculpted rose, studying it.

As Clara studied the rose, Jack studied her, not quite able to look away.

He didn't know what it was, but there was something about the way that Clara studied the icy rose in her hand -- the rose that honestly looked like a blue version of the real thing -- that made a blush come to his cheeks. Maybe it was because she was studying something he had made, or maybe it was something else.

After all, Clara may have just said that he was amazing, but he didn't feel so amazing at the moment -- not compared to *her*, anyway.

Jack couldn't ignore how strange and unique the girl standing in front of him was -- how interesting, intelligent, focused, curious she was. Clara had lived all of her life in a place and way that was unstable, nearly unfeeling, having no regard for what she herself wanted, and yet she had grown up to be the most interesting person in the world.

And not only was she *interesting*, but she was also *interested.*

Clara looked at the world around her and saw it not only as a thing. She wanted to know how everything worked.

She wanted to know how things functioned, connected, felt. She wanted to know any and every thing she could, though she really had no reason to be curious about any of it.

She should have been a miserable person. She should have hated life. She should have scorned her parents and grandparents and every living thing that walked the planet for the way she'd been treated--

But she *didn't*.

Despite everything and everyone, Clara was a completely wholesome, caring, life-loving person. Through all that she had been through in her life -- the death of her mother, her stepmother's wrath, her father's ignorance -- life had managed to steal nothing from her. She was--

Perfect. Clara was perfect.

Jack didn't notice he was staring at Clara until she looked up at him, her eyelashes fluttering like butterfly wings. "What is it?" she asked, curious. "What are you looking at?"

Jack's mouth answered without him. "You," he said, voice strangely quiet. "I was looking at you."

To Jack's surprise, Clara blushed when she heard that, her eyes widening again, her hands trembling ever so slightly. He didn't know why she reacted like this, getting all embarrassed, because he knew she didn't like him that way.

How had he been so stupid? What was he thinking? He couldn't be telling her things like that! She would get the wrong idea!

He did *not* like Clara Claus!

Jack looked away from her as quickly as possible, annoyed with himself for being so honest. "We'd better get going," he said, starting once again towards the *Empty Flake Pass*. "Or we'll be late to meet North, and goodness knows he'd hate that. He's so OCD about time," he looked to see if Clara was coming.

She was, though at a slow pace, her head bent in thought and what looked like worry. Jack watched her for a moment before she finally caught up with him, and they stepped into the Pass, trudging up a small hill.

The Empty Flake Pass was perhaps the only place in all of the North Pole (well, in the town, anyway) that was desolate, holding nothing but a small not-quite road and a view—

A view of the North Pole.

"Wow," Clara breathed when they reached the top, which sat just over the trees of the park, overlooking Santa's little town in all its wonder. "You can see *everything*! There's the theater, the café, the workshop! It's amazing," a serene smile graced her lips as she stared, snow falling in small flakes around her. "Isn't it beautiful?"

Jack smiled, enjoying the scenery, his confusion over Clara's earlier expression pushed aside. "Yes, it is beautiful," he said softly, the word feeling strange on his tongue -- since it was so used to throwing around insults instead of complements.

It wasn't until Jack blinked that the fact that he was looking at Clara, not the town, sunk in.

Jack wanted to smack himself yet again as he looked away from her towards the town, trying to focus on something.

What was he *thinking*? He couldn't be doing this -- getting attached to Clara, making her ice sculptures, calling her beautiful. He just couldn't. It would ruin all of his plans, ruin his promise -- and he couldn't allow that to happen.

He only had one chance left. Only one more Christmas to try and destroy. If he couldn't implement his plan this year, there would be no trying again. If he couldn't rid the world of Christmas by sunrise on Christmas day, then St. Nick would banish him from the Winter Council, from his role as Jack Frost, since he wouldn't -- and couldn't -- fulfill St. Nick's proposed task.

He had to destroy Christmas this year, even if it meant destroying Clara as well. He couldn't afford to wait.

He had promised himself, and Molly--

He couldn't let his sister die in vain.

"Clara," Jack cleared his throat, trying to find a way to approach the subject of Santa, pushing his strange emotions aside, hiding them just as he hid every other emotion that happened his way, "what do you think of--"

Just as he was about to say Santa's name, a cold gust blew by, making Clara shiver convulsively, Jack not even flinching, since he was more than used to the cold. Distracted by the wind, Jack didn't get to finish his question, and before he could ask another, Clara spoke, shivering again.

"It's so *cold*!" Clara shivered a third time as she gasped, obviously not liking the wind. "How do you stand it? Is it because you're Jack Frost, or because..." she turned towards Jack, cheeks red — this time from the wind, which was starting to pick up.

She hadn't been able to say *"immortal"*.

Jack shrugged, deciding to leave the topic of Santa for later. *Again.* "Part of it is because of my job, and the fact that I'm...immortal," he tried to judge Clara's reaction to the word, but she didn't flinch, "and impervious to the cold, but part of is just because I'm accustomed to it. I'm around the cold all day, all week, all year," he grinned at her as they started down the gradual slope that sat on the opposite side of the Pass, leading into Santa's town. "If you're around the cold that much, you start to ignore it. I could probably freeze myself and not even notice," he sniggered at that thought, turning to make sure Clara wouldn't slide down the slope.

That was the last thing he needed. Sliding down the slope would be, while it was fun, a bad idea. Not only would they get covered in snow, having fun would start to make him forget his mission again, and he didn't want that.

He had to stay focused, no matter what.

I'll ask her about Santa. Jack thought as they continued down the slope, stepping carefully, about halfway there. *I'll ask her...*

Jack never got to ask Clara about Santa as they traveled down the slope, however, because just at that moment the wind picked up, blocking out his voice, and Clara slipped, completely clumsy. Jack refrained from making a comment on her climbing and falling skills (though she wouldn't have heard him, anyway) as he reached out and caught her, grabbing onto her arm just as he had done earlier that day.

And that was when everything changed.

Jack helped Clara to stand again, taking the greatest of care, and as she blinked into the harsh wind, he offered her his hand, not even thinking about it.

Before he could take the action back, Clara grasped his offered hand, smiling shyly as they continued the rest of the way down the slope towards the café and their lunch date with North--

But Jack didn't mind so much.

He kept hold of Clara's hand all the way down the slope, and even into the town. Part of him said he was stupid for it, and part of him didn't care.

But all of him was happy, wanting to hold onto Clara's hand as long as he could...wanting to keep her as close as possible until he had to let her go.

****

When they reached the café, North was already there, waiting outside, staring at the sky and looking as thoughtful as ever.

He looked down just as they stopped in front of him, smiling slightly when he saw Clara. "You must be Miss Claus," he said, tipping his head a little as a bow. "It's wonderful to meet you," Jack wanted to beat North's head in as he kissed Clara's hand, but he refrained because Clara didn't seem to mind.

"Thank you," Clara said with a smile, cocking her head at North. "You must be North, then?"

North's smile didn't widen, which wasn't surprising, considering it was shocking for him to smile at all. "Yes," he said in his near-monotone voice, glancing towards Jack. "I'm North. I assume Jack told you about me?"

Jack felt his chest tighten in anticipation when he saw North glance at him, knowing his friend was just itching for the chance to push his buttons. Unfortunately, he probably would be able to. Jack was having a hard enough time with his emotions already.

"Well, isn't it obvious? Of *course* I told her!" Jack snorted as he crossed his arms, glaring at North. "Don't be stupid."

North's smile tightened, and his eyes curved upwards ever so slightly; it was his mocking expression. "Of course. Of course, Jack. No need to get yourself wound up. I'm sure you didn't mean to make Miss Clara *late*."

"We're not late!" Jack felt his fists ball as he checked his watch, Clara jumping at the loudness of his voice. "We're right on time! Or can't you *read* time?"

North pretended to be uninterested then, looking up at the sky once more. "Of course I can read time," he said in monotone. "You're the one with the *digital* watch."

Jack probably would have tackled North had Clara not interrupted then, stepping in between the two boys.

"Like I said," her voice was cheery, forced. "It's very nice to meet you, North, but I'm actually starving, so could we, uh..." she glanced at Jack, and he felt his temper fade, seeing her big doe eyes. "Could we please go in?"

Even if Jack had wanted to say no, he couldn't have. The look in her eyes was just pleading for peace, and though peace wasn't really his thing, he knew he had to oblige.

He couldn't stand for her to be unhappy now, especially since he was going to ruin her life later.

"Alright, alright," Jack sighed, glancing at the café door. "Let's go in already. I'm starving, too," he saw Clara smile then, making everything worthwhile, and--

Before he could step into the café, North stopped him. "Aren't you going to let Clara in first?" he asked, an eyebrow perking ever so slightly. "You know -- *'hold the door; ladies first.'* Any of this ringing a bell?"

"What are you--" Jack started, but North cut him off again.

His navy-haired friend sighed, taking Clara's arm. "Don't mind him," he said as he opened the door for her, admitting her into the café. "Jack doesn't have much training as a gentleman. In fact, he's more like a *mongrel* than anything. I blame it on his parents, personally," Jack felt anger itch at him when North mentioned his parents. "I don't think he had any good role-models growing up..." North seemed to question this in his mind as he walked in behind Clara, letting the door hit Jack as he tried to squeeze through. "Or maybe he's just lazy..." he trailed off then, asking Clara which table she'd like to sit at.

"Mongrel!" Jack's anger was back as he glared at North, pushing past him to pull Clara's chair out for her, ignoring the way she tried to cover her laugh. "What do you mean 'mongrel'? What are you trying to say?"

North simply shrugged as he went to sit next to Clara, pulling out his own chair. "Oh, nothing," even his monotone voice was slightly smug as he glanced back at Jack, who glared at him.

How dare North call him a mongrel! Sure, he wasn't as well learned as North was, but it wasn't his fault! He'd grown up in a family that hadn't cared anything for values.

And how dare North sit next to Clara! He'd just met her!

"We should have just had lunch by ourselves," Jack growled as he sat down, wedging in between Clara and North before North could start a conversation. "It would have been so much better!"

When Clara blinked at him, confused once again, she cocked her head. "Why?" she asked, the perfect picture of innocence. "Didn't you want me to meet North?"

Jack was just about to answer when North cut him off. Again. "I think he's just jealous, Clara," North said as he picked up the menu, flipping through it, Clara's face turning pink. "He wants you all to himself."

It was then that Jack lost it. "What are you t-talking about?" he sputtered, feeling flustered at North's mention of his jealousy. "Don't be stupid! I brought her here so she could meet you and--"

"Alright, alright," North's smug smile was back — even bigger now than normal, which kind of scared Jack. "Let's simply order, shall we?" he cast Jack another smug smile as he stood and crossed to the other side of the table, leaving Jack sitting next to Clara, unbearably close.

Clara nodded, looking from one to the other. "I think that's a good idea," she said, glancing down at the menu again.

She may not have said anything, but Jack could more than catch the disproval in her voice. Normally Clara didn't seem to mind his outbursts to an small extent, wonderfully patient, but now...she was upset, obviously annoyed with their boyish bantering, since North was egging him on purpose.

North did that on numerous occasions, saying things he knew would upset Jack, just to see his reaction, how he handled the situation. And Jack knew that, though this was annoying, he was the one choosing to get upset. He was the one who was going to have to control his frenzying emotions, because otherwise, he would say something he'd regret.

And he didn't want to say something he would regret — especially around Clara.

"So, Clara, have you seen the Pass?" it was North's voice that broke through Jack's thoughts, addressing his oh-so-dear Clara Claus. "Isn't it extraordinary?"

Clara's features brightened at this, and Jack felt his heart pound in his chest. "Oh! Yes. Yes, I have," Clara said as she sat her menu down, looking up at North. "It's wonderful. I'd like to go again sometime," she glanced over at Jack then, asking silently if they could go.

"We can't," Jack hated to tell her no almost as much as he hated the fact that he hated to tell her no, but knew he had to. "Remember that wind we ran into today? It's the pre- Christmas wind. North brings it up every year before Christmas Eve, to prepare for the holiday," he grimaced as he said the word "Christmas", but Clara hardly seemed to notice.

She was looking at North now. "The pre-Christmas wind?" she asked, raising an eyebrow, as cutely curious as always. "What's that?"

"Oh, it's fantastic," the words sounded strange coming from North's mouth, since they weren't fluctuating but monotone, though Jack knew North meant them. "Every year I bring in the pre-Christmas wind. It brings snowstorms to the area, so that no planes or helicopters will try and find Santa's town; it works in accordance with the barrier, which from outside appears as an afterimage, though it's not seen on any human equipment," he shook his head at that, frowning just a tad bit.

"Every year some new team tries to find the North Pole, so they can watch Santa's takeoff, prove he's real. The Pole is protected the rest of the year, hid from human sight, but the day before Christmas Eve its protective shield – different from the barrier, mind you – is taken away, so that Santa won't have any problems leaving," his slight frown turned into a slight smile then, as he looked at Clara. "So it's my job to bring in a snowstorm, so that no one can get close. If you were to try and go to the Pass after today, you'd freeze."

Clara's eyebrows wound at that. "Oh," she said, looking defeated. "That's too bad. I wanted to go and see the Pass again. The town and snow are just beautiful from up there," she stopped speaking after a moment, frowning again, and Jack looked at North, irritated.

He'd truthfully been hoping that Clara would forget all about the Pass once they left it, since he couldn't stand telling her no (a fact which was still bothering him). But no, North just had to bring it up, dashing all of Clara's premature hopes.

Though that was better than what he was going to do. At least North hadn't told Clara that Santa was evil, destroying the dreams she had of a loving family.

That was what *Jack* was going to do.

"So, Clara, what do you think of Santa Claus?" it was North who popped the question, surprising Jack to no end. "I know you haven't known him that long, but..." he trailed off, looking at Clara but glancing at Jack, as if to egg him on.

And egg him on it did.

Jack glared at North icily — a look that made most people's hearts stop beating — but North didn't even flinch, though he lost his slight grin, probably seeing his error. Jack was just about to yell at him again, not caring if Clara saw, when Clara suddenly spoke--

"Santa?" she asked, her voice strangely small, almost distant. She looked off for a moment, staring at the wall before she replied. "It may sound strange, because I've only known him a few days, but..." her blank expression was replaced by a warm, soft smile, and Jack felt his heart sink to the bottom of his chest, wishing for all the world that she'd look at him like that -- though he didn't understand why or how. "I love my grandpa."

Jack was shocked to hear this news, as was North, though it didn't show on his face nearly as much as Jack's.

She *loved* him? She loved Santa? Already?

It just wasn't fair.

I thought it would take more time. Jack felt his heart sink even further into his chest, all but evaporating, though he was trying so hard to smite his emotions. *I thought I had more time.*

How could this have happened so quickly? She had just met Santa!

How was it possible? How could someone learn to love someone else in less than a week?

It just didn't make sense!

But...wasn't that what had happened with Clara? Though Jack didn't *love* her necessarily, hadn't he grown to care for and become attached to Clara in a short amount of time? Hadn't she surpassed all of his expectations of her in the relatively small time she'd been near him, amazing him with her wonderful, intriguing personality? Hadn't Clara attached herself to him like a leech, all without his approval?

Yes, Jack had to admit.

Yes, Clara had attached herself to him in the time he'd spent with her, even if it was without her knowledge or planning. He *cared* for her, though he had promised himself he wouldn't. He cared for her, though he knew he shouldn't.

He cared for her, and that in itself was a miracle.

Why couldn't she care for Santa also -- a blood relation who was everything she wanted to hold near and dear, the very essence of her beloved holiday?

But, *still.*

Jack looked at Clara one last time, wondering what he had done to deserve this.

He'd only been expecting to crush her dreams along with Christmas...not her *heart*.

Chapter Fourteen: Clara

"So, are you going to tell me what it is now?" Clara looked up to see Jack studying her face, waiting for her answer.

They had left their lunch date with North (which had taken forever) perhaps ten minutes ago, and were now walking around Santa's North Pole town as it started to grow dark, window-shopping more or less.

Clara was amazed by all of the Christmas decorations and displays that were set up in the tiny shops of the little town, looking just like New York's Times Square (only considerably smaller). She watched as little elves bought Christmas gifts for their families, rushing from shop to shop, just like people did...

It was strange how much this world was like the one she knew, only so different.

I remember Christmas shopping. Clara thought as she watched a little elven girl and her elven mother walk down the street, both carrying bags.

They had been out shopping that fateful night, her and her mother had. They had been looking for a last minute gift for Clara's father, who was nearly impossible to shop for. They had been going from store to store, looking in windows, gaping at displays. They had been happy, jumping in the car to make their way to their next destination. They had been--

They had been thirsty when they'd stopped at that gas station, where the man had suddenly appeared, holding a gun...where Clara had screamed, her mother lying lifeless on the ground.

"Clara!" it was Jack's voice that broke through her thoughts, seemingly a million miles away. "Hey, are you--"

Clara cut him off as she blinked, realizing that she was starting to sway, unstable. "Oh...yes..." she said slowly, shaking her head, gaining use of her feet. "I'm fine..." she wished it were the truth.

Jack didn't say anything in reply, but the way he stared at her, his icy blue eyes boring into her brown ones, told her that he knew she was lying, that he knew she wasn't alright.

"I'm sorry," Clara sighed as they stopped at a particularly large shop window, holding all sorts of Christmas cheer. "I'll tell you now..." she trailed off, staring into the glass.

Clara had been trying to figure out what exactly to tell Jack all day, knowing that he wouldn't be able to keep his curiosity stable for too long.

Since she had decided to tell him about her mother that morning, a million different scenarios had played through Clara's head -- a million different ways for her to tell him the truth -- but none of them had seemed to fit quite right, and they still didn't.

But, as Clara peered at the window, an idea suddenly popped into her mind.

"Jack," she said, eyes widening, "do you know what that is?" she pointed towards the window, singling out a single Christmas-like object.

Jack didn't even look at the display, snorting. "It's Christmas junk, of course," he said, as though it were obvious. "They cram it in these windows every year, taking up valuable space," his arms crossed as he shot her a grimace, probably annoyed that they were even referring to the holiday he so ardently hated.

But Clara shook her head. "No," she said, pointing to the glass again. "I'm not talking about the whole display. I'm talking about that," she pointed once more to the object that she wanted Jack to see, hoping she sounded a little more forceful this time.

This was her plan, after all. She was going to tell Jack about her mother -- her wonderful, lovely, deceased mother, who had always kept Christmas Spirit best. Maybe if she could get Jack to understand her mother -- to understand what she had taught Clara about Christmas, and what Christmas now meant to Clara -- then maybe, just maybe, she could get him to give Christmas another chance.

I sure hope so. Clara thought, watching as Jack took a second glance at the display, scowling now. *I hope I can get him to understand.*

She wanted him to be able to look past the commercialism of Christmas, really see the heart of it. She wanted him to be able to put away his hate for the holiday.

Maybe then, he would tell her what had happened to him. Maybe then, she would discover why it was that he hated Christmas. Maybe then, he would really start to understand what hope was all about.

"Are you talking about that shiny thing?" Jack once again broke Clara from her thoughts, pointing towards the display. "Over there, on the right?"

Clara's eyes lit up when he finally saw it, and she smiled. "Yes," she said, looking at the object herself.

The object in the window -- the object that she was so attached to -- was none other than a plastic, sparkly nativity scene, much like the one her mother used to have, only bigger, brighter, more expensive looking. It was sitting up on a shelf in the display, a glowing star hanging above it, in its own little spot, far away from the Santa decor.

Clara felt her chest constrict when she laid eyes on it, even though she loved it instantly, thinking of her father.

She had talked to him maybe once since coming to the North Pole, asking him how things were going with the divorce, asking him if Isabelle was being her usual annoying self. He had answered all of her questions directly, leaving no room for discussions, and after a moment of checking up on her, had ended the conversation, leaving Clara in the Claus' living room, phone held to her ear.

She'd stayed there with the phone to her ear for more than a few moments, her father's voice ringing through her head, wishing she could hear it again, but by then it had been too late. Her father had already informed her that he probably wouldn't make it back to the Pole for Christmas, so Clara had known that she was going to be all alone, the only portion of her parents with her being the nativity scene her father had given her before he'd left...the nativity scene that had been her mother's.

It wasn't like Clara didn't appreciate her newfound family or anything, but it would have been nice to have her father home for Christmas.

But, that was alright. He had things he had to do, and she understood that, even if it made her sad sometimes. Her father already missed out on so much because of his work, why should he have to miss out on Christmas, too? It wasn't like Clara was a little girl anymore. She would be turning eighteen in a few days, her birthday being the day of Christmas.

Clara looked over at Jack as she began her explanation, taking a deep breath as she focused on the present.

"My mother's nativity scene is almost like that," she said, pointing once again at the window display. "Only smaller. She made it one year when she was younger, as a Christmas present for her dad -- Santa -- and then he gave it to her before she left home. My father has had it for years, and this year he gave it to me before he left the North Pole."

Jack raised an eyebrow at this, but didn't really look all that interested. "How fascinating," he said, sneering as he looked at the display again. "But what does this have to do with what you wanted to tell me?"

"*Everything*," the word rolled off Clara's tongue in a breathy state as she looked at the nativity scene again. "Because it was my mother's, and she died on Christmas Eve...because of me."

Clara remembered that single, solitary memory no matter where she was, what she was doing. It stuck to her mind so hard that she could scarcely think sometimes, seeing the image of her dead mother over and over and over again.

She remembered what had happened when they'd pulled up at the gas station, both of them hopping out of their car to get a drink at the convenience store. She remembered what had happened when the man with the gun had come out, waving his weapon as if it were a flag. She remembered what had happened when her mother had gasped, pulling her out of the way, hoping that the man hadn't seen them. She remembered what had happened when --

BANG!

Why had they stopped at the gas station? They had been headed to the mall! Couldn't they have gotten a drink there! Why had it been the gas station? Why not somewhere else? Clara found that tears were dripping down her face as she related the tale to Jack, who was now staring at her, the same expression on his face as when he'd first seen her cry. But this time, she didn't mind. This time, Jack wasn't a stranger.

He was a *friend*.

"She would have been alright if I hadn't screamed," the words burned at Clara's throat, wanting her to take them back. "The man with the gun didn't even see us. But then I screamed and he shot her, and—"

Clara's words stopped forming then, and the night was silent, the wind blowing in the snow, all of the little elves shopping, not even seeing Jack and Clara.

And Clara tried to slow her pounding heart as she closed her eyes, wishing her tears would stop…but the moment she felt Jack's hand brush at her cheek, wiping her tears away, she felt it speed right back up.

When she opened her eyes she saw Jack was staring at her with a sad, pained expression, looking at a loss.

"I'm sorry, Clara," he said, and in that moment he sounded more sincere than he ever had. "I'm sorry for everything. I wish it hadn't happened, and I wish that I could do something to change it for you," his eyes settled strangely on her then, and he looked like he'd just realized something. "And, I wish I had the same strength as you do."

The words confused Clara, and she felt more teardrops fall from her eyes as Jack swiped them away once again before pulling his hand away -- though Clara honestly wished he would just hug her instead, the biting sadness she felt over what she'd just told him still spreading.

What had he meant when he'd said she had "strength"? Clara had never felt strong, not once in her life, so how was it he--

"I understand what you're trying to do," Jack's words came faster now, as if all of the thoughts were rushing straight from his head to his mouth. "I know you're trying to get me to not hate Christmas by telling me the truth, making me realize how you've reacted to it even after tragedy, but..." he stopped for a moment, sighing, and looked sorry once again. "*I can't stop hating it.* It's too important somehow, and I don't have the type of strength you do -- I can't just stop hating something that ruined everything."

His icy eyes were penetrating as he said: "I'm *not* like you."

Clara stared back at Jack as he admitted this, and she once again felt sad. She'd wanted to change his mind, but that was when Clara realized something, just as Jack had--

Maybe it was time, Clara thought, to let Jack sort out his own problems. Though she wanted to help him, she couldn't fix everything -- she realized that now. She had her own problems to sort out too, and though it was hard, she was just going to have to let him discover his own reasons for things.

So, she hadn't changed Jack's mind, but she had told him the truth about her mother, and now she felt better. She had told him the truth, when she couldn't bear to tell anyone else.

After her mother had been shot, the police had been called -- along with her father, who had gotten to the scene faster than the law enforcement had. He'd been frantic when he'd arrived, and Clara knew she'd been crying, on the ground next to her bleeding mother, yelling for her to get back up. By the time the ambulance had gotten there, it had been too late to save anyone.

Clara had spent months upon months at rehabs after that, seeing psychologists, psychiatrists, and every other kind of "trist" there was. But nothing had helped to erase the image of her dead mother from her mind. Nothing had helped to erase her guilt...In fact, Clara had never told anyone about her role in her mother's death--

No one but Jack.

How was it that she could tell Jack -- someone she had met less than a week ago -- her deepest, darkest secret, when she couldn't even tell her own father? What was it about Jack Frost that made her feel so connected to him, so able to tell him, well, *anything*?

Clara wasn't sure, but in that moment it didn't matter, because the fact was that she could tell him.

Clara blinked from her thoughts, looking up at Jack, who was still staring at her, closer than before. She felt her eyebrows knit in confusion as she spotted the look on his face, which now mirrored hers.

Jack was confused? *Why?*

"I don't understand you, Clara," he said in a strange, foreign tone, the look in his eyes pained once again. "I don't understand you at all," the words rang in Clara's head before he continued. "We each have the most grandstanding reason to hate Christmas -- to *hate* it! -- and yet you don't, and I can't understand that."

Clara felt bafflement take her as she stared at him, trying to decipher what he was saying.

Was he hinting that someone else -- someone he loved -- had died on Christmas, just like her mother? Was that why he hated the holiday -- because every time he thought about it, he thought about the person he had lost, the person who he would never get to hug again, never get to smile with? Was that why he hated Christmas, because instead of receiving a wonderful gift on the holiday, he had been thrust into a nightmare?

Was that the reason he hated Christmas?

Jack seemed to sense that he had said too much as he looked into her eyes, frowning now. "Don't ask me about it," his voice was cold again, though not as cold as it had been the last time he'd said it. "I don't want to say anything."

"Okay," Clara felt the blossom in her heart begin to bloom as she reached out, taking Jack's hand. She was going to let him deal with this, but that didn't mean she couldn't help a little bit. "I won't, but can you at least listen to what *I* think about Christmas?"

Jack's eyes flicked down to their intertwined hands before he gave her a rueful smile. "Fine," he said, the anguish disappearing from his face. "I suppose I'll amuse you."

"Thanks," Clara couldn't help but smile at that, turning once again towards the Christmas display. She was going to let Jack's hand go, but she decided against it, realizing that she rather liked the feel of his hand in hers.

Was that normal?

"I know you think that Christmas is nothing but commercial -- toys, and gadgets, and *stuff* -- " Clara giggled as she recited Jack's previous accusation, and he glared at her mildly, wordlessly telling her to move on. "But to me, that's not what Christmas is about at all. Christmas is all about that -- " she pointed to the nativity scene again, her eyes lighting up.

Jack followed her gaze, grimacing. "*That?*" he repeated, eyebrows rising. "So, what you're saying is, Christmas is all about a *piece of plastic?*"

"No!" it was Clara's turn to glare, pointing harder towards the nativity scene. "Look closer."

Jack did look closer, and he grimaced yet again. "Oh, I'm sorry," his voice was mock- polite. "You're saying that Christmas is all about a piece of plastic *in the shape of a child.* My bad."

Clara glared at him again, her lips pulling together, though she wasn't really mad. "That's not what I'm saying at all, Jack. I'm saying that Christmas is all about *Hope*. That's why people give gifts, to be reminded of that," she felt herself calm as she saw Jack's eyes widen, taking another look at the nativity scene in the window, zeroing in on the plastic Christmas child. "The world was given the greatest gift, and that's what started Christmas."

Clara remembered her mother telling her the original Christmas story, reading it to her from a book, a serene smile on her face.

Even though her mother had been Santa's daughter -- Santa, who for many was the epiphany of all Christmases -- she had still been able to see the hope that the real Christmas gave, the hope that her father worked hard to remind people of.

After all, Santa didn't give people gifts just because they were naughty or nice (though Clara was sure that was part of it). He gave them gifts because he was trying to remind them of something, trying to get them to really see past the commercialism that so many people -- like Jack -- saw in Christmas. Clara's grandfather wasn't only trying to make the kids of the world happy, but to remind them of what Christmas was really all about.

"Hope," when Jack said the word, it rang through Clara's ears, making her heart beat fast. "Hmm, I'm not sure I remember what that word means."

Clara turned towards Jack then, sure he was playing a game, when she realized something...he wasn't.

Jack was being *serious*.

"You've never felt hopeful?" Clara asked, her eyes widening as she gaped at him, horrified.

Jack's smile was wry when he looked at her, squeezing her hand. "I guess I can't say that," he said, his blue eyes seeming to turn cold again. "But it certainly isn't what I think of when I think of Christmas..." he trailed off then, jaw clenching at the word "Christmas".

Clara felt then was the time to be truthful.

"I didn't use to think so, either," Clara admitted, looking down as she felt a gust of wind pass by her, feeling something akin to regret. "When my mother first died, I blamed Christmas too -- and I also blamed myself...and sometimes, I still do," Clara felt Jack's eyes on her, but she didn't look up. Instead her eyes found one of the Christmas decorations near the bottom of the window display -- a plaything of a family laughing as they opened presents -- and she focused on that.

"I think the only reason I stopped hating Christmas was because I thought of how sad that would have made my mom," Clara continued, eyes feeling suddenly misty. "And once I finally stopped hating Christmas, I eventually stopped hating myself, and then I started to see Christmas for what it really is," when Clara looked up again, Jack was staring at her wholeheartedly, blue eyes wide in shock.

And Clara smiled at him. "I'll never forget my mom. And when I remember her, I want the memories to be full of *love*, not hate."

It seemed like the whole world spun in slow motion as Jack continued to stare at Clara, wide and frosty blue eyes hiding turning thoughts behind them. And Clara didn't mind the wait, because as they stood there, in the swirling snow, something in her began to change.

She finally felt whole now, like some chain that had been binding her had lifted -- like there wasn't a weight above her head anymore. She felt like she could truly move on now that she'd shared her secret, had truly realized what it was she'd been feeling all this time.

Because, even after Clara had decided that she wouldn't hate Christmas or herself -- had finally given up on the rage she'd felt after losing her mother, the overwhelming sadness that had accompanied her loss -- there had still been something sad there, lingering. The fact that she had never told anyone the truth had begun to haunt her, an empty ache in the pit of her stomach, but now...

Now she felt freed from that. Now that she had finally taken the blame she'd placed on herself away, told the truth about what had happened, she felt relieved. And maybe now that he seemed to be thinking what she'd said over in his mind, maybe Jack--

And that was when Clara had her brilliant idea.

"Of course!" she exclaimed, grasping Jack's hand tighter as she made him gasp, blinking quickly as he stopped staring. "I know! I have a great idea!"

Jack smiled strangely then, seeming to still be thinking. "What is it?" he asked.

Clara grinned at his willingness, the whole world seeming like it was falling into place. "I have a proposition, Jack. I think that we should *both* help Santa in the workshop tomorrow. Maybe if you see things up close, you'll get a better idea of what Christmas is to me, to us."

Jack seemed to process this, and Clara could see the gears of his mind turning, turning, turning, trying to figure things out yet again.

She wasn't going to force him to love Christmas; she couldn't change him, and she wasn't going to try -- he would have to make that decision himself, if he wanted to change. She was going to let him figure things out on his own, let him truly discover what Christmas was, what it could be...and what better place to do that at than Santa's workshop?

When Jack finally answered her, he was smiling strangely again. "I'll come if you want me to," he said, and Clara felt happy to hear it.

"I *do*," the words rushed out of Clara's mouth. "I really do."

And, she did. She wanted him to come with her more than almost anything else. She wanted him to see the real side of Christmas, to understand the way she felt.

She wanted Jack to be *happy*.

Was that so wrong?

"Tomorrow, then," Jack finally said as he let go of her hand. "Tomorrow I'll go to the workshop...but only because you asked me to," he smiled wryly then, offering the sky a *"what can I do?"* look. "Don't forget that," and then he was gone, disappearing into the snowy night.

It wasn't until Clara looked up that she realized they had walked away from the Christmas display and shopping plaza, the door to Santa's townhouse standing right next to her. Clara blushed as she realized that Jack had walked her home, reaching for the door.

"*...but only because you asked me to.*"

Clara stopped as the words rang through her head.

Suddenly she felt that if she had asked Jack to do anything -- anything at all -- he would have...but only because she'd asked him to.

Chapter Fifteen: Jack

Jack tried to calm himself as he balanced a tea mug in his shaking hands, feeling strangely frazzled...and annoyed.

He wasn't annoyed for the obvious reason, though. No, it was a completely different reason altogether, a reason he'd never thought, in his wildest dreams, that he would ever come across...

He'd *lied* -- To Clara. No, it hadn't been a horrible lie -- he hadn't told her he loved Christmas, which, for Jack, would have been the most horrific lie of all -- but he had still lied to her, and that made him feel horrible. Though everything in him was trying to fight the feeling, he still felt like he'd betrayed her, though he didn't know why he should care.

Jack sighed as he sat back in his chair, closing his eyes for a moment.

But it was alright. So what if he felt horrible? So what if he'd lied to Clara? He would just ignore it. He'd had enough of feelings and attachments -- what had they ever done for him, anyway? He'd only become attached to two things in his life, and one had already vanished, the other not far behind...

Though, he had to admit, detaching his feelings from Clara was going to be a hard task. It wasn't so difficult to think of her as nothing but Santa's granddaughter -- a pawn in his plan -- when she wasn't around, but when he saw her face...then something happened, and he couldn't ignore what he felt for her.

But that had to stop, no matter what. He'd already lied to her, anyway -- set her up as part of his new, devious plan -- so why not cut all ties with her? It would make things easier.

It would make him fulfill his promise.

Jack nearly jumped out of his seat when the door to his room flew open, admitting North, who he was (for once) very glad to see. His friend cocked his head ever so slightly as he sat down across from Jack, his unfeeling eyes holding a strange light. He stared at Jack for a moment before he glanced at the tea mug Jack held in his hands.

"Are you going to drink that?" North asked, probably noting (along with a million other things) how the mug was still full. "It's peppermint, right?"

Jack nodded, and then shook his head. "Yeah, it's peppermint, and no, I'm not going to drink it. Do you -- " his words were stolen away as North reached for the mug, not even asking.

Jack tried to ignore his annoyance at the gesture, instead turning to the topic at hand -- the very topic that he had asked North to discuss with him.

But, before he could ask North anything about the new Christmas-destroying plan he had put into place, another question flew out of his mouth: "Why did you ask her about Santa?"

"Pardon?" North's eyebrows barely rose at this, curious. "What was that?" he stopped just before taking a sip of tea, the mug in front of his lips.

Jack shook his head, trying to clear it, but the words came out yet again. "Why did you ask her about Santa?" he asked another time, angry at his mouth, wishing he could staple it shut.

"Oh," North's expression turned just a hint smug as he took a sip of tea, making Jack wait for an answer, his eye starting to twitch. "Oh, yes, that. Well, you know..." he trailed off, paying more attention to his tea than to Jack.

Jack couldn't take it then. All of the annoyance and anger and confusion and -- and -- *feelings* -- that had been building up inside of him suddenly exploded, bursting forth from him like a destructive tornado.

He felt his face turn red in fury as he jumped from his chair, facing North, who was quiet, looking into his tea mug as if he were having a private conversation with it.

"Why did you ask her about Santa?" the question burst forth from Jack's lips yet again, and he glared at North, who still didn't look up. "And don't you *dare* tell me 'well, you know' again! I want the truth! The *truth*! You hear me?"

He didn't know why he was getting so upset over the Santa issue, but...then again, maybe he did know.

Jack had been fighting with himself for the past almost-week, wrestling with something he didn't normally wrestle with — something that bore the name of "feelings".

Ever since Molly had died, Jack had all but forgotten about emotions, freezing his heart (so to speak) so that he could feel nothing but the anger that he kept towards Christmas -- feel nothing but the need for revenge. And he had done a good job of keeping his feelings frozen--

He'd kept hating Christmas, devising ways to destroy it, working endlessly on plans for revenge, adapting his icy demeanor. He'd kept hating people, becoming distant and distasteful to anyone but North, who was so unfeeling himself that he didn't even flinch at Jack's insults. He'd managed to stay on the Council, managed to remain the official Jack Frost, even though everyone knew he would stop at nothing to destroy their precious Christmas holiday.

He'd done everything in his power to remain the revenge-seeking person he'd become, to keep the promise he'd made to himself and to Molly to destroy Christmas forever, ridding the world of it.

He'd taken everything into calculation, plotting and scheming and making sure that nothing -- not even St. Nick's threat to expel him -- would stop his plot to rid the world of Christmas. He'd examined every inch of every plan, making sure that no one would stand in his way, that no one would ever be able to warm his icy heart. He'd taken every precaution, but--

Jack suddenly felt as if he were melting, falling back into his chair.

He'd never counted on meeting Clara. The Claus girl was the only bump in his plans, the only thing he had never foreseen.

She'd simply landed in his life without notice, smiling her way through every defense that Jack had put up against her. She'd barely spoken, and he'd been under her spell, quite unable to stray from it. And that in itself was something.

After all, if he had ever expected anyone to break through his emotional bound, it wouldn't have been Clara. Clara was the exact opposite of what he was normally interested in. She was simple, overly curious, and extremely naïve, and yet...she was also the most interesting person in the world; sweet, shy, forgiving.

And perhaps it was these facts that had made her so appealing, that had made Jack take a second look, which had led to his downfall.

Yes, he'd never expected to meet Clara, and now, even if he tried his best to forget her -- to detach himself from the feelings he felt towards her -- he'd still never be able to win. Even if he blocked her out, used her as a pawn in his new Christmas-destroying plan, he still wouldn't be able to forfeit what he felt.

No matter what, Clara would always have a hold on his heart. There was no stopping that.

Jack grimaced as his eyes clamped shut, feeling a burning pain -- anguish -- in his chest. "Why did you have to ask her about Santa, North?" he asked yet again, unable to let it go. "*I was supposed to ask her. I was going to ask her, but now...*" he groaned as his head fell into his hands, his shoulders hunching.

He couldn't do it. Not anymore. He just couldn't do it.

I thought it would be easy. Jack's shoulders hunched even more as his fingers tightened around his head. *But I was wrong...*

He couldn't do it.

Jack shook his head, wanting to drown in despair. "I can't do it anymore, North. I just can't tell her that Santa is bad. I'm not even sure if I believe it myself anymore..." he trailed off for a moment, his eyebrows knitting. "And if I told her, she'd *hate* me. She'd never speak to me again, and I don't want that. And then, Christmas--"

And then it hit him -- a revelation so large that he could hardly contain it.

Jack pulled his head away from his hands, staring at North with wide eyes. "I can't do it," he repeated, the finality of the words sinking into his mind. "I can't destroy Christmas because -- because then I'd be destroying something she *loves*. I'd be destroying her very heart, and that isn't..."

Possible.

It wasn't possible.

Jack smiled at North ruefully, the anguish he felt worsening. "I can't destroy something she loves. I'm not even sure if I still hate Christmas. I wish they would change it, make it less commercial, but that doesn't mean I can destroy it, because she..." he winced as the pain in his chest grew, his fists balling so tightly they turned white, "I know I promised myself -- promised Molly -- but," his eyes widened as he looked at North, "If it's for Clara, I would do *anything*."

Jack sat there as the words sunk in -- both to his head and to North's.

The room was quiet for a while as they both contemplated, Jack trying to relax, North trying to reason.

Just when Jack felt as if he were about to faint from the anguish he felt -- the conflict over what he'd promised Molly, and what he wanted for Clara -- North stood, crossing the room almost silently. Jack was about to ask what he was doing, when he came back, handing Jack a fresh tea mug, steam drifting off the top.

"Here," North said in a commanding yet monotone voice, handing Jack the steaming mug. "Drink this. You're too tense. It's bad for the body," Jack ignored the comment, wanting to throw the drink at North, but taking the steaming mug instead.

After a moment or two the tea had cooled down a bit (mostly thanks to Jack's frosty powers), and Jack finally felt his tense frame relax as he drank it, sighing in exasperation. He had just raised the mug to his lips when North finally spoke, still staring at him.

"I think I know what's going on here," North said, his voice monotone, but Jack could see a new expression -- a real expression -- on his face, one that North never showed. It was *pity*. North felt sorry for him. "I think I know why you're having such a hard time with this."

Jack sighed into his tea, feeling stiff now. "What?" he asked, almost dreading the answer. "What exactly is wrong with me?"

There had to have been something. This wasn't normal for him at all. He'd never gotten so attached to someone in such a short amount of time. He'd never been unable to let someone go.

It just didn't happen. It just wasn't right. Why couldn't he ban Clara from his heart?

"There's nothing 'wrong' with you, Jack," North's monotone voice was quiet now, thoughtful. "There's nothing wrong with you at all. It's just that I wasn't expecting this to happen," he almost looked confused. "I was *never* expecting this to happen."

Jack shot him a glare, his whole frame tensing, wanting to know what it was. "Just spit it out already!" he nearly yelled, teeth grinding together. "Why can't I just destroy Christmas and not care!"

He had been trying to destroy Christmas for so long now, it almost didn't seem possible that he could suddenly not want to destroy it, that something else -- *someone* else -- could suddenly become more important. And yet...

And yet, Clara *was* more important, more important than anything had ever been before.

Jack blinked then, feeling suddenly nauseated, his chest constricting so badly that he was finding it hard to breathe.

Panic. Was that what this was? Was he really so upset that he was panicking? It couldn't be. Not him. Not Jack Frost. He never felt panicked.

But, if it wasn't panic, then what was it? What else could be this painful?

When North finally spoke again, Jack was taking another sip of tea, trying to relax, his whole frame still stiff. "Jack," he said, his monotone voice quieter than ever now, a lot less monotone and a lot more understanding, "the reason you can't destroy Christmas and not care is because...well, you *do* care. You care quite a bit, my friend. A lot, if I may say so," Jack raised an eyebrow at this, still drinking his tea. "And the reason that you care is because," North seemed to be weighing his options, but he pressed on, seeing Jack was starting to get agitated, "because you're *in love* with Clara."

Jack stared at him for a moment, unable to comprehend what North was saying, before he finally got it, the words hitting him like a brick.

Love? North thought he was in love? With *Clara?* That was ridiculous!

"I am not!" Jack almost spit his tea out, hopping up from his chair, his face instantly red. "That's -- that's -- that's -- it can't be true! I *cannot* be in love with Clara Claus!" he couldn't believe North had even thought of it.

And, Jack was right. He couldn't be in love with Clara, not at all. Not only would it complicate things for him, but it would also complicate things for her, and he didn't want to complicate things for her any more than he already had.

He didn't want her to hate him--

Even if it meant *lying* to himself in the process?

North raised an eyebrow at him, shocking Jack by his expression. "Oh?" he asked rather calmly, sounding almost like his normal self. "So, I was wrong, then?"

"Of course you were wrong!" Jack snapped at him as he turned his head towards North, but then he sunk back into his chair, hanging his head. "No. I'm lying. You're--" he stopped himself before he could say it, his chest tightening again.

How could he admit that North was right -- that he really *was* in love with Clara?

Jack had never encountered this problem before, the only thing in life he'd ever truly loved being his sister Molly, who was now dead, her smiling face never to grace the earth again.

He had hated his young life, before he'd become the official Jack Frost, and he had hated his parents, who had been so messed up they hardly classified for the title. He had hated school, hadn't had any friends, and his only pleasure in life had been spending time with Molly, listening to music, and reading. He hadn't cared about anything but keeping his sister safe and happy, not even planning for his future.

And when Molly had died, he'd started to hate everything -- Christmas most of all.

He'd hated the Winter Council and their stupid meetings, with their stupid members, all of whom (minus North) had hated him in return. He had hated the North Pole with all its luxuries, which he only got to see a few times a year, banned to roam the globe on his "frosting" travels. He'd hated the elves and all their little toys, preparing for the big Christmas holiday -- the holiday that had stolen his sister.

He'd hated everything and everyone (minus North)...all until he'd met Clara.

What was it about her that had changed him so thoroughly? Was it simply the way that she saw the world -- marveling at the tiniest of objects, seeing snow as though it was the crown jewels? Was it the way that she tolerated him -- laughing at his snide remarks, not minding when he dragged her around? Was it the way that she let her curiosity overtake her -- always asking him questions, wanting to know any and every thing she could fit into her lovely little head? Was it the way that she had cried that first day, the night before -- shedding her tears without even thinking about it, not turning away or trying to hide?

Or, was it that smile of hers -- that smile that reminded him so much of his own sister's smile?

Jack didn't know what it was that had made him fall in love with Clara, but whatever it was, he was glad that he had...no matter what it cost him. Because falling for Clara had made him realize something else--

He didn't want to destroy Christmas.

It seemed almost silly now, but Jack knew it was true. He'd spent more than half of what would have been his life (had he been mortal) devising his plans to destroy a holiday, and now he was giving up on his revenge. When he thought of all those years he had spent planning, scheming, seeking revenge, it made him sad, and for the first time in his life, he actually felt like he wanted to do something.

Jack didn't want revenge anymore -- he'd extinguished that need -- but it didn't mean that he wanted life to be meaningless, either. He'd spent so much time thinking of revenge that he had never stopped to think of what he wanted to accomplish, other than ruining Christmas.

But now, he was starting to think of things — things he wanted to do with his (soon to be mortal again) life before it was over.

He couldn't say that he hated Christmas anymore, because, when Jack thought about it, he realized that it wasn't Christmas that had killed his sister...but the *celebration* of Christmas.

It had all happened so quickly, his sister's death. He'd been the official Jack Frost for a few years by then, and he loved his job, actually getting along with Santa and the elves (though he'd still been completely cynical and obnoxious). His sister had invited him to come visit for Christmas that year (yes, they'd kept in touch, even though he was an Immortal), and the Council had given him leave for a few days, so that he could go.

But it had already happened by the time he'd gotten there; he'd had to hear about it second-hand, from a halfway coherent man who barely remembered what had happened.

Jack's father had been having a party on Christmas Eve, all of his strange friends invited, and his sister had been present, hiding in her room, away from the "festivities". His father had been out for the moment -- had gone to the store to pick up more beer (like they'd needed any) -- and that's when it had happened.

Jack had always known that his father had rowdy friends who liked to drink, but he'd never suspected that one of those friends would bring about his sister's demise.

Jack's father had been a man involved in most illegal activities, and had more than one gun stored away at his house. While he'd been out at the store, one of his friends had found a loaded gun and, completely drunk, had caused it to misfire...just as Jack's sister had walked out of her room, tiptoeing through her father's drunken friends. The shot hadn't been immediately fatal, but it had been bad, and yet no one had called the police...and by the time Jack had gotten there, it had been much too late.

Jack had never been able to erase the vision of his sister, lying on the floor amidst drunkards -- who hadn't even seen her! --

a huge puddle of blood around her, her eyes still open, not seeing anything.

Jack had been immediately furious at the sight, a strange sense of rage overcoming him, and he'd wanted to strangle the man who had done this...but the killer had already been gone, disappearing into the night well before Jack had arrived.

After that, Jack hadn't known what to do or who to blame, so he'd started to blame Christmas.

If it hadn't been for Christmas, he'd reasoned, then his dad wouldn't have had the party, and his sister wouldn't have been shot. If it hadn't been for Christmas, he'd thought, then he would have been by Molly's side, and not at the North Pole, helping Santa prepare for his big flight.

But now, sitting in his chair, staring at the floor and nothing, Jack realized that he'd been wrong all of those years. It had never been Christmas that had killed his sister, it had instead been a *man* -- a stupid, drunk, greasy little man.

But he had been blaming it on Christmas all these years, trying to destroy something that made so many people (including Clara) happy.

How horrible of him.

"Are you alright, Jack? *Jack?*" it was North's strangely worried voice that brought Jack from his gloomy thoughts. "Did I say too much?" Jack almost laughed at that, surprised.

North never thought he said too much.

Jack finally looked up, feeling much lighter now, much... happier. "No, no," he said, waving it off. "You think I would let what you say bother me?" he snorted. "Don't be ridiculous."

"You seem to be back to normal," North's smile was slight, but it was there. "I'm glad. I was afraid I'd shocked you so thoroughly that you were going to stay all bottled up the rest of your years."

Jack rolled his eyes at that, annoyed. "Oh, yes," he said, grinning a fake grin. "That sounds just like me," he rolled his eyes again then, frowning. "Honestly, North, you make it sound as if you've just met me."

"I honestly think I have..." North's voice was quiet when he spoke, shocking Jack into a stupor. "You've changed since you met the Claus girl, and I feel...I feel as if I'm meeting you for the first time," his smile widened a smidge more. "Though you're still completely obnoxious."

Jack had to laugh at that, the sound ringing through the room, though he knew that North was right.

He *had* changed since he'd met Clara -- changed for the better, hopefully -- but he was still himself.

Jack rubbed his temples, his head suddenly hurting. "What am I going to do?" he groaned, for once unable to concoct a plan since, well, there wasn't really anything left to concoct. "I don't want to destroy Christmas anymore, but I still hate the way that it's displayed. And," he sighed again. "I'm supposed to meet Clara at the workshop tomorrow morning, to help Santa prepare for the 'big day'."

He was glad that he would be able to spend a little more time with Clara -- his oh-so- curious, adorable girl -- but he was kind of regretting signing up for "Santa time" since, while he didn't hate Christmas anymore, he also didn't like it.

Jack still thought the Christmas season was too commercial, too focused on things instead of people. He knew that, deep down, Santa meant well, but when the obese man still delivered toys to bratty kids in expensive houses, Jack had a problem.

After all, what about all of the children that didn't get Christmas presents? What about all of the children who didn't send Santa cards, or leave out the customary milk and cookies gig? What about all of those people -- children or not -- who needed food, shelter, clothes? Did they get anything on Christmas? Was Santa helping *them*?

Jack didn't think so, and that bothered him.

And what was so great about toys, anyway? Did children really need a box full of toys? Couldn't they be grateful with just one or two? Why did they need so many? Couldn't Santa give them a variety of gifts, a variety of the things they needed? Weren't there more important things than toys?

Jack knew that Christmas needed to be turned around. He couldn't stand it anymore, seeing people suffer while others ripped open presents they didn't even need. He'd seen too much of that in his own life...with his sister.

Growing up, Jack and Molly hadn't had much of anything -- let alone toys and gadgets and *stuff*. Their dad had made plenty of money in the black market, selling God knows what, but most of it had gone towards the drugs their mother had bought, the drugs she had all but lived off of. They'd had a car, but their dad had always taken it, leaving for days upon days, weeks upon weeks, never driving them to school. They'd had a place to sleep, but it had been so rundown that their father hadn't even stayed there, choosing instead to stay elsewhere -- except when he'd had company, since they'd always trashed the place, anyway. They'd had a mother, but she'd never been coherent enough to really interact with them, not that she'd cared.

In short, Jack and Molly had had almost...well, *nothing*. Nothing but each other, anyway.

And Santa had never helped. They'd never gotten gifts on Christmas (since, as Jack found years later, Santa had never been able to find them), and even if they had gotten gifts, what would that have done? No toy would ever have been able to replace what they hadn't had, what they'd needed...though Molly had wished they could receive gifts on Christmas.

Jack knew that Santa tried his best, and he guessed he could appreciate that, but there had to have been *something* else, something that could be done about all of the people who were left out. After all, all the shelters and organizations in the world couldn't do it alone. They had to have needed help.

And who better to help than Santa Claus?

"That's it!" the idea popped into Jack's head at that moment, the idea that would change everything in his life from that point on. "That's it! Tomorrow morning, when I go to the workshop, I'm going to have a talk with that fat--"

"--obese," North interjected, mouth curving slightly.

"Whatever!" Jack sighed, glaring at him. "Tomorrow I'm going to have a talk with dear old Santa, give him a good kick in the pants."

North frowned at that. "Somehow, I don't think *Clara* would appreciate you doing that to her grandfather."

"It's a figure of speech, North!" Jack grimaced once again, throwing his friend dagger eyes. "All I'm saying is that, since I don't want to destroy Christmas, I'm going to do something else."

North's eyebrows raised a hint. "And that is?"

"The hardest thing of all," Jack grinned deviously, a plan forming in his mind. "I'm not going to *destroy* Christmas, I'm going to *change* it."

"And Clara?"

"What about Clara?"

"Are you going to tell her?"

Jack paused when he heard that, not sure how to answer.

Was he going to tell Clara? Should he tell Clara? What if she didn't like him back, and it ruined their friendship? He only had a limited amount of time left; he didn't want to waste it.

And what about St. Nick's trial? He had fallen in love with a human, but did it count if that human was Santa's granddaughter? Would he still be able to keep his job? Would they let him off the hook?

Jack didn't know, so he decided to wait, to see what the morning brought.

He would make his decision tomorrow.

****

Jack never truly got to decide whether or not to tell Clara the truth. The unexpected came the next morning, when he arrived at the workshop.

It was still early when Jack got there, stepping into the main toy room, looking around at all of the different playthings and gadgets. There was no one around when he first walked into the large room -- dodging its long wooden tables, gears, and plastic parts -- but after a moment of silence, someone appeared...

It was an elf, short and tired and generally un-merry looking in his grungy and unwashed, red and green clothes. He glared up at Jack as he went over to the far wall and clocked in for work, saying something nasty under his breath.

This annoyed Jack, and he frowned at the elf, crossing his arms. "Well, aren't you a bucket of sunshine," he said, and the elf turned towards him, still glaring.

"What are you doing here, Frost?" the elf didn't even have the courtesy to call him "Jack", crossing his arms to mirror Jack's pose. "I thought you hated Christmas," the elf sneered then, eyes boring holes. "Or is that why you're here, to make my life harder -- again?"

Jack felt himself bristle at the words, angry that the elf was trying to single him out, making him somehow responsible for his having to work overtime, but he didn't say anything. He simply glared at the elf harder, not caring what the small man thought.

Jack knew why he was there, and it wasn't to destroy Christmas.

It was for *Clara*.

Though Jack had told North he'd have a talk with fat old Santa, he was truly there for Clara, to make her happy -- as well as spend some time with her before he was sent away. He wanted every second he could get, and though trudging around the workshop and hearing "ho, ho, ho" one too many times wasn't exactly his idea of fun, he would still do it if it meant he could see Clara.

"Not answering, huh?" the elf's tone was grading when Jack didn't say anything, and he took a step forward, pointing a finger at Jack. "You just don't want to take responsibility, do you? You just want to act like you've never done anything!" Jack opened his mouth to speak, to tell the elf to calm down already, but the elf was persistent, coming forward again, making Jack step back. "*You* want to act like Christmas doesn't mean anything since you don't care about it! You want to forget everything you've done and act like you're a good person who deserves to be happy, don't you?"

Jack found himself taking another step back as the elf advanced again, overtired and overworked, obviously feeling he needed to get his frustrations out. He tried to speak again, but the elf wouldn't have it. The little man was so angry now that he could have probably lit a fire with the glare in his eyes.

And, though Jack felt he didn't deserve to be paraded, he knew the elf was right.

He hadn't wanted to take responsibility for his actions of trying to destroy Christmas, not before -- but now, now that he'd met Clara and he'd changed, he didn't mind. He knew it was all his fault, knew that he'd made everyone's lives so hard, and he was *sorry*.

And he wanted to change Christmas, make it better.

Why wouldn't the elf give him a chance to speak, to relay that?

Why wouldn't he *listen*?

Jack decided then that he'd had just about enough of the elf's bantering. "Just shut up and listen!" he yelled, trying to get some silence, and then--

A crash.

Yelling at the angered elf, Jack's gesturing arm had run into one of the wooden work tables, sending its objects flying harshly, most of them landing on the hard floor. More than one thing broke as it hit, but nothing sounded louder than that one, single crash.

Jack felt an ominous feeling wash over him when he heard the sound, somehow knowing it wouldn't be good. And, when he turned to see what had crashed, his fears were confirmed, and he gasped, bending down to look at the thing--

"*Jack!*"

And then he heard Clara's cry. Jack's head snapped up as he realized that he was now holding the broken object, looking guiltier than he ever had in his Christmas-destroying lies. He found her eyes immediately, wishing he could speak and tell her it had all been an accident, pleading her understanding.

Clara simply stared at him from the doorway to the room, tears in her eyes, her eyebrows knit in confusion. Her mouth formed a frown as she looked at him, and then...her eyes filled with even more tears, narrowing dangerously as she looked at the broken pieces in his hands, catching glimpse of what she didn't know was a mistake--

And Jack felt horrible, still unable to speak, still unable to actually tell the truth for once in his life.

After everything he had done to Clara -- yelling at her, threatening her, lying to her -- this was the worst. After everything he had done to try and keep her close to him until he had to leave, to make her like him instead of hate him, she ended up hating him anyway. After all he had done to protect her...

Clara's anguished eyes met his once more before she turned, running out of the room.

After all he had done to prevent it, he'd still broken her heart.

"Clara!" Jack's cry came too late.

She was already gone. He sighed as the door slammed shut behind her, wishing he could take everything back.

His chest felt weighted as he looked down at the broken pieces in his hands -- the broken pieces that had made Clara so upset, made her run out of the room, sprouting tears--

It was the nativity scene that he had broken -- the one Clara had been talking about, the one that had been her mother's. It was cracked, broken into so many pieces there was not even a possibility of repair.

Clara. Jack's thoughts were spinning in his head as he looked towards the door, the stupid elf he'd been fighting with having shuffled away, feeling despair once again. *How am I supposed to fix this?*

What could he do? He'd broken her nativity scene -- the one heirloom she had from her mother, her most prized possession. She was going to hate him.

Forever.

Jack felt his hands rest the broken and shattered pieces of the nativity scene on the work table near him as he stood, heading for the door, knowing he had to try something to reach Clara -- tell her he was sorry, that it had been an accident.

Though Jack didn't actually reach the door, unable to get that far.

"I don't think you should follow her, Jack," it was Santa standing in his way, the obese man's belly looking like some overly blown balloon. "It seems to me you've done enough already," his gaze was stern for once, and Jack felt annoyance as he stared at him, though he tried to push it away.

Santa thought that he'd actually broken the nativity scene on purpose, as did Clara, so Jack couldn't really blame him for being angry. Now all he had to do was tell Santa the truth, get him to move out of the way, then he would be able to fix things--

But, when Jack opened his mouth, for once, Santa wouldn't let him speak.

"You've done a lot of things over the years, Jack," the obese man said, his eyes sad yet reprimanding, and Jack felt himself take a shocked step back, "but this is by far the worst. How could you do this to poor Clara, and after everything that's happened?" for once, Jack felt like Santa was looking down on him, disappointed in someone who nearly everyone else had already given up on.

And he should have been disappointed and angry, had Jack actually done the damage he'd done on *purpose* -- but he hadn't.

Jack tried to relay these things to Santa. "But you don't understand -- " he started, but the obese man cut him off.

Santa was shaking his head now, and Jack felt a prick of anger at this, not liking being cut off. "I don't need to understand, Jack. I've seen the evidence. I know what you did. And unlike most times in the past, there's no covering it up."

Jack tried speaking again, desperately: "But--"

"But nothing!" it seemed that everyone -- not just the elves and St. Nick and the Sugar Plum -- had had enough of Jack. Even Santa couldn't seem to stand the sight of him now. "You never take the blame, Jack, and numerous times I've covered for you. But this time, it won't happen. This time, you've gone too far. This time, all of the blame is *yours*."

Jack felt his throat freeze, his words dying, when he heard this, uttered so harshly, and then he felt anger flare in his chest, stronger now than before.

How dare Santa blame him for this! It had been an accident! He hadn't wanted to break Clara's nativity scene -- he cared too much about her for that. He'd come to the workshop to help; he'd come to the workshop to try and change Christmas, not destroy it; he'd come to the workshop for Clara.

Why was it when he tried to do things *right*, only pain came from it?

He'd agreed to the job of "baby sitter", though grudgingly, and now he was attached to Clara. He had befriended Clara, and then upset her. He had come to the workshop to help, and broken Clara's nativity scene.

No matter what he did, good intentions always seemed to be tragic -- and not only that, but nobody else but Clara would actually *listen* to him.

Jack's anger radiated throughout him, hate eating at his insides, as he suddenly glared. "Shut up!" he bellowed at Santa, just as he'd done to the elf. "You never listen to me! You never take the time! How can you blame *me*? This is all *your* fault!" he couldn't stop the words as they started to flow, pointing a finger at Santa accusingly. "If you would have done your job right, then none of this would have happened! I wouldn't have hated Christmas, I wouldn't have upset Clara, and -- " the weight returned to Jack's frame as he tried to breathe. "Molly would still be alive. My sister would still be--"

If Santa had taken more care with his job, then he would have gotten Jack and his sister out of their parent's house -- placing them in better custody -- in the first place, solving all sorts of problems.

"You just don't understand Christmas," Jack was shaking now, so overwhelmed with emotion as he stared into Santa's wide blue eyes. "You don't understand anything!" his yell echoed off the walls. "You ride around in your stupid sleigh, delivering stupid presents, giving stupid hope. What about all the people you pass by? Don't think there aren't any! What about all of the families who need so much more than presents? Have you ever thought of that -- of *them*!"

Jack was out of breath completely by the time he stopped yelling, all of the color draining from his face as he sank to the ground, pale and panting. It was a few moments before he could even blink, could even think of looking up at Santa.

When Jack looked up at the old fat man, he saw something he thought he'd never see. Tears. Santa was shedding tears, truly upset. He gave Jack a saddened smile as he shook his head. "I have thought of those things, Jack," he said, sounding sincere. "Truly, I have. It's just...I know there's a lot of pain and suffering in the world, but I'm only one person, Immortal or not. I can't fix everything. I wouldn't even try, but," he smiled another smile then, one that looked so happy, Jack almost forgot he was crying, "that's why I do what I can, lighten the load. Just because I can't do everything, I'm not going to stop doing *anything*."

Those words pierced Jack to the very core, right down to his icy heart.

He'd never heard anyone say anything like that before. Why, most people thought Santa could do anything -- thought Santa was like God -- but now Jack realized he wasn't. He may have been Immortal, living much longer than the average human, but he was still *human* himself, only able to do so much, only able to make a small amount of difference.

But he didn't let that stop him. Even though he couldn't help everyone -- couldn't save all the sick and dying, helpless people who needed so much more than toys and gifts -- he helped the people he could reach, and even that little bit made a big difference, a graceful impact.

Those kids who he delivered toys to, maybe some of them didn't deserve the things they got, maybe they already had everything they'd ever need, but...then again, maybe they didn't, either. Maybe Clara had been right.

Maybe Hope was the real gift that Santa was giving -- reminding everyone of the greatest gift the world had ever been given, the start of Christmas.

Maybe life wasn't measured in how much you did, but in how much you *changed*. Santa had certainly changed many lives, all through his thoughtful gifts.

And if Santa could change lives by delivering gifts, then what could Jack do? Jack was caught up in the midst of this revelation when it happened--

"Santa!" the door to the workshop room burst open, admitting a small little elf with a bent hat, who was panting, his face white. "Sir, we have a problem!"

Santa was immediately alarmed, which was strange to see, since he was normally so jolly. "What?" he asked, his eyes wide. "What is it, Frank?" If Jack had been in a better mood and not suddenly panicked, he probably would have laughed at the elf's name, which he thought was just hilarious, not to mention completely un-elflike.

But, Jack wasn't in the mood for laughter just then, his mind automatically jumping to horrid conclusions--

Clara.

What if it was about Clara? What if something had happened to her? What if he had really messed up this time -- worse than before?

"Well?" Jack's voice was even more frantic than Santa's had been. "Spit it out, midget! We don't have all day!" the little elf jumped in fright as he yelled, ducking behind Santa, who raised an eyebrow at Jack.

Jack knew he should have been worried -- what if Santa realized how protective of Clara he'd become? What would he think? But at the moment, he didn't care. He just wanted to know what was wrong.

He just wanted to know that Clara was *safe*.

"It's...it's about Miss Clara, sir," the little elf turned even paler as he stepped away from Santa, trying his hardest to ignore Jack, who was glaring at him now, his worst fears confirmed. "She -- she ran off!" he shouted, earning a gasp from Santa, a stiffen from Jack. "She was upset, you see. We tried to stop her from leaving, warning her about North's storm, but she wouldn't listen," the little elf glanced at the door then, shivering, as if caught in the storm.

If Jack hadn't been panicked before, he was panicked now. A snowstorm? Caused by North's wind? If Clara was caught in that--

"You idiot!" he snapped, growling at the little elf, who cowered again, hiding from his icy glare. "How could you let her just waltz outside, unprotected, without anyone! What were you thinking! She could be trapped now! And with that storm--"

With that storm, Clara would never make it...and he would never see her again.

"Jack, do you know where she is?" Santa's voice was frantic and forgetful of their little fight as he turned towards Jack, who felt like his heart was being ripped out repeatedly. "Do you think you can find her? If you know where she is, I can get the sleigh, and gather a team. I'll follow you there."

Jack nodded, not having to think about it as he started for the door. If anyone could get to Clara, he was the one. If anyone could find her, he was the one. But, what if he couldn't save her? What if he lost her for real this time?

Jack stopped at the doorway. "I know where she is," his lips formed a thin line as he glanced back at the frightened Santa. "She's at the Pass...because of me," he rushed out the door then, ignoring Santa and the elf's shocked gasps.

He really was no good for Clara.

All he seemed to do was cause her pain, confusion, and grief -- no matter how much he cared about her. All he seemed to do was trash her hopes and dreams.

But, after this, I'll never hurt her again. Jack promised himself as he sprinted down the hall and out the doorway of the workshop, into the wind-blowing snow. *After this, I'll only have a few more days, and then I'll be gone...*

St. Nick didn't need to know that he had completed his task -- that he had learned to love a human. He would just walk away. He would give up his job, become mortal again, find something new. He'd try to forget all about the North Pole and Clara, try to leave everything behind. He'd pretend as if it had never happened, as if he'd simply woken up from a dream.

He would never hurt Clara again.

He would find her. He would make sure she was okay. He would make sure she was alive -- and then, in a few days, he would be gone, never to see Clara again, never to lay another finger on her fragile heart.

Yes, soon he would leave her alone, leave her to be happy, but, right now--

Right now, she *needed* him.

Chapter Sixteen: Clara

Clara tried to blink through the snow and swirls as she was blown around, her boots sliding beneath her with her uneven footing, every breath she took aching in her chest.

Why had she acted so stupidly?

I was upset. Clara's thoughts were billowing like the snow, making her feel even dizzier. *And I stopped thinking.*

The last thing she had expected to see when she'd opened the door to the toyshop had been the sight of Jack and her broken heirloom. The last thing she'd expected to feel was agony, agony at seeing her mother's broken nativity scene — which she'd given Santa to show to the elves, as a token to his legacy. The last thing she'd expected to do was run from the room, sprinting until the town was behind her, landing herself in the middle of a snowstorm on the Pass.

How had she been so stupid?

Clara shook her head, trying to clear it as she continued along her path, wishing she could find Santa's town again, but it was no use. She could already feel hypothermia starting to set in, her limbs aching from the shivers, her mind feeling strangely sluggish. Clara managed a few steps more, looking around desperately, trying to find a way home, but once again it was no use, and she tripped and fell, landing back in the snow.

Clara felt tears start to sting at her eyes as she gazed up at the swirling snow, feeling strangely alone. The thing that she had once deemed beautiful seemed almost malignant now that she was losing focus, her shivers starting to subside as she felt the faint, sluggish feeling overtake her.

Only one thing lingered on Clara's mind...

Death.

Am I going to die out here? Clara wondered fearfully as the edges of her eyes started to display black. *Am I going to die?*

She couldn't die! Not now! Not when she still had so many things to do, still had a full life to live!

She couldn't die now! If she died now, then she would never get to see Santa again, never get to help him prepare for Christmas. She would never get to help her grandmother, Mrs. Claus, make Christmas dinner. She would never again give her father the extra hug she knew he always needed. She would never be able to—

"Jack," Clara breathed just before she passed out, one lonely tear still falling down her face. "I'm sorry," her eyes closed almost peacefully as her head lolled to the side.

And then she was gone, disappearing into a void of darkness.

"I'm sorry."

Chapter Seventeen: Jack

The air was harsh and whipping on the pass, blowing Jack to and fro, tossing him about like he was a toy it didn't care about or want anymore. And though the wind and the cold and the snow didn't bother him -- he being immortal and impervious to the cold -- there was something that bothered him to the point of breaking as he searched frantically through the snow, his eyes threatening to close as the harsh wind bit at him...

Clara. Where was Clara?

Jack didn't know. He couldn't find her. And with every step he took, he prayed he was getting closer, knowing that all too soon, he would be too late -- if he wasn't already.

His heart felt like it was going to shatter like an impacted icicle as he searched the wind surrounding him, holding out a hand to shield his eyes, and then--

There she was, right in front of him.

Jack was on his knees next to Clara as soon as he found her, having spotted a glimpse of her nearly snow-covered figure through a break in the wind, one of her arms poking out of the snow along with her head. He felt despair eat at him as snow whipped around the two of them, knowing he had to get her out of the harsh weather somehow, and trying to think of a way to do it.

He had to be logical about this. As much as he wanted to tear Clara out of the snow and grab her and shake her awake, screaming out, he knew it wouldn't work, that it wouldn't cause any hypothermia to break. But, maybe it he could get her to some sort of shelter, find a way to warm her, maybe...

But how was he going to do that? He had to remind himself that he wasn't Jack *Fire*, but Jack *Frost*.

He didn't know what he should do, but he had to do something, so he did the first thing that popped into his mind--

Jack's heart raced as he set to work, freezing the snow that was swirling around them before it could even try and move, permanently binding it together. It took him less than two minutes to solidify an igloo-like covering to shield them from the cold, and he felt himself relax just a hare, hoping Santa would be able to see them from the sky -- crazy as he was for trying to fly his sleigh in this weather.

When Jack was finally satisfied that his makeshift igloo would hold and not fall in on their heads, he turned to the unconscious Clara, who was still buried in the snow, his breath hitching as his heart raced again.

He felt his frantic rush back as he saw her, and dove into the snow once again, shoveling it aside as he desperately tried to reach her, hands shaking worse now than before, barely managing to push the snow away. After a good amount of snow was gone, and he could finally pull her out of her little hovel, his eyes connected with her unconscious face and closed lids, his beating heart sinking.

"Clara..." his voice seemed to come from miles away as he dusted snow off of her, noting how limp she was as he held onto her wrist, hoping to feel the rhythmic beat of her pulse, though he knew it was a lot to ask. "Clara, please don't..." and there it was, her heart-rate, beating softly...

Bah-dum.

Bah-dum..

Bah-dum...

It was getting slower, her pulse was, slowing down, losing its fluttering rhythm. It was getting slower, her heart pumping less blood, her fingertips looking frozen. It was getting slower, telling him it was time, time for her to--

"No!" Jack wanted to scream, wanted to fight this, but when he spoke his voice was barely a strangled whisper.

"Not yet..." he looked up at the roof of the igloo pleading, not able to look at the sky, his teeth grinding together. "Please don't take her from me yet!"

He wasn't ready. Not now. Not yet -- He was supposed to have more time! And he was the one who was supposed to leave -- not Clara! She was supposed to be happy! She was supposed to stay in the North Pole with her grandparents, while he was banned from his job! She wasn't supposed to *die*!

I can't. Jack felt like he couldn't breath as he dropped Clara's wrist, a gut-wrenching agony playing in his chest. *I can't even--*

He couldn't even think of it -- of death -- and yet he had no choice.

Clara was lying there, on the snow, right in front of him. Her pulse was slowing faster and faster, dying off like a nipped rosebud. She was losing color, fading fast, and if he didn't do something, he was going to lose her forever -- and not only him, but everyone else, too.

But what could he do? He once again had to remind himself that he was Jack Frost. His powers were in no way useful in this kind of circumstance. He was meant to kill and freeze, not restore life. And there was no way that Clara would last long enough for him to carry her down to Santa's village, not in the current weather.

CPR wouldn't do anything for hypothermia.

Santa would never make it in time.

Jack couldn't stop the incessant wind.

There was nothing.

He could do *nothing*.

"Unless..." Jack's eyes widened as he remembered something -- something that hadn't been used in a while, yet just might work to save Clara. "Unless...it might work..."

He didn't know what had reminded him of it -- maybe it was just a miracle, a work of God? -- but at the moment he didn't care, either. Even if his plan didn't work, he still had to try.

Jack pushed all of his agony and heartache aside as he gazed down at the pale Clara -- who still looked hauntingly beautiful, despite her appearance -- brushing her hair from her cheek, taking her hand. "Clara, I'm sorry I did this to you..." he could feel it through her hand -- her pulse, still fluttering slightly, barely there. "I'm sorry for everything, but after this...after this, I promise I'll never hurt you again. I'll leave, and you'll never see me, and then you can go on being happy without--"

Jack swallowed the rest of that sentence as he leaned towards her, nearing her face. "After this, I promise I'll disappear, but until then..." he looped his fingers through hers, squeezing her hand as their noses touched. "But until then, please stay by my side if you can."

And then all room for talking was gone. Jack met Clara's cold lips just as the wind spiraled by outside, creating harsh sounds, making even him feel cold. He begged and pleaded with the force that worked miracles as he kissed Clara, wishing for all the world that she were alright.

Please, let her be alright. Jack thought desperately, wanting to but not wanting to pull away. *I'd do anything.*

And he would.

Jack would do anything if it meant that Clara could be alive again -- well, happy, safe. He'd never felt that way about anyone but his sister before -- and even then not as strongly -- but somehow that didn't scare him anymore; somehow, he didn't mind.

Because Clara, who was the most important person in his life, was in trouble, and he had to do something about it.

Jack pulled away by just a few inches as his once-closed eyes slid back open, and he stared at the all-too-close Clara, fighting the urge to breathe, as if the moment he did she would shatter.

He waited a moment -- still staring, still hoping -- before he finally let out a breath, feeling Clara's chest rise ever so slightly beneath him. Jack gasped as he grasped her wrist with his free hand, feeling for her pulse again.

Bah-dum...

Bah-dum..

Bah-dum.

Bah-dum, bah-dum, Bah-dum!

Her heartbeat was quickening, returning blood-flow to her body! She was going to be okay! His plan had worked! He'd saved Clara. Jack let out a shaky breath, feeling an overwhelming joy enter his heart. He couldn't believe that the plan had worked. It had been so long since someone had tried it -- since someone had succeeded -- that he'd been worried.

But, it was okay. Clara was alright. The Immortal's Kiss had worked.

Jack had learned about the Immortal's Kiss shortly after coming to the North Pole, completely by accident. It had been after one of the Winter Council meetings, when he'd snuck into Santa's library, trying to get a few moments of peace and quiet (and trying to prove North wrong, since his friend had been convinced that he couldn't sneak into the library). Jack had been in the library maybe ten minutes when he'd stepped on a book, smashing its pages beneath his foot.

Jack had always loved reading, strange as it seemed, so he'd been completely appalled with himself for stepping on something as precious as a book. He'd picked it up immediately, leafing through it, and that's where he'd found out about the Immortal's Kiss...

Jack had always wondered about it, anyway. He'd always wondered how Immortals had friends and family who were Immortal too, even though their friends/family really didn't do anything extraordinary or useful. After all, it wasn't like Mrs. Claus delivered presents to the world or anything. So why was she Immortal, too?

The book had told him.

If an Immortal were to kiss a human being, half of their immortality would be transferred to that person, not only binding the two together, but also ensuring that said human would live forever...or, well, for seemingly forever, since no one could truly live *forever* on earth.

The Kiss had its rules, though...

1) The human-turned-Immortal could still, just like every other Immortal, be killed (not even Immortals were invincible, after all).

2) The human who would receive the Kiss couldn't be brought back from the dead (they had to still be alive when receiving the Kiss).

And, 3) The newly-turned Immortal had to use their immortal life to somehow aide the formulations of holidays/seasons, even if it was only cooking and cleaning for another, more prominent Immortal (such as Mrs. Claus did for Santa).

Jack had never expected to even try and use the Immortal's Kiss, but...

But that was alright, because he had saved Clara, and he wasn't exactly complaining about the kiss part.

Jack felt his once light heart start to ache as he blinked, staring down at the too-close Clara again. "Clara," he said, his voice riddled with pain -- pain because he knew that, no matter how happy he was that she was alive, he knew he would have to leave her too soon for his comfort. "I wanted to tell you--" Jack stopped before he could say the rest, swallowing hard, still staring at Clara.

Could he really confess his feelings and not fall apart at the seams because of it? Yes. Jack decided, sighing again as he stroked Clara's cheek, which was starting to gain some color now, his hand still intertwined with hers. Yes, I can. If he didn't tell her now, then he would never get to tell her. He had already decided that he wouldn't say anything to her before he left. He didn't want to cause her any more trouble or pain, and telling her how much he cared about her was sure to bring both of those.

So he would tell her now, while they were on the Pass, the snow swirling around outside their igloo, Clara's new immortality still kicking in. He would tell her now, and she would forget...but Jack, he would remember--

He would *always* remember.

"Clara," Jack started again, smiling slightly now, almost glad that Santa wasn't there yet, "even though it's crazy, and it makes completely no sense..." he almost laughed at his own phrasing, his nose touching Clara's yet again, his hand still holding hers, the warmth returning to it. "*I love you.*"

And then he kissed her, right on that snowy day, right under the force of the full winds that were tormenting the North Pole, right when perhaps he needed it most. And it was a real kiss, the kind that you could get lost in, the kind that altered you forever--

The kind that altered Jack more than it had ever altered anyone before. Jack pulled away after a moment, feeling lost in what had just happened, and then: "Jack?"

Jack felt his heart melt when he heard the voice, turning his head towards Clara, who now had her eyes open, looking around in bewilderment. He forced the urge to reach forward and kiss her again away as his eyes connected with hers, and he put on his normal, slightly cynical grin. So what if he was changed? No need to let Clara know that.

He would be the only one.

"My dear Miss Claus, you've returned to us," Jack said as Clara blinked at him. "And here I was afraid you might leave us for good..." Jack trailed off before he could stiffen, knowing the truth of those words.

He had been terrified. He'd thought he would lose Clara--

Forever.

But, she's alright now. Jack reminded himself as he helped Clara sit up. *Everything's alright now.*

Yes, everything was fine.

Absolutely everything.

"What happened?" Clara asked in a small voice as she shivered. "I feel...*different,*" she stared at her hands for a moment then, and Jack could tell that by "different", she meant more than not being frozen.

Jack wanted to tell her just how "different" she was now, but he knew he couldn't. If he told Clara, then it would come back to haunt him later, when the Winter Council started asking questions. They couldn't know that he'd completed his mission or that he'd saved Clara, because if they did, it would ruin everything.

He'd just have to act innocent -- something he was good at.

Jack smiled at Clara as she looked around at the igloo, eyes wide. "Santa's on his way to get us," he said, and Clara smiled as well.

"Santa," she said as Jack followed her gaze, looking at the igloo too, hearing the sound of loud sleigh bells as Santa neared them, and then: "Jack."

Jack didn't want to admit that he felt a mix of extreme pleasure and extreme pain when she said his name, however stupid that was. "Yes?" he asked, seeing that Clara was suddenly crying, which alarmed him. "What--"

"I'm sorry," those two words canceled everything he'd been about to say. "Jack, I'm so, so sorry. I shouldn't have gotten mad at you and run off. I should have just stayed and listened to--"

This time it was Jack's turn to interrupt. "It's fine," he assured her, putting a finger to her lips in order to silence her, which ended up being a bad idea. Jack felt his head swim slightly as he stared at her lips for a moment, before shaking his head. "I'm just glad you're...safe."

Clara seemed to buy that, nodding as the sleigh bells echoed again, Santa drawing nearer.

Jack fell strangely quiet as the snow twisted around outside, but when the sound of the sleigh bells grew to an all-time high, he noticed that he was still holding Clara's hand, that their fingers were still intertwined.

"Don't let go," Clara held onto him as her eyes began to close and began to fade, exhausted. "Please, don't let go."

As Jack looked at her, reaching out to keep her from falling back as her eyes slid fully closed, he found he couldn't refuse. "Alright," he admonished, feeling joyful yet pained. "I won't."

And he wouldn't let go, not right now. He would hold onto Clara while she still wanted him to, while he was still there. He would be there for her to hold onto.

Until Christmas came.

On that day nothing -- not even Clara -- would be able to make him stay.

Chapter Eighteen: Clara

Clara could hear everything and nothing. The world was as void as it was full, beautiful...silent...

Until her grandfather spoke. "Clares?" his voice was soft, unsure of what it wanted to say. "Clares, are you there?" Clara wanted to respond -- wanted him to know that, yes, she was there -- but for some reason, her mouth wouldn't work. It was glued shut, just like her eyes, and no matter how hard she tried, she couldn't get it to open.

There was a moment of silence before Santa repeated again: "Clares?" this time it was more of a question than it had been before. "Are you th--"

"Of course she's there!" Clara would have jumped when she heard the shout, but her body was still immobile. "She's just out of it. She probably can't even hear you," Jack's voice was quiet on that last note, as if it pained him to say it.

Santa seemed to consider this before he replied. "Really?" he asked a moment later, his voice a little further away than it had been last. "You don't think she can hear us? Because I've always been told that sleeping people can hear you, they just can't say anything because they're -- well, you know, they're not awake, and--"

"Alright, alright!" Jack's voice was more annoyed now, more like the voice Clara was used to hearing. "Maybe she can hear us. I don't know. The point is that she's not awake, and until she wakes up, we're not going to be able to get on with--"

Jack stopped as Clara's eyes opened, and she looked up, catching the faces of Santa and Jack, both of whom looked astonished. Clara blinked for a moment, before Santa's gaping mouth stretched into a smile.

"Welcome back, Clares," he said in his overly jolly tone. "I was beginning to think I'd lost you..." Clara was about to try and ask him what he meant when she suddenly remembered--

Snow. Ice. Wind. Cold.

She'd been about to freeze, about to leave the world forever, and then suddenly she'd woken up...and everything had been fine...and Jack had been there.

****

Clara felt almost dazed as she was ushered into the circular room that contained the Winter Council, more than one person talking to her at once. She watched people pass by as she struggled to focus, seeing faces that she never remembered seeing before, some of them smiling...some of them not. She kept hold of her grandfather's arm as the doors shut behind them, and her grandfather kindly told her to take a seat.

It wasn't until Clara sat down that she realized she was directly across from Jack.

He was staring at her now, an unreadable expression on his face. Clara opened her mouth to say something -- to say anything -- but before she could utter one word, the man at the head of the conference table stood, silencing everyone.

"Καλωσο ορισμα," he said, reciting what Clara assumed to be a greeting. "Welcome. Let the five-hundredth and fifty-seventh Winter Council meeting officially start," Clara thought she saw him glance her way before he sat down, but she couldn't be sure.

When St. Nick had all but demanded that Clara join the next Winter Council meeting, Clara had been sort of scared...well, okay, *really* scared. And now that she was there, the feeling had returned to its full force, leaving her legs shaking, her hands clasped tightly in her lap.

She knew why they'd asked her there, why they'd wanted her to attend the meeting that was scheduled only for Immortals. She had learned the reason from her grandfather right after she'd first awoken at his house, safe and sound and out of the snow at last.

Santa had been mystified, filling her in. "*Clares, I don't mean to frighten you, but we've been summoned to a meeting. You're an Immortal now. I can see it!*" he'd said, shocking Clara as he relayed the information, showing her a pair of what looked like reading glasses, which supposedly cast a strange light around a person if you looked through them, if that person was an Immortal. *"I don't know how it happened, but it's a miracle!"*

He'd looked at Jack then, probably searching for an answer -- since Jack had been the last one to see her "normal" -- but Jack had been staring out the window, looking almost irritated.

Just like he did now.

Clara tried to send Jack some sort of message -- using her eyes, since her hands were shaking, and since she couldn't speak at the moment, St. Nick referring the "problem" to everyone -- but he didn't catch it. Jack was staring at St. Nick now, paying attention for once, and Clara could see the gears of his mind turning.

He was plotting something. She could tell.

But what could he possibly be plotting now, at the Winter Council meeting? Hadn't he decided that he liked Christmas? Hadn't he decided to help Santa make it better? Wasn't he done with trying to destroy the holiday? Isn't that what Santa had told her after he'd explained the nativity scene incident?

Clara hoped so, but wasn't sure. The last twenty-four hours had passed in a strange blur for her, and though she knew that Jack had been by her side, she hadn't gotten the chance to talk to him.

Ever since she'd woken up at Santa's, he'd been...*distant*, like he was trying to figure something out, like he was trying to work around something.

He's probably just shocked like everyone else. Clara thought as she sighed, her heart sinking. *I mean, this isn't the way it's supposed to happen.*

People weren't supposed to become Immortal by getting caught in a snowstorm, nearly freezing to death. They were supposed to be chosen for a job, come to the North Pole to start their new lives -- just like Jack had.

Nothing about Clara's "transformation" was normal.

"...so, you see our problem," Clara caught the end of St. Nick's speech, her heart sinking again. "Miss Claus has obtained Immortality through an unnamed gesture, and that is strictly forbidden," he looked over at Clara then, catching her eye, his gaze stern.

Clara's mouth fell open in shock as she looked back at him, and beside her she could hear Santa gasp, just as shocked as she was.

St. Nick thought she'd *stolen* her new Immortality? Was that even possible?

"Listen here, Nick. I know we can't explain what happened, but that doesn't mean that Clares has done anything wrong," Santa looked disappointed when he spoke, but Clara couldn't tell if it was St. Nick he was disappointed in, or if he was more disappointed in her.

Did Santa think she'd cheated, too? Did her own grandfather not believe her? Was she really seen as such a liar?

Clara felt tears start to form in her eyes as she thought of this, her hands clasping even more tightly in her lap — so tight they nearly bled.

She didn't know what to do. How could she explain what had happened when she didn't even know herself? She barely remembered anything, and what memories she did have of her time on the Pass were blurry, incomprehensible. How could she explain things when they didn't even make sense?

It wasn't like she'd wanted immortality, anyway. And now that she had it...she still wasn't sure that she wanted it.

What good was it to live forever when everyone hated you for it?

"I know this is hard for you, Kris," St. Nick was speaking to Santa now, a saddened look on his face. "But you have to think of the facts. We cannot explain what happened at the Pass, since she hasn't become immortal by normal means. And if Miss Clara won't tell us, then I'm afraid we're going to have to..." he trailed off then, not finishing his sentence, but Clara was sure that it had ended on a bleak note.

They believed that she had lied. They believed that she had cheated. They believed that she was a fraud. What were they going to do to her now?

A million horrible, torturous things flew through Clara's mind as she sat there in that circular, spacious room, feeling like all of the air was being sucked from her lungs. The room started to spin as each of the Immortals (minus her, Jack, and North) started into the feud, each stating their own opinions, almost all of them against her. Clara felt the color begin to drain from her face as she started to lose consciousness, starting to tip towards the table.

How could they not believe her? How could they think she was bad? How could they want to get rid of her? What had she done to them?

Clara was about to just give up -- give into the horrible, deafening loneliness that had suddenly set in on her -- when she suddenly heard it--

Jack's voice.

Somehow, the sound of Jack's voice made everything better, centering Clara's world until she could see again, could feel, could breathe. Somehow, the sound of Jack's voice made all of her loneliness melt away, as if he was telling her that everything was okay, even though he wasn't actually speaking to her...

He was talking to the Council.

"Hey!" Jack's shout caught the attention of everyone, the chattering conversation that had been going on around them coming to a halt. "Listen up -- I have an idea," he looked completely serious, staring at the Council with determined eyes.

The Sugar Plum Fairy, who Clara had just barely met, was the first to speak. "Ha!" she laughed, smiling a smug smile at Jack, who bristled at her cackles. "*You* have an idea? I don't even want to hear it. We all know what kind of ideas come from *you*."

Clara gasped at the Sugar Plum's words, as did Santa, but Jack for one didn't stay fazed for long. He glared at her for a moment before he composed himself, his lips pursing into a thin line. Despite herself, Clara had to gasp again when she saw this, noting how much Jack had changed in the last week.

When she'd first met him, he would get angry at nearly anything; he had no qualms about yelling at people who made him mad -- and he certainly wasn't afraid to threaten to freeze people, to use his powers to his advantage. When she'd first met him, Jack had been such an angry person, mad at the world and its people, not caring for anyone but himself, but now--

But now, he was different. Now he was able to shake off other's comments. Now he didn't hate people -- or even Christmas. Now he was standing up for someone other than himself--

He was standing up for her.

"You may not like me, but courtesy dictates that you listen to what I have to say," Jack was so calm, controlled when he spoke to the Sugar Plum that even she was silenced, falling into a shocked stupor. "Now, about Miss Claus," Jack ended the sentence with a triumphant grin, his gaze flicking over to St. Nick, who was equally astonished, "I don't think we should question her motives. After all, since she's been here, hasn't she proved herself to be a good, honest, and yes, Christmas-loving person?"

St. Nick seemed to consider this a moment before he nodded. "Yes. Yes, she has."

"Well then, why on earth would you suspect her of foul play?" Jack frowned on this note, and the Council gasped, probably never having seen someone stand up to their leader.

St. Nick was quiet when he answered, humble if anything. "Well...you see," he seemed to be struggling for an answer, "it doesn't make sense."

"It doesn't make *sense*?" Jack repeated slowly, as if he were talking to a child. "Do you know how many things in this world don't make sense -- even to us? Why should Immortality be any different? Did you ever consider that Miss Claus -- " he motioned towards Clara calmly, but Clara could have swore she saw him wink at her, making her blush, "was purposefully made Immortal? Maybe our Big Boss has a job for her."

The word "job" brought St. Nick back to reality, and he shook his head fiercely, everyone staring at him. "A job? No, no way. There aren't any Immortal jobs open right now."

"There aren't?" Jack was prepared for this excuse, raising an eyebrow as he put an elbow on the table, his head in his hand as he leaned forward. "*Really*? You can't think of any job openings?" there was a smug smile on his face as St. Nick gasped.

"Snow!" St. Nick said joyously, laughing now. "Of course. Forgive me, Jack. You're right. The Snow Queen position is open!" Clara wasn't the only one who gasped when St. Nick said it.

Snow Queen? Jack wanted her to become the *Snow Queen*?

It would be perfect.

I love snow. Clara thought as a smile broke out over her face. *I love snow! I could do it!*

She loved snow more than anyone, and she was a good artist -- she could design snowflakes. She would love to design snowflakes. It would be a dream come true.

But.

Things would change if she became the patron of snow. Her whole life would change -- no more school, no more normal family, no more career planning and paper writing. She would have to coop herself up in one space all year, designing snowflakes day and night. She would never get a break. She would never be able to just go somewhere, have a vacation. She would--

Her relationships would change; her relationship with Jack--

"So, what do you say?" it was once again Jack's voice that broke Clara from her thoughts, making her jump. When she looked up she could see he was directing the question towards St. Nick, though he was looking at her. "Is that a good fit?"

St. Nick didn't even notice that Jack wasn't looking at him. "Of course!" he laughed in agreement, and everyone else joined in, though Clara wasn't sure if they were actually happy or not. "That's a perfect match. Why didn't I think of it?"

"I don't know. Why didn't you?" Jack's mouth formed a frown as he looked down at the table, back to his normal sarcastic self. "It wasn't that difficult..."

As was normal it seemed, St. Nick ignored him, looking at Clara instead. Clara marveled at how quickly he had changed his mind as he extended his hand to her, smiling. "Well, Miss Claus.

What do you say? Do you accept the position?" everyone leaned forward as his smile widened, waiting for her answer.

Clara simply stared at them, suddenly afraid to speak -- suddenly *afraid*.

What should she do? She didn't know whether or not she really wanted to be the Snow Queen. How could they ask her to decide now? She needed more time to think. This wasn't some small decision. It would change her whole life--

She wasn't sure what she wanted.

Nearly all her life, Clara hadn't been the one to choose. She'd never gotten to choose what outfits she wore, what classes she took -- what color her birthday cake was, even. She'd always been told what to do by her stepmother, or her teachers, or her father (when he was around)...she'd never had a choice of her own, not until coming to the North Pole.

But when she'd gotten to the North Pole, suddenly everything had changed. She'd had choices. People had begun to ask her what she wanted -- even Jack, who had been as frosty as his name at first. No one had ordered her to do anything. No one had bossed her around (well, except when she hadn't made a decision, and they got annoyed with her). No one had made her decisions for her.

And for the most part, Clara had liked it. It had allowed her to grow -- and grow she had, turning into a completely different, yet still keenly herself, person in only a few days. But, now...

Now, they were asking her to make the biggest decision of her life. They were asking her to make a decision about something that would change her whole existence. They were asking her to do something crazy.

What should she do? Did she want to become the Snow Queen? Well, yes, but what would her parents think? Her friends? And ultimately, what would *she* think? Would she like the job? Would she regret taking it? Would she wish that she could go back, make a different choice, live her life the normal, human way?

What would her mother have done? Clara felt a pang in her chest as she thought about her mother, St. Nick and everyone else still waiting for her answer.

She was sure that if her mother had been there, she would have told her to do what she thought was best, to go after what her heart was calling for. And for the most part, Clara would have agreed with her, but--

But, even though she wanted to take the job, to be the Snow Queen, the thing she was most terrified of was being alone.

Clara heard a few inconspicuous coughs as her throat began to tighten. She could see St. Nick's eyebrows bunch as she glanced his way, sure that he was getting tired of waiting. She could feel the Sugar Plum Fairy's glaring smile as she waited, hoping Clara would be too afraid to say yes. She could sense her grandfather's soft smile, begging her to say something.

She didn't want to be alone.

But she could see Jack's why-not-give-it-a-shot shrug when she looked up, meeting his eyes.

I'm not alone. Clara realized as her gaze locked with Jack's, and she suddenly felt braver. *Not anymore.*

She had friends now, and family -- more than before. She had people she could count on, people who would be there for her through anything. She had support and love, and all she needed, right there...in the North Pole.

"Have you decided?" when St. Nick spoke, Clara was ready, setting her jaw. "Do you know what you want?"

Clara looked over at him, her eyes shining. "Yes," she said, sure of herself. St. Nick raised an eyebrow at this, and Clara felt a little frightened again, so she looked away, her eyes once again landing on Jack.

And then, she felt stronger.

Why was that? Why was it that, despite everything they had been through, Jack was the one to always make Clara feel stronger, more confident -- like she could do anything? What was it that had happened to make them so close that they could be a shield for each other, fending off fears and woes? What was it that fueled that strength, so that when Clara looked into Jack's eyes, she didn't feel any fear at all?

What had happened?

"I decide..." Clara saw Jack smile before she did, "to accept the job. I'll be the new Snow Queen."

****

Clara lay on her bed later on that night, opening up the journal she'd been given by her grandfather, unable to get that day's events out of her mind.

How had everything changed so suddenly? How was that possible? Could a person's life really turn upside-down in twenty-four hours?

Yes, Clara had to realize.

It could. It had.

It *did.*

Clara felt her heart beat wildly as she mentally went through the events that had taken place that day, wanting to remember as much as possible so that she could catalog it in her journal.

She was just thinking about Jack's speech when she opened the journal up, her fingers fumbling from the excitement she felt, and the pages turned, revealing the first written page.

About Jack Frost...

It said, neatly written in her handwriting, trailing off at the end.

Clara stared at it for a moment as her thoughts rushed away, suddenly feeling lightheaded.

She hadn't been able to finish that sentence when she'd first written it, what seemed like a million years ago now. She hadn't been able to clearly define Jack then, having just met him, having just stepped into his world. She hadn't been able to think clearly about her "tour guide", more confused and fearful of him than anything.

Clara smiled, picking up her pen.

Now, she felt she knew him better. Now, she felt that maybe -- just maybe -- she knew Jack enough to actually define him, to give his unique personality a name.

Clara's smile slipped as she raised her pen to the paper, feeling lightheaded all over again. Her whole world began to spin as the pen touched the paper, and she began to write.

About Jack Frost...

I have come to the conclusion that...

But she stopped, unable to write any more.

Chapter Nineteen: Jack

When Jack saw Clara the next morning, waiting for her on the steps just outside her abode, he couldn't believe his eyes.

It really should have been illegal, to be that pretty. It really should have been illegal, to make someone's heart leap into their throat, all without their say-so. It really should have been illegal, to change yourself so suddenly, making your friends and family fall into shock.

It really should have been illegal to make someone love you.

"Y-You look," Jack tried to hold his compliment in, not wanting to say the word "beautiful", though it was just on the tip of his tongue, "*different...*" Jack wanted to smack himself at that, feeling stupid.

Different! He'd called Clara *different*! How stupid of a comment was that?

Clara looked suddenly self-conscious, her splendid smile vanishing. "Different?" she repeated, frowning. "Don't you like it?"

Did Jack like it? Of course he liked it! Though he would never tell Clara exactly how much...

It was a custom with the newly rendered Immortals to change something about themselves, to tack a new feature onto their identity, to show that they were now different than the rest of the human race -- part of a secret, elite group of never-aging people.

These changes came in many ways. When Kris Kringle had become Santa, he'd stopped wearing glasses and had started wearing contacts, not even Mrs. Claus recognizing him at first. When the Sugar Plum had started her job, she'd began to drink nothing but tea, always carrying a pot with her, even when she was walking. When Jack had become Jack Frost, he'd swapped out his old wardrobe for a new one, taking North's lead in fashion, wearing nearly the same old fashioned, Gothic type clothing.

Clara twirled a lock of her hair nervously, waiting for Jack to answer her.

Clara, she'd changed her hair.

"When I said 'different', I meant -- good!" Jack stated quickly, suddenly feeling like Jell-O, wobbly, and sick, and not in control of himself. "It looks good...different, but good," he sighed then, rubbing his temples, and Clara giggled amusedly. "Okay, okay, so I'm bad at complements. Just shoot me, why don't you?"

Clara giggled again as she shook her head, her brown hair, which now hung loose, showing off her new, bright blue highlights. "I can't shoot you," she said. "I don't have a gun."

"Oh. Ha, ha," Jack managed to glare at her, grimacing as she giggled a third time. "I honestly think I've had enough of guns and shooting for a lifetime. Which reminds me..." he saw Clara's eyes darken as she stopped laughing, and he reached out his hand, offering it to her.

There was something he had to do, and if he didn't do it now, he would never get the guts again, not to mention the time. If he didn't do it now, he would be gone, pushed back into the human world he'd grown up in, forced out of his job, and as much as he was okay with leaving (though, if he'd had a real choice, he would have stayed), he wasn't comfortable with leaving if it meant that he couldn't tell Clara what he had to tell her.

If he couldn't tell Clara about his life.

Clara took his hand without even thinking about it. "This is our next to last day together," she said, and Jack felt a pang in his chest, knowing all too well how true that statement was, even if Clara didn't. "I'll let you choose where we go."

"Thank you," Jack managed to smile then, though it was sad. "I suppose we should head over to the park."

****

When Jack and Clara sat down at the park bench, Jack could barely breathe, let alone talk.

Though he wanted more than anything in the world to tell Clara the truth — to tell her what had set him off, what had made him start hating Christmas — he was almost...*afraid* to.

What if she was repulsed by what had happened — by the fact that he'd let his hate for his sister's killer develop into his hate for Christmas? What if she never spoke to him again, too appalled by the fact that he'd started hating Christmas because that's when his sister had died?

What if she *hated* him?

Jack could bear a lot of things — losing his job, saying goodbye to everything and everyone he had known forever...giving up Clara — but he would never be able to bare that.

Jack stared out at the late afternoon ahead of them as he tried to gather what he wanted to say, snow blowing by them mildly. Though North's wintry wind and snowstorm wasn't going to vanish until after Santa returned on Christmas morning, it had moved away from the inner regions of the North Pole, where Santa's was town was, in order to assure that the obese man had a safe flight out the next night.

So now the air around them was simply light with falling snow, floating gently down from the sky above, not too cold or heavy for sitting out on a park bench and talking. Plus, now that Clara was immortal, the snow and cold didn't bother her anymore.

"This — what you wanted to tell me — is about your past, isn't it?" it was Clara's voice that broke Jack from his thoughts, the strange warmness in it making him feel more edgy, though it should have made him feel just the opposite.

When Jack looked up at Clara, he could see that she had that look on her face -- that overly curious look she always wore whenever she wanted to know something. It was the sight of that look that made him sigh. "How did you know?" he asked, not remembering having told her.

"I didn't," Clara bit her lip almost sheepishly as she shrugged, her newly highlighted hair swaying in the chilly wind. "I just guessed," her eyes darkened then, and every inch of happiness vanished from her face. "I knew from the beginning something happened -- something sad."

Jack felt a pain stab through his heart when he saw that look, hardly able to bare it. As much as he wanted to be honest with Clara -- which was something he was still trying to come to terms with, something he'd never had to deal with before -- he was also unsure.

How could he hope to tell her something so horrible without her hating him for it?

Please don't hate me. Jack's mind begged as he looked at Clara, trying to get his mouth to form words. *I never said you had to love me -- and honestly, I don't want you to -- but...*

But, he didn't want her to hate him.

Not ever.

He would never survive that.

It was alright if she didn't love him -- better, in fact. Because, if she had loved him, it would have made things much harder for the two of them, Clara especially. If she had loved him, it would have been even harder -- near impossible -- to leave the North Pole, his job, and most of all, Clara.

If she had loved him, he would want more than ever to stay with her, and he simply couldn't do that.

Jack bit his lip as a pain leapt through his chest, trying to silence it. Even though he had promised himself to give up Christmas day -- to leave the North Pole and his job without a fight -- he was finding it increasingly difficult to stay true to. The more time he spent around Clara, the more time he wanted to spend around her, even though he knew that, after Christmas morning, he could never see her again.

But, the thought of leaving her now -- hiding away in his room until he had to come out for his sentence -- was even more unbearable than leaving her on Christmas. So, Jack concluded, he would simply have to pull a tighter rein on his emotions, try and forget about Christmas...no matter how hard it was.

"Please, Jack. Tell me about your story," Clara's voice broke through Jack's thoughts like a pick broke through ice, causing him to turn and look at her again. "I want to know..." she trailed off, frowning, and Jack was sure she was thinking that what she'd just said was uncalled for.

But Jack was grateful for the distraction. It pulled him from his aching thoughts -- back to the present, where Clara was.

He shook his head. "No, No," he said, and Clara looked at him. "It's fine. Don't feel bad. I wanted to tell you. I still do."

And so, tell her he did, sitting there on the bench in the park, no one around, the elves all busy at work.

He told Clara every excruciating detail of his life that he could remember -- growing up with a father who relied on everything illegal, a mother who relied on everything drug-related; trying to protect a younger sister, working to make sure she was alright; becoming Jack Frost and leaving his sister behind, returning on Christmas Eve to find her dead; blaming Christmas for his sister's murder when he couldn't find the real murderer...

And Clara sat there through the whole story, her eyes wide as she took in every detail, her facial expression giving nothing away for once. She didn't interrupt him with questions as she normally did, choosing instead to stay nearly silent, and Jack found himself grateful for that as well -- grateful that someone was finally taking the time to listen, after all these years--

Another reason why he loved Clara: she *listened* to him.

"So," when Jack was finally done relaying his tale, he was nearly out of breath. "That's what I wanted to..." he trailed off as he looked at Clara, realizing that she was crying.

Jack felt himself freeze with fear when he saw the tears dripping down her face, every inch of him crying out, telling him of his stupidity.

This was it -- he'd been right. His worst fear had come true! Clara hated him. He'd known it would happen. He'd known she would think the worst of him after hearing his story. He'd known that she would hate him for trying to destroy Christmas because of it, but...he hadn't been prepared for it.

Nothing could have prepared him for the loss he felt now.

"Clara — " Jack tried to say something — anything! — to make things better, to make her not hate him, but no matter what, the words wouldn't flow from his mouth. "Clara..." he reached out a hand towards her, wanting to comfort her in some way, but it died down before it could reach her.

And then, she caught it.

"Jack," Jack stared at Clara in disbelief as she looked up at him, now holding his hand tightly. "I'm so, so sorry."

Sorry? Had she just said that she was sorry?

What had she done? He'd been the one to make her cry.

Jack was taken aback. "W-What?" he managed, still staring at her teary orbs. "You didn't--"

"I'm sorry about what happened. About your sister -- about everything," Clara clamped her eyes shut then, more tears falling down, shaking her head -- and Jack just stared at her, unbelieving. "I'm so, so sorry. You've been through so much. And here I was thinking about the meeting, afraid of--"

"Afraid?" Jack caught onto the word, his eyes narrowing as something constricted in his chest. "What are you afraid of?"

What had he done now?

He'd only wanted to help Clara reach her dream; to help her fulfill what he figured was probably her purpose in life. He'd never imagined that he would make her afraid. He hadn't wanted that at all.

He'd only been trying to help.

Clara must have seen the look on his face -- the look of utter horror -- because she gasped, shaking her head fitfully, letting go of his hand. "That's not what I meant!" she assured him, and Jack felt himself relax ever so slightly, sighing. "It's just that..." she peered out at the snowy town for a moment, lost in thought.

Jack didn't take his eyes off of her, immersed in her wandering, far-away look.

When Clara spoke, her voice was small. "It's just that, before coming here, I had all of my choices made for me. No one ever asked me what I wanted, and then suddenly," he saw a flicker in her eyes as she smiled softly, and it started to snow a bit more heavily, "here I am, making every choice on my own -- making the *biggest* choice on my own. I guess I'm just worried that I made a bad one."

"But, isn't it what you wanted?" Jack jumped to inquire, not even thinking about what he was saying. "Didn't you say you wished you could become the Snow Queen?"

She had said that, hadn't she?

Clara nearly giggled when she looked over at him, her too-long eyelashes waving hello as she blinked. "Yes," she said. "I did say that. And you were listening, and you stood up for me in front of St. Nick. I guess I still have to thank you for that."

"It's no big deal," Jack tried to wave it off, frowning as he thought of St. Nick. "That guy has it in for everybody," he stopped speaking as Clara smiled wider, shaking her head.

She reached out to touch his arm, and Jack felt the whole world spin. "Again, that's not what I mean," she said, her eyes all seriousness. "I have a lot to thank you for. After all, if it wasn't for you, I wouldn't be here."

Jack's whole body froze when she uttered those last few words, his mind reeling, hoping that Clara wasn't saying what he thought she was.

She couldn't know that he'd saved her, could she? She couldn't have known that he'd shared an Immortal's Kiss with her, could she? She'd been asleep, nearly dead when it had happened. There was no way.

Or *was* there?

Had Clara somehow been awake, even at the near-end of her life? Had she somehow opened her eyes when he hadn't been looking (much more occupied with other matters)? Had he messed up that badly?

Jack didn't know, but he sincerely hoped not.

He'd worked too hard to pry himself from Clara, he didn't want to give up now. And if she knew about the Kiss, then he'd have some explaining to do, some explaining that would break both of their hearts.

I can't let that happen. Jack vowed, waiting for Clara to say more, hoping to God that she wasn't going to say what he was dreading. *I can't tell her that I love her...*

And, he couldn't. If he did, it would ruin everything, all of the careful plans he had put in place.

He wouldn't be "fired" from his job if he told Clara. He wouldn't leave the world of the Immortals forever. He would see her every month at least, if not every week.

And as much as he wanted that, in one way, he also knew that he couldn't have it. All he was capable of was causing others pain, grief...death. It was his lot in life, both as Jack Frost and as himself.

He was built for pain, not pleasure.

"Jack? Are you alright?" Clara's voice was like a bell tolling off in his head, telling him to wake up, come away from his thoughts, back to the real world.

Jack blinked as he looked at her, still not used to her bluely highlighted hair. "I'm fine," he said stiffly, still fearful of what she might say. "But, you were saying..." he trailed off, almost not wanting to remind her.

"Oh!" but it seemed Clara remembered. "Yes, I was saying," she looked at him shyly as he braced himself for the worst, her long eyelashes moving as she blinked, "if it weren't for you, I wouldn't even be here. You volunteered to be my tour guide this week. Without you, Santa wouldn't have been able to keep me, and then I would have been..." a frown lighted on her otherwise beautiful face, and Jack felt himself relax, breathing normally again.

So, she didn't know what he'd done, after all.

He was safe--

For now.

"Do I have to live in the North Pole?" the question came from Clara's mouth as all other questions did -- unexpectedly. "I mean, you don't live here, right? So do I have to?" Jack shook his head, grateful for the distraction, finding her questions amusing as always.

"No," he said as he tried to hide a chuckle. "In fact, you don't live at the North Pole." "I don't?" Clara seemed mystified by this, probably thinking that, since she was a Claus, she would be allowed to stay, unlike the rest of the Immortals.

"Well, where do I live then?" Jack turned towards her, surprised by the look on her face.

"You don't know?" he asked, and Clara shook her head, her doe eyes widening. "Oh, well, I suppose I'll have to tell you then…"

Jack watched Clara's eyes widen more and more as he told her about the Snow Queen and her duties once again. He couldn't help but think of the old Snow Queen as he recounted the various duties, and he felt a shiver travel up his spine.

It had been a while since Jack had seen the old Snow Queen, whose real name had been Rosaline. He'd never much liked her, since she was too cold and cruel for even him to stand, but the dislike hadn't been mutual. Ever. It was well known between the members of the Winter Council that Rosaline had had a "thing" for Jack.

Needless to say, he was glad when she'd been "fired".

"So, that's basically it," Jack sighed as he finished explaining the Snow Queen's duties to Clara, conveniently leaving out what he knew about Rosaline. "You draw snowflake designs, send them to the Snow-elves, and they make the snow. But you don't stay at the North Pole. Only Santa does that," he grimaced on that note, his nose wrinkling at the mention of Santa.

Clara laughed at the jab, but her eyes were still wide with wonder. "So I'm free to go wherever I want?" she asked, and Jack nodded. "Then I must only come to the North Pole for Council meetings, just like you. Where did the other Snow Queen stay?"

Jack sighed as she asked him the question, not really wanting to answer.

He tried to think about Rosaline as little as possible, because when he did think of her, it made him feel uncomfortable. He'd lived through her "reign" with enough problems to last a lifetime, and even though she was gone, it sometimes felt like she was still present, watching him, waiting for the day she could pounce--

Though of course, that was completely ridiculous.

"The old Snow Queen had a castle in the South Pole," Jack sighed as he answered Clara, the wind starting to kick up a bit now. "It was underground, really fancy. I think she moved there just so she could pretend that she was more important than the rest of us," he snorted in disdain. "She always was a snooty one."

Clara laughed again. "Reminds me of someone," she said, and Jack glared at her. "But, that's okay. I'm actually kind of glad that I don't have to live at the North Pole. Maybe I can -- " she stopped abruptly as her eyes lit up, wider than before, and Jack's heart leaped as she grabbed his hand again, suddenly excited.

"Maybe I can travel!" Clara breathed. "Just like you! *You* travel, don't you?"

Jack simply nodded, unable to actually say anything, too overwhelmed by Clara's bright eyes and happy smile.

"That would be perfect," Clara finished, looking away from him now, marveling at the sky and the falling snow. "I could see everything then, and," she turned towards Jack, and he just knew by the way that her smile widened that she had an idea, "then we could be partners! You could use your ice-sculpting talent to show me what my snowflake designs look like -- so I know that they're good before I send them to the elves -- and I could..." Jack saw her eyebrows furrow as she frowned, thinking no doubt. "Well, I'm sure there's something I could do for you."

Jack felt his head swim as he looked back at her, trying to gain control of his emotions. He could think of quite a few things that Clara could do for him, though he wasn't about to say any of them out loud -- in fact, he was appalled at himself for thinking of them in the first place.

But, Clara and him, partners?

No! It wouldn't work!

He wouldn't *let* it work.

He could never let it happen. He was giving up. Come Christmas, he would be gone, and they would find a new Jack Frost, and then *he* could be Clara's partner, travel the world with her.

Jack didn't want to admit it, but he felt a horrible jealousy seize him when he thought of that. He didn't want another Jack Frost to be around Clara, though he had no choice, since, come Christmas, he wouldn't be able to be around her himself ever again.

No matter what. Jack thought. *I can never see her again.*

It was Clara's yawn that broke Jack from his thoughts this time, making him blink and turn towards Clara, who suddenly had all looks of sleepiness.

"Are you tired?" he found himself saying, and then looked up at the sky. "I guess I didn't notice, but it's getting darker," it certainly wasn't nighttime yet, but close enough to it.

Clara yawned again as she rubbed her eyes. "Yes," she said. "I am tired," Jack felt his heart beat wildly as she closed her eyes, placing her head on his shoulder as she sighed.

A moment or so later, she was asleep.

Jack sat there on that park bench, with Clara asleep next to him, for a long time before he could move. He stared at Clara's face in that time, trying to commit to memory every inch of it, not wanting to ever forget the face of Clara, the person that he cared so deeply for...even if he would soon never see her again.

Jack sighed as the wind blew.

Even if all it did was make him suffer.

When Jack finally did move, it was only an inch, only a tilt of the head, so that he could look at Clara's face better. "My dear Miss Claus," he said, reaching out to sweep the sleeping girl's bangs from her face, "you're being cruel," he sighed on that note, leaning in to kiss her forehead. "And, like a fool, I'll be basking in your cruelty until the very end."

And he would be caught in her cruelty until the very end, because she would keep being kind to him, keep smiling at him, keep being her wonderful self. And he wouldn't run away. He couldn't run away.

Jack felt a wrenching pain pass through his heart as he placed his head on top of Clara's.

Because, after all, he only had one day left.

Chapter Twenty: Clara

Clara felt nervousness run through her like a spear as she poked her head around the corner of the pillar, searching the thronging crowd for Jack.

It was officially Christmas Eve, and everyone had been hard at work that day, making last minute preparations for midnight, when Santa would leave to deliver his gifts to the world. Nearly everyone had been enlisted in the "Christmas Help", and Clara hadn't seen head or hair of Jack all day.

She'd searched for him in the halls, the building room, the wrapping room, and even Santa's Multi-Mapping Room, but he had been nowhere. She'd also searched the town as best she could, on the few breaks that she'd had, but he was nowhere to be seen.

It wasn't until that afternoon, when the announcement had been made, that Clara understood.

Jack had been helping set up for the party -- the party that, while it was held every year to kick-off Christmas, would this year be held especially in her honor.

The news had come around one thirty, shortly after she'd finished helping wrap the last of the Christmas presents. It had been announced over the intercom, Santa's voice ringing, but invitations had been issued as well, floating to every elf (and Clara) on little parachutes.

Annual Celebratory Christmas Party Tonight

The invitations had said.

Join us as we all welcome our new
Snow Queen, Miss Clara Claus.

Clara had blushed profusely as the elves around her had burst into applause, not really wanting to be praised, since she hadn't actually done anything yet.

Santa had told her that morning that she was off snowflake-making duty until New Years, her designing duties being held by the Snow-elves just a little longer. At first Clara had protested to this, wanting to get to her job right away, but then she had agreed with Santa, figuring she probably needed some practice.

As good an artist as she was, making snowflakes was going to be different for her, something she'd never (really) tried before. She wanted to make sure her talents were as perfect as possible before she started officially, so that she could do her best—

Plus, she had to see how Jack's ice-carving went -- see how well they worked as a team.

Clara felt herself sigh again as she peeked around the pillar once more, trying to calm her raging nerves. Her grandmother had helped her prepare for the party that afternoon, after she was done setting up for Christmas, bringing in some sewing elves to help with her dress. She had seen Santa not long after her dress was finished, and he'd beamed proudly, but that didn't mean that she wasn't nervous.

What if they didn't like her? What if all of the elves thought she was too young, too incompetent? She'd already run into a few people who thought that -- the Sugar Plum Fairy and St. Nick mostly, though St. Nick tried to hide it.

And what if they were right? What if she was wrong for this job? What if--

Clara felt her breath catch in her throat as she spotted Jack, who was looking around (for her no doubt), some of her fear vanishing at the sight of him.

What if she couldn't handle it?

Can't think about that now. Clara told herself as she gathered her puffy dress-skirt. *I've already been named the Snow Queen. Besides, I've been practicing.*

And, even if she was bad at the job, even if everyone hated her, Clara still wanted to do this.

She had been dreaming of something like this for so long -- of real happiness, a place where she could belong -- she didn't want to give up the only chance she had. And, if it turned out that she was horrible at it, then she would quit, go back to her normal life.

But until then, she refused to give up -- No matter what. "J-Jack," Clara felt herself wobble in her heels as she quickly made her way down the stairs towards Jack, who had his back turned, not having noticed her yet. "I'm right -- " Clara let out a shriek as she tripped on a carpeted stair, tumbling down the last step, and--

Jack caught her.

"My, my. You certainly do know how to make an entrance, don't you, Miss Claus?" he laughed in a smug sort of way, having caught her by the waist. "And here I was wondering if you'd arrive normally."

Clara felt suddenly out of breath. "Sorry," she said as she started to pull away from him, steadying herself. "I'm just..." she trailed off as he let her go, and she noticed he was staring at her, his eyes wide.

Clara felt her face turn hot in an instant.

When her grandmother had called the sewing elves in, Clara hadn't really known what to expect. She'd been informed that the celebration was to be formal -- as in, formal attire -- so she'd expected something nice, maybe a simple prom-like dress, but that was far from what she'd gotten.

The dress had ended up being much more extravagant than any simple prom dress, though lovely and classy at the same time. It was white in color, made out of satin, though the skirt had a second skin made out of a sheen-like material, tiny sparkling snowflakes born as its design, flowing down the bottom of her dress in four layers, every other trimmed with white lace. The dress itself was slightly billowy at the bottom, but thin everywhere else, hugging but not choking Clara's figure, the top a modest sweetheart, also adorned with lace. Instead of being simply strapless, the dress had one strap to hold it up, and three small "straps" crossing from the left side of the dress's top, connecting with the main strap, all various shades of blue, and bearing their own lacy accent, as well. Wound around the waist of the dress was a light blue ribbon, ending in a long, loose bow at her hip, a sparkling snowflake adorning its middle, matching Clara's dangling earrings.

In short, Clara had thought she looked pretty -- not *amazing*, but pretty.

Her blush worsened as Jack continued to stare at her.

Obviously, Jack thought differently about how she looked.

Clara took an unwilling step back, feeling suddenly fearful again, but in a different way -- in a confusing, heartbreaking way. "*What?*" she asked Jack, her shoulders hunching. "Why are you looking at me like that?"

"Like?" Jack blinked, and his eyes connected with hers, strangely sad. "Does it bother you?" he asked softly, taking Clara off guard.

Why was he asking her that?

Did it bother her, the way he'd been looking at her?

Clara wasn't really sure — she didn't know how she felt about it. It was confusing, the way her skin was starting to tingle, the way she suddenly felt like she couldn't breathe. It was strange, the way her heart had been racing only a moment ago, seeing Jack's strange stare.

Clara shook her head, banishing that thought before it started, tears springing to her eyes.

"Clara..." Jack's voice was smaller now, more sensitive. "Please answer me. Does it bother you?"

Clara wrapped her arms around herself, shaking her head again. "I — I don't know!" she managed, feeling unsteady on her feet, like the world was spinning around her. "I don't know."

"You don't know?" Jack seemed disconcerted by this, but Clara could see the hurt on his face, plain as it was. "What do you mean you don't know?"

Clara looked at the floor then, unable to look at Jack.

What *did* she mean? What was she talking about? Why was this so difficult? He'd just been admiring her new dress! There was nothing more to it! It shouldn't have made her feel so strange.

She shouldn't have felt anything.

Clara sighed in defeat, dropping her arms as her face reddened even more. "I just..." she started, looking for the right words. "I don't want to talk about this."

"Alright," when Clara looked up again, Jack was smiling, back to his normal self. "We won't talk about it, then," Clara let out a sigh of relief as he glanced at the party, which was well underway, and then Jack offered her his hand. "Would you, by any chance, care to dance, Miss Claus?"

Clara didn't have to think. She took his hand, letting him lead her towards the dance floor, already occupied by spinning elves.

"Yes," she said, pushing her worry, fear, and strange feelings aside. "I would," she smiled at him. "Thank you."

When Jack smiled back, the smile didn't reach his eyes — couldn't cloud over the secret agony they shared.

****

Clara felt strangely lightheaded as she and Jack danced on the terrace, alone for once.

They had been inside with the rest of the dancers — the Immortals, the elves, the reindeer — but when Santa had taken off for his midnight flight, Jack had suggested that they go out onto the terrace, which was right outside the party room, in the open air. Clara had readily agreed, feeling lightheaded from the crowd, and they had both watched Santa take off, Clara smiling up at her grandfather as he'd left.

That had been hours ago, at midnight. It was now nearing sunrise, the cloudy, windswept sky calming down, and the moon starting to move away.

"Everyone's supposed to gather to watch the sun," Clara found herself saying as Jack spun her around once slowly, keeping time to the music they could hear coming from the party room. "It's almost time," she glanced at Jack, and found he was frowning.

For some reason, that frown scared her. It wasn't his normal annoyed frown, or even one of his angry frowns; it was something else. It looked almost—

Pained.

Clara felt her breath freeze in her throat. "Are you not coming?" she asked, referring to the sunrise show. "Are you not...?" she trailed off, the look on Jack's face stealing her breath completely.

"No," he answered, smiling a smile so fake it might as well have broken. "I'm not. I have a meeting."

Clara's eyebrows pulled together at that. He hadn't told her anything about a meeting. And why would they be having a meeting at sunrise, just as Santa got back? Wasn't that a bit soon? Was the meeting really that important that they couldn't wait a little while?

They stopped dancing as she looked at him seriously. "What meeting?" she asked, feeling dread now. "With who?"

"The Winter Council," Jack's expression turned blank, and he stepped away just a tiny bit. "Since your duties don't technically start until after New Years, you're not really part of the Council yet. That's why you weren't invited. And it doesn't really concern you, anyway. They're just meeting to...decide some un-snow-related things. I'm sorry," he frowned on that note, not looking sorry in the least bit.

Clara felt her heart sink when she heard this information, feeling a deepening sense of confusion.

What Jack was saying, it didn't make any sense. Santa hadn't told her anything about a meeting, either! Why would they keep secrets from her? Why would Jack keep secrets from her?

Unless...

Clara found it hard to voice the question she was faced with. "But," her voice came out soft, wisp-like, panicky, "you're coming back afterwards, right? I mean--" she didn't have to finish her sentence. She knew the answer as soon as she looked into Jack's eyes.

No.

He wasn't coming back.

But, how?

Clara felt her breath quicken as she looked down at the ground, feeling lost now, trying to capture her racing thoughts.

How did this happen? How could this be happening? *How?* It just wasn't fair! She didn't want Jack to leave! She never wanted him to leave.

"Please, don't be upset," when Jack spoke, Clara felt like she was in a dream, her head spinning so quickly she felt sick. "I was hoping you wouldn't find out. I didn't want to upset you."

Clara's head shot up then, disbelief in her eyes. "You didn't want to *upset* me?" she repeated, gasping, shaking her head. "What does that even mean? Why didn't anybody say anything? I mean --

" she felt tears pool in her eyes as she grabbed Jack's arm. "You can't go!"

He couldn't go! He couldn't leave her! She--

She *needed* him.

What was Clara supposed to do without Jack around? He was her friend, her confidant, her -- what would she do without him? How could she hope to travel the world by herself? It would be too scary. She wasn't ready for something like that. Not alone!

She never wanted to be alone.

Please, don't go. Clara begged in her mind, staring at Jack, hoping he would tell her that this was all some huge, cruel joke, that he wasn't serious. *Please, don't leave me...*

Clara felt the tears start to fall from her eyes as Jack sighed, gently freeing his arm from her grasp. He gave her a sardonic, sad smile as he shook his head. "Please, Clara," he said, "don't make this harder than it already is."

Clara closed her mouth at that, biting back all of the questions she had, all of the answers she wanted. She couldn't ask him now. It didn't really matter, anyway. There was nothing she could do.

Nothing besides ask: "Why?"

Jack seemed almost confused by the question. "Why what?" he asked, taking another step away from her, probably wondering if he should run for it, make it to his stupid meeting.

"Why are you leaving? Are they making you?" the hard look in Jack's eyes told Clara yes, and she gasped. "Why? Why would they make you leave? Why--"

She was cut off by Jack's chuckles as he suddenly laughed, looking like his normal smug self. "You really are amazing, Clara," he said, and Clara felt herself blush, though she was upset by the comment. "Here we are, moments from sunrise, talking about a topic like this, and you still find time for questions."

"It's not *funny!*" Clara felt her fists ball, more tears springing to her eyes. "I want to know why! I want to know--"

Clara was cut off by a loud chiming sound, coming from above. She felt herself start to shake as Jack looked at her coolly, not even moving.

"How about *when?*" he said, his icy blue orbs penetrating her to her very core. "How about *now?*"

Clara felt her shoulders start to shake as the tears flowed from her eyes, staining her cheeks, and then -- the edges of her vision blurred for an instant, and she felt her legs give way, though she didn't fall.

Once again, as if it were habit, Jack caught her, his arms winding around her waist as he held her up. Clara blinked the tears from her eyes, trying to look at him, but his head was over her shoulder, so she couldn't see his face. Above them, the bell that signaled the start of his meeting chimed over and over, sounding like a gong of death rather than a sweet melody.

Clara couldn't get the sound of the bell out of her mind. "Right now?" she repeated. "You have to go *right now?* This instant? This second?"

"Yes," even though Clara couldn't see Jack's face, she knew he was smirking, obviously finding her questions darkly amusing. "Yes. Of course, Miss Questions. Right now is the time."

Clara felt her shoulders shake as she fought off sobs. "Right now," she repeated again, looking up. "That bell..." but when she looked up, it wasn't the bell that she saw at all, but something else.

Something green.

"Mistletoe?" Clara's voice was disbelieving, her eyes widening as she took in the plant. "Is that really mistletoe?" the second time she said it, Jack looked up too, perplexed.

But, Clara was right, it was mistletoe, hanging directly above them from a long pole, which had once borne a flag no doubt. Whether it was there naturally or by design, Clara couldn't be sure, but she felt suddenly shaky as she looked at it.

She was standing under mistletoe.

With Jack.

Outside.

On the Terrace.

Under mistletoe.

With Jack...

Is he going to kiss me? Clara felt a strange sensation when she thought this, snaking through her chest, both painful and elating. *Would he really..?*

Would Jack even do that? Did she even want him to? Clara wasn't sure, about either question. She wasn't sure about anything anymore.

Everything was confusing. She almost wished that she had never come to the North Pole.

When Clara looked down, she realized Jack was staring at her, face only inches away.

But, no, she didn't quite wish for that.

"Clara, I'm going to kiss you," Clara felt her whole body go rigid when Jack said this -- so calmly, too! -- taking her face in his hands as he grinned. "You can beat me up afterward, if you want to, but..." the rest of his sentence was never heard, however, because at that moment there was no room left for talking--

At that moment, Jack was already kissing Clara.

Clara's mind fell numb as soon as Jack's lips touched hers, so soft and warm and inviting. And, for a moment, she was glad. For a moment, she didn't want to think. For a moment, nothing seemed wrong.

For a moment, Clara wished she could freeze time, stay still in this lingering memory she was being faced with, but then--

Jack pulled away, and the moment was gone, and Clara knew she would never be able to get it back, though she wanted more than anything to.

Jack didn't look at her when he spoke next, choosing instead to stare at the ground beneath them. "Thank you Clara, for everything. But I'm afraid," she saw him take a deep breath, "I have to go now. Goodbye," and then he was gone, walking away, their eyes never connecting again.

Clara stood on that terrace for what felt like the longest time after that, her body frozen, but her mind racing, full of all of the things that had just happened.

When Jack had kissed her, he'd been sincere. She'd known it. She'd been able to tell. He hadn't been joking with her, playing around, treating her like every normal guy treated every normal girl who they just happened upon. He'd been serious. To him, she hadn't been just some other girl, only there for the taking, she'd been...*real.*

He'd *meant* it. Which meant...

Clara found herself shaking when she was finally able to move, raising a hand to her lips. "Oh, my," her breath was shallow when she blinked. "Jack..."

And that's when she saw it, the thing that changed everything. It started to smile upon her as she gasped, looking up, its rays just peeking out over the horizon--

The sun.

"Sunrise!" Clara was already on her way as she gasped, knowing what that meant. "The meeting! I have to -- I have to--"

She had to find the meeting! She needed to see Jack!

She had something to tell him...

Chapter Twenty-One: Jack

The last remains of Clara's kiss lingered in Jack's mind as he glowered at the Winter Council, awaiting his sentence.

He couldn't say he was exactly happy with the way things had ended, but he couldn't say he was exactly sad, either. He had been hoping to spare Clara the pain of telling him goodbye -- because, he knew, even if she didn't love him, they were still close friends -- but in the end, Jack found that he thought it better that she had been there, better that he had been able to say his farewell in person.

Hopefully now Clara would be able to move on, enjoy her life for once.

"Καλωσο ρισμα. Let the five-hundred and fifty-eighth meeting of the Winter Council officially come to order...The sentence of Jack Frost has finally come to start," it was St. Nick's voice that broke Jack from his thoughts, making him sigh. "Do you know your sentence, Jack?"

Jack rolled his eyes, feeling the cold stares of everyone across from him. He really thought St. Nick was being too overzealous about his punishment.

When he'd first entered the Council room he'd been immediately ushered to the opposite end as everyone else, standing in the proverbial spotlight like some kind of traitor — which, he supposed, in the eyes of the Council (well, everyone minus Santa and North, who weren't present yet), he was.

Jack sighed as he looked at the Council members. "Yes, I know my sentence," he said in a bored tone, and then: "Can we just get this over with? You don't have to be all symbolic about it. Just let me go on to my normal, human life, and forget about me."

"You would like that, wouldn't you?" it was the Sugar Plum who spoke up, glowering at Jack as if he were a rat. "But personally, I'm enjoying seeing you sit there."

The other members of the Council started to snigger as St. Nick sighed. "Now, now, Sugar Plum," he said in an unconvincing voice. "I'm sure Mr. Frost isn't looking forward to his sentence *too* much," Jack grimaced, glaring at him, knowing that St. Nick was just as eager as the Sugar Plum to be rid of him.

Some great guy he was. Though, Jack supposed, if he'd been in St. Nick's position, he would have acted the same.

After all, Jack had tried to destroy and destroy and destroy again St. Nick's beloved holiday -- the holiday he had spent so many years working towards, the holiday the Winter Council had been formed to watch over. Jack found it hard to scorn him overly for protecting what it was he cared about.

But still, St. Nick and Sugar Plum, they made his sentence sound as if it weren't that bad, instead of the horror-filled reality that it was. They made it seem like he was just going off on vacation, instead of being expelled from the Council, from his job as Jack Frost. They made it seem like he wasn't losing the only person he'd ever truly loved.

But, Jack realized with horribly finality, he *was*.

He was losing all of those things. And it was going to be horrible. He wasn't even sure if he knew *how* to start a new life. He'd been Jack Frost for so long, he wasn't sure he knew how to do anything else--

He certainly didn't *want* to do anything else.

Jack's gloomy thoughts were interrupted by none other than Santa, who burst into the Council room just then, panting. Everyone turned to look at him as he "ho, ho, ho"ed, sauntering over to St. Nick.

"Sorry I'm so late, Nick," he said with a ragged smile. "I got caught up in Japan. What's...?" then he spotted Jack on the other end of the room. "Don't you think that's a bit much?" he asked, mirroring Jack's complaint.

St. Nick just shook his head. "Not now, Kris," he said lowly, and Santa backed off, sighing, sitting down in a chair as St. Nick turned back towards Jack. "Now, as I was saying, your sentence--"

It was then that St. Nick was interrupted, Jack's pulse pounding in his ears as he heard a voice he never thought he'd hear again.

"*Wait!*" it shouted, loud and gasping. "Please, wait!"

And that's when he saw her.

She burst into the room much like Santa had, panting and red-faced, tired from running. Her brown doe eyes scanned the room frantically until she found Jack, her face contorting into a look of horror when she saw him ostracized from everybody else. She quickly rushed over to him as the other Council members gasped, all of them recognizing her.

St. Nick was the first to speak. "Miss Claus -- " he started, but Clara wouldn't give him the time of day.

Instead, she stepped in front of Jack, putting her arms out in a defensive position. "You have to stop," she said, her voice strangely strong. "You can't send Jack away," he caught her eyes as she glanced back at him. "You just can't do it."

Jack's pulse raced as he stared at Clara, feeling an intense mixture of emotions, none of which he could describe.

How was it possible that Clara was there? How was it possible that she had come, to defend him of all things? How was it possible that she cared enough to stand up to the Council for him? Sure, he'd done it for her, but that was different. She didn't love him like he loved her.

Jack noticed something strange when he looked into Clara's eyes.

Or, did she?

"Miss Claus," St. Nick started again, drawing Clara's gaze away from Jack. "I would like to know the meaning of this. You're interrupting an important meeting, I hope you know," St. Nick frowned at her, growing angry now.

But Clara didn't budge. She stared at him coolly, and Jack just knew that she was going to ask questions, as always -- though he didn't quite expect the first one out of her mouth to be: "What did he do?"

Why was Clara asking St. Nick that? Shouldn't she have been asking "Why are you doing this?" or "Why is Jack being singled out?", or even "Why aren't you firing me for interrupting your meeting"? Why did she want to know, out of all of the things she could have asked, what he had done to deserve this?

It wasn't like she didn't know already.

Jack saw St. Nick sigh as he took a seat at the meeting table. "Well, Clara," he said, his eyes fixing on her, "as you know, Jack has tried to destroy Christmas countless times, and the Council has decided that it's becoming a problem, so we're expelling him."

"But you can't do that!" Clara was frantic as soon as she opened her mouth to speak. "I mean, you didn't even give him a chance to--"

But St. Nick wouldn't hear it. "We've already given him a task to complete, and he has failed at it. So, Miss Claus, if you would kindly step aside and let me do my job," Jack watched as St. Nick frowned at Clara, who wouldn't move.

"What was it?" she asked instead, still as still as a statue. "What was Jack supposed to do?"

Jack held his breath as he waited for St. Nick to answer -- to tell Clara what he'd thought was the impossible (not to mention embarrassing) job St. Nick had given him...the task that had turned out to not really be so impossible, after all.

He felt himself sigh as he watched Clara's eyes widen as St. Nick relayed the information, barely catching the thoughtful look in her eyes as St. Nick finished, still waiting for Clara to move.

But, when Clara turned to face him, a near pleading expression on her face, Jack found he couldn't breathe at all. He could barely think.

"He said '*love*'," Clara's big doe eyes were shadowed by her too-long eyelashes as she blinked. "In order to keep your job, you had to fall in love with a human. Don't you think you accomplished that?" Clara blushed as she looked down, and the Council members gasped before she looked shyly back at him. "I mean...you love *me*, don't you?"

If there was any color left in Jack's face, it drained away then, leaving him weak and dizzy feeling.

What was Clara asking him? How had it come to this? He was supposed to leave and never see her again! He was supposed to do what was best for her, so he would never hurt her another time! He was supposed to *leave*.

Though he didn't want to.

Would it really be so bad to stay by Clara's side? Would it really be so bad to start to like Christmas again, to finally do things the right way? Would it be so bad to really have a family -- Clara's family -- around?

Would it?

No. Jack had to admit. *It wouldn't. In fact, I think I'd almost like it...*

He didn't want to leave. He wanted to stay.

Always.

He wanted to stay with Clara, because she was the one he cared about most--

And he knew that he couldn't lie to her.

Jack watched Clara as her eyes began to tear, still waiting for a response. "My dear Miss Claus," he finally said. "As you know, I've always been a wonderful liar, but not to you," he sighed then. "Never to you..."

And then, the hardest, most heartbreaking, most wonderful part--

Jack smiled. *"I do love you."*

It was at that moment that everyone in the room gasped, including Clara, who looked happier about the news than the rest as Jack took her hands in his. The Sugar Plum Fairy fainted as she watched the two smile fondly at one another, St. Nick gaping, Santa chuckling as if he'd known everything all along.

In short, the whole occasion was rather joyous until St. Nick spoke up, interrupting Clara and Jack just as they were about to kiss.

"Hold it!" he shouted, rising from his seat quickly. "Hold everything!" everyone stopped to stare and gape at him, all flabbergasted, Jack managing to glare.

St. Nick stood to his full height as he looked at Jack and Clara, disbelief in his eyes. "This still doesn't mean that you completed your task," Clara opened her mouth to protest, but he cut her off. "Your task was to fall in love with a *human*," St. Nick pointed out, and then pointed at Clara, "which *she* isn't."

Jack was just about to tackle St. Nick, annoyed with all these technicalities, when the door to the Council room burst open once more, and in walked--

"North!" Jack gaped at his best friend, who was looking strangely smug -- though only a little bit. "Where have you been, you bum? You're missing everything!"

North simply regarded him coolly, yawning as he sat down in a chair. "I was directing the last bits of the storm away from the North Pole," he said matter-of-factly. "*Some* of us have important jobs to do, Jack," he smiled slightly when he saw Jack's eye twitch. "But that's not really what I came for..."

Everyone was surprised when North stood up, making his way over to St. Nick, who he stared at blankly, not the least bit intimidated. "I understand you're unconvinced that Jack has completed his task?"

"Yes, but," St. Nick actually looked flustered, "how would you know that? You just got here."

North smiled another tight-knit smile. "That doesn't really matter at the moment," he stated as he sighed. "The fact is, though I have no physical evidence of it, that Jack did complete his task," he turned away from St. Nick, motioning to Clara, who was now in Jack's arms. "He's been in love with that girl practically since he met her. You have no idea what I've been through just trying to keep him sane," Jack glared at North on that note, but his friend just shrugged slightly, still monotone as ever.

And then he turned towards St. Nick again. "So, whether we have evidence or not, do you really think you have the right to break those two up? After all, there has never been a better Frost than Jack, and we haven't had a Snow Queen in a long time. Do you really want to go through hiring new recruits, and the trouble of *paperwork* again?"

"I think you're just fine the way you are. You are free to stay, Jack," St. Nick nodded his head in agreement, though no one was sure if it was the smiles of Jack and Clara that had changed his mind, or the mention of paperwork...

Probably the paperwork.

Either way, only one thing clicked in Jack's mind when he heard the news:

"I'm free!" he shouted, grabbing Clara and spinning her around in the air. "I don't have to leave!"

Clara laughed in response and then, as he set her down, said: "*I love you, Jack.*"

Jack felt his heart throb at hearing that, a grin spreading across his face. In all his years, he'd never thought he would hear someone say something as precious as those few words -- that someone would care enough about him to say "*I love you*".

But, he'd been wrong, because here he was, standing with Clara, hearing those words exactly.

Somehow the Claus girl had managed to break down his icy barrier and see down to the very heart of him. Somehow, Clara had managed to change his whole world in only a week, working a secret brand of magic that only she possessed. Somehow, he felt happier now than he ever had.

Jack smiled as he gently took Clara's face in his hands, leaning down to kiss her.

And he was glad for it.

Jack and Clara were rocked from their moment as a voice suddenly rang out from the crowd of Council members, and they pulled away from each other, startled. "No!" the voice shouted, just as Mrs. Claus entered the room. "Clara got her first kiss, and I missed it!" Jack groaned inwardly as Mrs. Claus produced a camera, her expression frowning when she laid eyes on him. "Although..."

Clara was the one to cut her off, giggling. "Actually, grandma," she said, leaning on Jack. "It's not my first kiss. It's my *second.*"

Her grandmother started to gape at that, and Jack felt his heart sink, knowing what he had to do.

This telling the truth thing is really getting annoying. Jack thought as he cleared his throat, everyone looking at him in wonder of what he had to say.

"Actually, it's her third," he corrected, and Mrs. Claus gaped, her eyes bugging. "No, wait..." everyone was staring at him as he counted on his fingers. "*Fourth*, actually..."

Jack was met with silence as everyone stared at him, various looks of disgust on their faces.

"Don't look at me like that!" Jack snapped, blushing. "I had no choice! She was *dying*! What was I supposed to do?"

Everyone developed a shocked face as soon as Jack said his outburst, but none was as shocked as Clara's, which had turned completely white. The only one who didn't look shocked was North, who was staring at Jack with a monotonely contemplating look. Jack felt his face turn red as he looked down, embarrassed.

He wasn't embarrassed by what he'd done, of course. He'd saved Clara — there was no embarrassment in that. But he was embarrassed by the fact that he was the one who had caused Clara's near-death in the first place, that he was the one who had upset her.

He had never meant to do any of the things he'd done, but in some ways, he was almost glad he'd done them. After all, if he hadn't, Clara probably wouldn't have been there, standing next to him.

If he had never accepted the duty of watching Santa's granddaughter, Clara would have stayed with her father for Christmas, and he never would have met her.

If he had never become Clara's friend, she would never have invited him to the workshop, and he never would have been able to speak his feelings about Christmas to Santa.

If he had never broken Clara's nativity scene, she would never have run away, and he would have never been able to save her, making her an Immortal.

If he had never spoken up for Clara at the meeting, he would never have been able to see her dream come true.

If he had never helped Clara become the Snow Queen, the North Pole wouldn't have had a party celebrating her...and he would have left without saying goodbye.

If he had never listened to Clara, he would have never learned the truth about Christmas.

"The world was given the greatest gift, and that's what started Christmas."

Clara's words rang through Jack's mind as he gazed at Clara, who was now listening to North's explanation of how she became Immortal, and he felt the truth of the words that she'd spoken.

He'd been given the greatest gift for Christmas. It may not have been a little baby lying in a nativity scene, and it may not have been the newest toy or gadget, but that was okay, because what he'd been given was much, much better—

He'd been given *Clara*.

Jack's thoughts were interrupted as Clara took his hand, holding it tight. "You saved me," she said as she smiled at him, now understanding what had happened at the Pass. "I don't know how to--"

Jack put a finger to her lips before she could finish. "You don't have to do anything," he said sincerely, staring into her eyes. "You're alive, and *I love you*. That's all I care about."

And it was the truth. Clara was alive, and she loved him -- that was all that mattered.

Epilogue

The North Pole,
Nearly A Year Later...

Clara was sitting at her desk when it happened, the journal Santa had given her the Christmas before open in front of her, displaying one page exactly.

About Jack Frost...

The page read.

I have come to the conclusion that...

Jack burst through the doors of the room just then, looking slightly out of breath.

I love him.

"Wow, that was loud," Jack realized, referring to the way he'd all but knocked down the door as he turned towards her, grinning. "Well, are you ready, my dear?" he offered her his hand.

Clara tried not to blush as she smiled at him, taking his offered hand as she stood, but it was hard not to. It was still hard.

"I'm ready," Clara admonished as they left the room, and she cast one last glance at her closed journal. "Is grandpa all set up yet?"

Jack snorted at that. "Oh, yes," he said grouchily as they walked through the halls, headed towards Santa's sleigh. "And your oh-so-lovely grandmother is coming with us..."

Clara giggled at that. Jack and Mrs. Claus were still having a hard time getting along, even after --

"Clares!" Santa greeted as they entered the sleigh-prepping room, coming to give her a hug. "Are you ready for the big night?"

Clara nodded as she pulled away, holding up a huge, rolled up map. "Yes," she said. "We've got the map. North marked it for us."

"Ho, Ho, Ho," Santa laughed as he looked at the map. "That North has always been so good with maps."

Clara smiled as he trailed off, thinking of the trip they were about to take.

It was Christmas Eve, time for Santa's big round-world delivery, but even though Jack and Clara were going to be taking a Christmas ride in the sleigh, they weren't going to be delivering toys.

Something quite different, in fact...

"Jack," Clara turned towards Jack as Santa finished prepping the sleigh. "are you ready yet?"

And Jack smiled smugly at her, taking her hand in his firmly. "*I'm ready for anything.*"

~The End~

Of Book One

Special Edition
Paperback Exclusive
Bonus Short Story:

North of Perfect

North Of Perfect

The Wind blows however it wants to, and is free – at least, that's what North, also known as the North Wind, thought before that one, fateful meeting.

North happened to be in New York City at the time. It was the day before New Year's Eve, and everyone was excited. Even the wind seemed happy as he directed it, doing his job.

The wind was blowing strongly that night, whipping North's dark, navy hair across his face. His long jacket moved as he walked down a strangely empty street, the streetlamps above him flickering. In the background, he could hear all sorts of noises – laughter, cars honking, people shouting, ads that were being displayed.

And then, he heard the shout, the silent cry for help.

"Wait!" a voice said, as if speaking to someone; it sounded distressed. "Come back!"

North looked up at that moment to spot a young woman flailing her arms nearby, looking like a *New York City Ballet* dropout who couldn't quite master the ballet positions. His Wind was flinging her scarf about, and she was trying to grab onto the plastic bag she'd no doubt been carrying, her eyes wide.

North didn't know why, but, for some reason, the sight of the girl flailing amused him.

He cracked a small smile as he stepped towards her, silently telling the Wind to settle down, to stop bothering the poor girl. The Wind rattled on for a moment, disobedient, before it finally obeyed, turning into a soft breeze that hovered in the air.

The girl finally caught onto the bag, a grin spreading across her face, but when the wind died, she tripped and fell, landing on her backside. Her face scrunched into a wince, the impact obviously hurting, before she placed a hand beside her and pushed, trying to get up.

That was when North decided to help the girl personally, though he knew that it was against the rules. Being an Immortal, part of the Winter Council, he wasn't supposed to interact with anybody on his travels. He was supposed to stay away from people – *humans* – so there would be no risk of one learning his secret, of them discovering who he was.

Normally, North stuck to the rules like glue – not because he was particularly fond of them, but because by sticking to them, he managed to stay out of trouble more than Jack; they had an ongoing bet, to see which could cause the least amount of ruckus, and North always won – but this time, North decided to disobey, to run free with his feelings.

He normally didn't allow his emotions to run away with him – thus giving off his monotone, boring personality – but the moment that North saw the girl fall, he knew that he couldn't ignore the emotion that was suddenly beating so strongly in him.

Because, there was something about this girl, though he didn't know what it was. He'd never talked to her, had never seen her face, didn't even now her name, but something about her called to him all the same.

Something about her seemed special, *important.*

"Would you care for some help?" North's voice was monotone as ever as he stopped in front of the girl, who was still trying to get up. When she inclined her head towards him, the first thing he took note of was the color of her eyes – aquatic green, like the sea. "I noticed that was quite a nasty fall," North put a small smile on his face for good measure, not wanting to scare the girl, though it wasn't a huge smile, by any means.

But, instead of being scared, the girl blushed, her sea-green eyes widening as her face turned red. North felt his smile stretch a bit wider at this, holding out his hand for her to take.

The girl looked tired, worn through her blush. She had on thin, purple gloves that were wearing at the ends, with a nearly threadbare jacket to match, her shoulders shaking as she shivered. Around her neck was that scarf that North's Wind had been trying to steal away, which looked as if it had been washed one too many times, pills blossoming across it. There were several rips in her jeans, and scuffs on her boots, but North didn't think that they were there by design.

The girl looked poor, cold, and perhaps hungry. Maybe a college student, or maybe a waitress trying to achieve her dream.

She had a multitude of freckles on her face, and her muddy, brown hair was in knots from flying all over the place. Her lips were almost pale, and her shape was neither thick nor thin. Her nose was crooked, as if it had been hit years ago, and hadn't grown back quite right, and her ears stuck out a bit.

But, something about her plainness was unordinary. Something about it made her unique, interesting, different—

Beautiful.

"Thank you," she blinked when she spoke, her voice small, yet somehow also loud. She took North's outstretched hand, and he could feel the scratchiness of her worn gloves spread across his bare palms. After he hoisted her up, she retrieved the plastic bag she'd been running after from the ground, which seemed to have a box in it – maybe food of some sort. "It was very nice of you to stop."

North nodded as his small smile stretched again – wider than most smiles that he shared. "You look a bit cold," he admitted, and when beckoned the wind around them to move, making the girl shiver. "Would you like to obtain some coffee, perhaps?" North raised an eyebrow slightly, and the girl laughed.

He knew that he was breaking the rules, but...

The girl laughed again. *"Obtain some coffee?"* she quoted, before she laughed another, louder laugh, which showed off her smile nicely. "Where do you come from, that you talk like that?" North noticed that she had a dimple, and that her accent made her sound very much like a New Yorker.

She must have been a resident of the City – had a permanent home, unlike him.

Not that he hadn't had a permanent home once, because he had. He'd spent his childhood there, had grown up in the same house as his parents...

North felt his slight smile deflate, a gloomy feeling overwhelming him.

But then, everything had changed.

There had been a fire, and his parents and home had been caught in it. It had burned to the ground – *everything* – and then he'd joined the Winter Council, since he'd had nothing left.

The girl saw his deflated look, and opened her mouth to speak, her sea-green eyes widening in what looked like regret, but North beat her to it, and spoke first, instead.

"If you would like to know more about me, then perhaps you should take my offer, and visit the coffee shop," North said as he offered her his hand once again, staring into her eyes steadily. She looked confused, but pleased, and...intrigued. "After all, it is a cold night, and you look as if you have nothing to lose. Am I right?" he knew he'd hit a sore spot, because the girl fidgeted.

She didn't have anything else to do, anywhere else to be – that much was obvious, though North had yet to figure out why. And it seemed, from the way that she was looking at him, eyes sparkling with curiosity, that she was just as interested in learning about him as he was in discovering about her.

North didn't know why, but they seemed drawn to one another, tugged there by curiosity. Maybe it was strange, and maybe it didn't make sense, but North had never been so curious about anyone in his life, or had anyone so curious about him.

Which I why, when the girl nodded and took his outstretched hand, he stopped thinking about how he was breaking he rules, about how he was initiating contact with the outside world. The thought was still lurking there, in the back of his mind, but as he looked into the girl's eyes, it didn't seem to matter anymore.

Because, for the first time in his life, someone was *interested* in him.

"What's your name?" when the girl spoke, her voice was light, the cold seeming to freeze around them.

North didn't wait to reply. With a small, upward tilt of his mouth, he told her: "Jack", using his best friend's name (which he would no doubt tease Jack about at one point).

And just before they started off to get their coffee, the girl's smile broke out into the world again, as she replied with a cheery: "I'm Holly."

****

A few minutes later, the two found themselves sitting in a small coffee shop, both with a cup in their hands. North's was small –

a cappuccino, no sugar or whipped cream, thank you – and Holly's was a large café mocha – plenty of sugar, whipped cream, and extra mocha, thanks so much; North had paid, of course, since it would be more than rude to let a Lady pay for herself, or worse, for him – he was more of a gentleman than that. Holly stared down at the cup in her now gloveless hands for a few moments, before she finally looked up at North. North thought of what was running through her mind.

Of course, he had no idea what she was actually thinking, but he could tell from the way that her eyes focused that it was most likely something interesting, or at least pressing to Holly. And though it wasn't normal for him in the least bit, he honestly hoped that whatever the thoughts were, that they were about *him*.

Not that it mattered, anyway, since he would only be visiting the City for a few more hours.

Holly finally looked up, her smile bright.

But, at the same time, North didn't quite want his visit to end.

"So, what brings you to the City?" Holly asked after a moment, already plotting how she could find out more about him, where he came from, who he was; it was evident in her eyes. "New Year's Eve is tomorrow night, are you planning to be in Times Square for it?"

North felt a smile curl his lips slightly. "No. Much too crowded, if you ask me," he said as he watched Holly take a sip of her drink, measuring the amount of mocha that would now be gone from her cup; he was extremely attentive to detail, and he knew it well. "I prefer to be at least somewhat secluded."

"*Secluded?*" Holly almost choked on the mocha, laughing again. She set her cup down. "If you like being secluded, then why are you in New York City? This has to be one of the least secluded places on Earth."

North had to admit that she had a point. If he'd been a normal tourist, only vacationing, it would have been an extremely strange place for him to be, since the City was known for being bustling, crowded, loud – all of the things he was rather un-fond of. But, he wasn't a tourist, wasn't there for pleasure, so...

"You must be here on business," Holly guessed, taking a sip of her drink again, turning slightly pink as she noticed North's eyes move with her movement. She turned her gaze away from his face, appraising his outfit, which was his normal, Victorian Gothic getup, with an added, sweeping coat. "You kind of look like you could be a C.E.O. A young C.E.O. – for a *morgue*," North felt his slight smile stretch just a bit, inching towards the real thing; Holly took this as encouragement. "So, what is it that you do?"

North honestly wanted to laugh at the question, though of course, he didn't, since laughing wasn't normally something he tampered with.

How shocked Holly would be if she knew what he really did – what he really *was*.

But, of course, he couldn't tell her. He could never tell anyone. It was too dangerous.

And North knew what happened when you did things that you shouldn't – when you cracked the rules too far, and made them broken. People got hurt, always in various ways – just like his family, who had been caught in the fire because of his rule breaking, because he hadn't cared enough to stay and help his mother tend to the overcrowded fireplace.

"Jack?" North blinked when he heard the name, remembering that right now, it was his. "Are you alright?" he looked up to see Holly's worried face, her large, sea-green eyes.

And he felt his heart sink, though he didn't show it. He didn't like to see that look on her face, this girl he had just met.

So, North ordered his slight smile to come back, ordered it to stretch into a real smile, ordered his emotions to respond visibly. "Yes. I'm quite alright, thank you," at his words, Holly brightened visibly, smiling again, cheeks just a tinge pink. "I was suddenly caught in the past..." he trailed off as he adjusted his coffee cup, which he hadn't drunk from yet, so that the label was positioned towards him.

"So far, you've been the only one to ask questions. I think that's rather unfair," North pointed out somewhat smugly as he looked up, Holly's mouth opening into a gape. "Perhaps I should be allowed to ask some now? Do you think that sounds quite...fair?"

Holly's eyebrows wound, and she looked at a loss for words, before she suddenly sputtered: "B-But – you haven't answered any of my questions yet! Doesn't that seem *unfair?*"

North's smile had to widen at her words, now dangerously close to being a Cheshire Cat grin. He leaned forward a bit, and put his head in his hands as he examined her face, thinking.

This Holly person, she reminded him of someone. Was that why he felt so magnetically drawn to her? Or, was it something else?

Is this what Jack had felt when he'd met Clara, had started talking to her, getting to know what she thought and felt about everything?

North wasn't sure, because it didn't make sense – not *logical* sense, anyway, and he was used to thinking logically. How could he feel magnetically drawn to someone? He'd never met Holly before, and though her face reminded him of someone, he didn't know her, at least not personally. She wasn't his friend – she was mostly a stranger.

So, why?

He wanted to know: *why?*

It seemed that Holly wasn't going to tell him. From the look one her face, she was just as confused as he was, though her confusion showed more than his did. Her mouth was open, gaping a little bit, reminding North of a fish – though a pretty fish. Her eyebrows were raised, as if she were expecting something, and her eyelashes were short and somewhat clumped together, though she wore no makeup.

North noticed again the bags under her eyes, the look of tiredness, and sat back, sighing.

Holly's next question surprised him. "What are you staring at?" she asked, and with a sinking, strange feeling, North realized that he'd been staring at her without even thinking about it.

What was wrong with him today? He wasn't usually like this...

Perhaps it was the start of the New Year, of new things? Or perhaps the ordeal he'd watched closely over Christmas had affected him more than he would like to admit?

It was the second, North knew. He couldn't hide it – not from himself.

It would be a sorry attempt to even try and hide it. North thought as he shook his head, and picked up his cappuccino for a heavy drink.

The events of that Christmas were still swirling in his mind, weighing heavily on him. Though he was immensely happy that Jack had finally found someone (else) who understood him, whom he loved, the idea was more than strange. And it left North feeling oddly empty, like he was missing something that should have been plain as day...

And, maybe he was. Maybe that was the problem – that he was missing something he shouldn't have been missing.

"Were you staring at *me*?" Holly answered her own question, blushing slightly as she set her cup down. She frowned, and North felt himself frown in turn, though his frown was nowhere near as deep as hers, shallow as all of his facial expressions were. "It's how tired I look, isn't it?" she moved her hand to stifle a yawn. "I've been up late lately, trying to prepare for my new semester of classes. I work the graveyard shift at a convenience store down the street..." she trailed off then, looking away, as if embarrassed.

But, North's interest was piqued, the puzzle that was Holly turning to fit together in his mind.

So, he's been right, in a sense; she was a student working late to pay for her tuition, her dream – and working hard, from the looks of it. But, what was she going to school for? What meant that much her to her, that she would work so hard for it?

Would could she simply not live without – what was it that caused her to breathe, to get up in the morning, to sacrifice so much?

"I'm a film major," Holly admitted after a moment, looking up shyly as North continued to focus on the conversation, sipping his cappuccino. Her eyelashes hid part of her eyes, but she was looking directly at him, willing him to understand what it was that she was saying, understand what it was to want something. "I want to be a director some day, maybe even write my own scripts. It's always been my dream," she smiled at him as his lips curved into a slight grin, but then her smile vanished, stolen away by something, and her eyes turned once again to the floor. "But, it's hard, trying to keep up with everything. I barely passed my classes last semester, and this semester...well..."

Her sea-green eyes were wide as she looked back up at him abruptly, wringing her hands. "But, I'm sure you don't want to hear any of this. I don't even know why I'm telling it to you," she laughed then – a nervous laugh – but the laugh soon turned to tears, and she began to cry.

And North watched her cry, fascinated. He wasn't fascinated because of her tears necessarily, more because of the look on her face, how the tears fell, how *much* she cried.

He'd seen true tears a few times – tears that were shed because of heartbreak, real sadness, real longing, or happiness – and North had always felt that real tears sparkled more than fake ones, had an almost iridescent shine to them, as if, though they were sad, they were also happy.

And as North watched those tears being shed, he was reminded of his mother, who had cried that day...the day the fire had stolen everything he had taken for granted from him.

He'd been so stupid then, hadn't thought of what he was doing. He'd gone to leave home that morning, off to see his friends, and his mother hadn't wanted him to leave. She'd needed his help that day, but he hadn't cared or heeded what she'd said. They had argued briefly, and then he'd turned to leave...and had caught the sound of his mother crying.

Her tears had been real that day, shining as they'd fallen down her face. They'd been crying out to him, begging him to listen, begging him to make up with the woman he had loved, though he hadn't liked to admit it. They'd been begging him to stay home – to *return* home, to truly become part of his family again...

But, he'd ignored his mother's tears, and he had turned away from then, and he'd regretted it, every single day.

Because, as much as North loved being North, he couldn't help but wish that he had been able to right things with his family, truly become human again...

So, he wasn't going to ignore the cry of tears this time. He wasn't going to ignore a plea for help, for acceptance.

Because, he knew what he was missing now, what he wanted, what had interested him about Holly.

North wanted a family, someone to care about, and for some reason or other, his heart had picked this person, just as his friend Jack's had picked Clara.

"You are very brave, willing to do everything on your own," when North reached across the table to brush away Holly's tears, he noticed that they were warm, coming from her heart. She stiffened, and then blinked at him, as if she'd forgotten that he was there, though there was something in her eyes – longing, maybe? "But I doubt that you wish to continue doing everything on your own, am I right?" North brushed one last year away, relishing the look in the confused and shocked girl's eyes, before he abruptly stood, knowing what it was that he had to do.

He had to get to the airport, be on his way to his next destination. He was already late, and unfortunately, there were no Wind Elves to fill in for him. However, he knew that he would be able to return to the City soon, and when he did, he would find Holly again.

He didn't know much about her now, but, North had a feeling that discovering more about her would perhaps be the most fulfilling discovery he had ever ventured upon.

W-Wait!" North was already out the door when Holly caught onto his coat sleeve, stopping him. He turned to look at her, mild confusion flickering across his face, as her wide eyes stared up at him. "What was all *that* about? What are you—" she wiped more tears from her face, shaking her head. She didn't look as though she wanted him to leave. "What are you doing? Where are you...going?" the last word brought tears to her eyes again, and North felt himself sigh.

He had been far from normal human contact for so long – had been kept to himself for so long – that he'd almost forgotten what it as like to interact with anyone other than Jack (and now Clara).

North reached out to brush the hair from her face, eyebrows pulling together slightly. "I'm sorry," he said in his normal monotone. "I ran away from you, didn't I? But, it can't be helped. I'm afraid that I have to leave now," as if to remind him of the truth in his words, the wind rustled then, pulling at them, swirling around them. North mentally told it to be quiet, and it quieted down a bit. Then, he looked straight into Holly's eyes. "The Wind is calling me," he said truthfully, and though she had no idea what he was talking about, she seemed to understand at least somewhat what he meant.

"But, I will be able to return shortly. Will you let me see you another time?" North asked the last bit with hope – something he never thought he'd feel again.

Jack had found hope during Christmas, and though North had seen it, he hadn't truly felt it – hadn't allowed himself to feel much of anything other than his happiness for Jack, and annoyance with the Winter Council and their ways.

But now, looking at Holly, so full of hope, and promise, and dreams, he truly felt some of the hope that Clara had been talking about, the hope that had come with the first Christmas, and had spread through the world from there.

He had something to look forward to now, something new to discover...some way to discover Hope.

"I'd like to see you again," when Holly admitted this, she didn't look the least bit embarrassed – her embarrassment seemed to have washed away now, evaporating, turning into eyes that resembled kindness, promise. "Please, don't forget to come find me."

North could have laughed at that, though of course, he didn't. Though he hadn't known it, he'd been searching for something for a while now, and now, he'd found it – even when he hadn't been looking.

And in light of that...perhaps Hope wasn't the only real thing – perhaps Miracles were real, too.

North felt so many emotions – real, true, heartfelt, and strong – bubble up in him as he stroked the side of Holly's face, before finally stepping back. The wind picked up again, as he drew away from her, and it even played with her hair, as if it had hands. Holly seemed to notice its strange behavior, and looked at him in question, her eyes wide again.

"Who *are* you?" she asked as the wind changed once more, per North's direction, and literally wrapped around her like a blanket. But, instead of looking scared, she looked happy, even laughed.

North smiled slightly, smugly, as the wind blew through his navy hair. "I am simply me," he said, then, after a pause, added: "But, I am also North, which is my real name, and I act as the Wind..." the wind blew in a gust then, and Holly gasped, closing her eyes.

North knew that when she opened her eyes, he would be gone, but he also knew that she wouldn't forget him, and that he would see her again, when he came back.

He had a promise to keep now – a promise to himself, and to Holly. Though he had broken the rules set by the Council, something good had come from it, and he was glad.

And now, he had promised himself that he would find the thing that he was after, would keep seeking hope of the truest kind, no mater how long it took him to find it.

And he would help Holly, maybe even come to love her as Jack loved Clara. To cover traveling expenses, and general duties, as a member of the Council, North was paid a handsome sum every month – and through the years, he had invested, growing the money until it was large, saving it for when he needed it – for now, for when he would meet Holly, so he would be able to help pay for her classes.

He would continue pushing on towards the things that he knew he needed, would help others achieve their dreams, all while keeping his job...

The Wind blows however it wants to, and is free – at least, that's what North thought, until he learned the Wind's true identity.

The Wind blew to wherever it was called, wherever it was needed...wherever it could help someone in need.

...Author's Note...
Of Frost And Snow

Third Author's Note:

I'm happy to say "Hello!" again.

The third anniversary of C.C. is coming up, and, as I'm penning this, I'm currently working on finishing up my first draft of *Clara Snow*, and editing *Sugar Plum Dreams*. The story has come so far since I sat down and first thought it up in 2009, and I'm thrilled that it's shifted into a series. I love Christmas so much, and to be able to write more than one story about it leaves me ecstatic.

This past year saw many changes for *Clara Claus*, including me deciding to make the book into a series, and it's fun now to look back, and see how much I've changed, and how much my writing style has changed, since this particular book was written. And now, I'm proud to be able to present the new cover for this book, and the official title of "series". There are many adventures left in store for Clara, and Jack, and the others, but for them...well, you'll just have to wait and see. But, I can tell you that they will be just as unique as this book.

One note: a special shout-out to the fans. Without you, this book would have never become a full-blown series. So, if you're new to C.C., then welcome, and, if you're an old friend re-reading, welcome back. I'm so glad to have all of you on my writing journey with me.

Also in this book is North's short story, the first of three that I plan on doing (to go with the consecutive books). It was originally published in 2011, as a special add-on only available in the paperback, and has returned in this Special Edition paperback.

I wasn't originally planning on writing anything from North's POV, but the idea hit me one day, and I just couldn't resist. So, with the story stuck in my mind, and with my best friends (who are both huge North fans) begging me to pen in, I wrote it down.

I have to thank them -- Dest, Ree -- for urging me to write the short, and for being the first ones to read it. I hope you've enjoyed reading it as much as I enjoyed writing it!

I'll keep writing, so, please, keep reading!

Alexandra ~ August 2012

Second Author's Note:

The tale of *Clara Claus* was originally released in November 2010, and I was very excited. The first run of the story did well for what it was, and I got some great feedback from it, thanks to my wonderful readers.

Originally, there was supposed to be a sequel released this year around Christmastime, but I've decided to leave Jack and Clara's story alone for now.

Clara Claus was released during a very hard month for me — November, in which I participate in NaNoWriMo, or National Novel Writing Month, which makes me even more proud of it. Not only did I write and finish a new novel while C.C. (my nickname for Clara Claus) was being edited and then released, I was also was able to publish my first novel!

I would like to take the time now to thank everyone who read that first copy. I hope you've enjoyed the new, updated version of Clara Claus. Thank you for all your feedback and comments!

Alexandra ~ 2011

The original Author's Note for Clara Claus:

"Everyone thought I was crazy when I told them that my first published novel would be a Christmas story...

Clara and Jack's story was the story I wasn't planning on writing for some years. I knew I wanted to eventually write a Christmas story, since I love the holidays so much, but I hadn't planned on it being so soon...

It happened around Christmastime '09, as I was getting ready to go visit my family up North for the holidays. I was watching Christmas shows when suddenly I realized something: there were hardly any Christmas shows involving Jack Frost.

Jack Frost has always been my favorite winter "character", so this made me kind of sad. It didn't seem right for him to not have a Christmas spotlight. So I decided to write a story about him, give him what he deserved...

And, a few months later, I began writing *Clara Claus*...

At first, of course, I had no idea how to write the story, despite the fact that I'd been thinking about it. I couldn't find very much info on Jack Frost. Every Christmas show I'd seen Jack in, he'd been basically focused on being jealous of other's Christmas fandom, and I didn't really want to write about that. And the internet wasn't exactly helpful in my search, either, so I had nothing to go on.

So I searched and searched my brain (probably the best search-tool), trying to come up with something else, trying to figure out how exactly I wanted to portray Jack, and then it hit me—

"What if Jack hated Christmas?" I'd thought. *"Wouldn't that be interesting? Wouldn't that be different? Would that be something I'd want to read?"*

So I began to think of a story where Jack hated Christmas and wanted to destroy it, all of his plans foiled (of course) by Santa and the others...

But, this still hadn't quite worked for me. It seemed too boring, and there was no one for Jack to really interact with, so I'd decided to add a character, someone no one would expect...

And so was born Clara, Santa's granddaughter.

Clara's character was drawn from my years of being a dancer, of finally getting to perform in my second favorite ballet, The Nutcracker. I knew from the beginning that I wanted to make her obsessed with snow, and I took some of her personality from what I remembered of Clara in the ballet (who was mystified by everything she saw), but I hadn't planned on her being such a lovable character...

And I hadn't planned on Jack falling so madly in love with her, either. I'd known from the beginning, of course, that I wanted him to like her, but...I hadn't expected him to like her that much. It's strange how stories can change on you, without you...

And when I realized just how much Jack had changed, that's when I realized what my story was really about—

Jack Frost.

Even though it's called *Clara Claus*, the story is truly about Jack Frost. He was the character I wanted to write about most, the character that was hardest to write. I spent hours upon hours just trying to figure him out, and I think for the most part, I did a pretty good job...maybe...

And through my shock I realized something else—this story, it's also about hope, maybe even more than it's about Jack Frost. I wanted to communicate what I felt for Christmas in this story, what I love about the holidays, and I think I did that. I think I succeeded.

A good story is the greatest gift *I* can give.

Yours in Writing,

Alexandra ~ 2010

Make a Difference!

Jack and Clara are all about spreading hope at Christmastime. Listed below are just a few of the organizations that help bring hope to the hopeless during the Holiday Season. See what you and your family can do for those in need!

    Operation Christmas Child: www.samaratanspurse.com
    Make A Wish: www.wish.org
    Toys For Tots: www.toysfortots.org
    American Red Cross: www.redcross.org
    Salvation Army: www.salvationarmyusa.org

...Thank You...

Many people inspire me. Here is a giant, thankful "thank you".

First, thanks goes to my wonderful savior and friend, Jesus. I couldn't have asked for a better talent.

Second, to my family and friends, who love and support: Mom, Daddy, Bubby, Gina, Destiny, Christina, Reneé. Extra thanks to: my mom, for reading and helping me edit; Gina, for being the first to read the published version; and Reneé, for extensive feedback and eagerness to read North's short story.

Thirdly, an extra rose of thanks to Dest, who read this for me first and laughed...a lot, and very hard.

To Mrs. Kester, the AWESOMEST creative writing teacher ever! Thanks for all of the support, from near and far.

To author Ridley Pearson, who gave me the best writing advice. I'm between the pages at last!

Again to Mema, who may deserve this story more than anyone else. We miss you lots. Last but not least: to my readers, new and old, who make every word worthwhile!

...About The Authoress...

Alexandra grew up writing. Since she could pick up a pen, she has scribbled in notebooks and binders, written on the computer. She draws inspiration from everything she sees, but her dreams are her main source of literary endeavors.

When not writing, Alexandra can be found reading, creating artwork, listening to music, and spending time with her family and friends.

Alexandra lives in Florida with her family and calico cat, Sanura.

Visit Alexandra on the web at www.AlexandraLanc.com
Visit Alexandra's blog: Words Of The Worlds
Follow Alexandra on Twitter @AuthorLanc

The Story Continues...

The realm of Winter has many Immortals, but only one delivers Dreams -- and that is the Sugar Plum Fairy.

The Sugar Plum, part of the Winter Council, has a severe disdain for fellow Council member Jack Frost. But, where did this loathing start?

Plunging into her memories, the Sugar Plum recalls her past -- how she became an Immortal, how she came to loathe Jack Frost -- and reveals how one unplanned meeting can lead to life-altering events...and life-altering consequences.

In Sugar Plum Dreams, a Snowflake Triplet novella, a history will be revealed, as connections are made, questions are raised, and the true meaning of love is remembered.

Sugar Plum Dreams

Book 1.5 in the Snowflake Triplet
Available In Ebook And Paperback Holiday 2012

A Dark Tale Begins...

Best friends Terren and Aura, two girls on the brink of adulthood, find their seemingly normal lives thrown into chaos when they are attacked by otherworldly creatures, and an evil plot begins to unfold...

The girls learn of Airian, a terrifying being bent on domination of the worlds, who seeks out Terren in order to fulfill his goal -- Terren, who learns the secret truth of her origins, as well as the mysterious connection she shares with the unknown figure lurking in her memories. Aided by an alien prince named Koren, whose group of warriors have been sent to Earth to defeat Airian, the future and reality become increasingly complicated -- especially for Aura, who possesses dark secrets of her own.

A tale of memories, loss, and the connections we form, Shadows of Past Memories is the first book in the Foxfire Chronicles, a breathtaking series that pushes beyond the normal to deliver an entirely new world, where nothing will ever be the same again.

Shadows of Past Memories

NOW AVAILABLE

In Ebook and Paperback

And Look For *Shadows at Midnight*, available 2013!

The Phantasmagoria Duet...

A world of wonder and imagination awaits you in the *Phantasmagoria Duet!*

In The Ending, book one, eighteen year old Melody is thrust into Heivion, the fantasy world that she created as a child — a world that has now become real. In order to save the inhabitants of Heivion from the Darkness that plagues them, Melody must go on a journey to recover her lost memories.

The Ending
AVAILABLE AUGUST 2012
In Ebook and Paperback

In The Beginning, book two, Melody returns to Heivion after four years, when her best friend Kay is stolen away. But, Heivion has changed, and in order to free Kay, Melody must join forces with Dais', who was once her game's villain, but who has supposedly changed. But, can Dias be trusted?

The Beginning
AVAILABLE SEPTEMBER 2012
In ebook and Paperback

Thank you for Reading!

Sincerely,

Alexandra Lanc

CPSIA information can be obtained at www.ICGtesting.com
Printed in the USA
LVOW06s2016151013

357047LV00001B/470/P